PEACE DIVIDEND

BOOK NINE OF ABNER FORTIS, ISMC

P. A. Piatt

Theogony Books
Coinjock, NC

Copyright © 2023 by P. A. Piatt.

All rights reserved. No part of this publication may be reproduced, distributed or transmitted in any form or by any means, including photocopying, recording, or other electronic or mechanical methods, without the prior written permission of the publisher, except in the case of brief quotations embodied in critical reviews and certain other noncommercial uses permitted by copyright law. For permission requests, write to the publisher, addressed "Attention: Permissions Coordinator," at the address below.

Chris Kennedy/Theogony Books
1097 Waterlily Rd.
Coinjock, NC 27923
https://chriskennedypublishing.com/

Publisher's Note: This is a work of fiction. Names, characters, places, and incidents are a product of the author's imagination. Locales and public names are sometimes used for atmospheric purposes. Any resemblance to actual people, living or dead, or to businesses, companies, events, institutions, or locales is completely coincidental.

Cover Design by Elartwyne Estole.

Ordering Information:
Quantity sales. Special discounts are available on quantity purchases by corporations, associations, and others. For details, contact the "Special Sales Department" at the address above.

Peace Dividend/P. A. Piatt -- 1st ed.
ISBN: 978-1648558603

"All candid economists concede the role of military expenditures in sustaining the modern economy. Some have held that expenditures for civilian purposes would do as well. The transition would be rather easy... [But] there is the problem of magnitude. For the price of a smallish fleet of manned supersonic bombers, a modern mass transit system could be built in virtually every city large enough to have a serious bus line. What would be built then?"
John Kenneth Galbraith, The Age of Uncertainty

"Some will say that these initiatives call for a budget windfall for domestic programs, but the peace dividend I seek is not measured in dollars, but in greater security."
President George H. W. Bush

"The West as a whole in the early 1990s became obsessed with a 'peace dividend' that would be spent over and over again on any number of soft-hearted and sometimes soft-headed causes. Politicians forgot that the only real peace dividend is peace."
Prime Minister Margaret Thatcher

DINLI

DINLI has many meanings to a Space Marine. It is the unofficial motto of the International Space Marine Corps, and it stands for "Do It, Not Like It." Every Space Marine recruit has DINLI drilled into their head from the moment they arrive at basic training. Whatever they're ordered to do, they don't have to like it, they just have to do it. Crawl through stinking tidal mud? DINLI. Run countless miles with heavy packs? DINLI. Endure brutal punishment for minor mistakes? DINLI.

DINLI also refers to the illicit hootch the Space Marines brew wherever they deploy. From jungle planets like Pada-Pada, to the water-covered planets of the Felder Reach, and even on the barren, boulder-strewn deserts of Balfan-48. It might be a violation of Fleet Regulations to brew it, but every Marine drinks DINLI, from the lowest private to the most senior general.

DINLI is also the name of the ISMC mascot, a scowling bulldog with a cigar clamped between its massive jaws.

Finally, DINLI is a general-purpose expression about the grunt life. From announcing the birth of a new child to expressing disgust at receiving a freeze-dried ham and lima bean ration pack again, a Space Marine can expect one response from his comrades.

DINLI.

* * * * *

Chapter One

Fleet Captain Oleg Kochav sat in his chair and surveyed the control room of the flagship *Colossus*. The view didn't thrill him like it used to, because he was alone with one other crewmember who manned both the propulsion controls and communications panel.

It is said the crew is the life's blood of a ship. In her heyday, *Colossus* had eight watch standers in the control room to operate the sensors, weapons, communications, and other systems. Now, she was an empty shell of her former self on the final leg of her storied career, worthy only of a bare bones crew. Kochav loved command, but he hated the death watch his tour had become.

The watch stander interrupted his reverie. "Captain, we're being hailed on the salvage orbit circuit."

"The salvage orbit circuit? Who's calling?"

"SOMO, sir."

The Salvage Orbit Management Office, known as SOMO, was the UNT agency that controlled the salvage orbit around Terra Earth and her moon. As space travel and exploration became more common, the UNT created SOMO and developed a system to maintain unused or derelict vessels for sale, repair, or breaking. Some owners placed their vessels into salvage orbit with plans to bring them back into service at some future date.

When the UNT government ordered the drawdown of military forces, Fleet Command decided to place *Colossus* and her sister flagships into salvage orbit, along with many of their escorts. The drawdown created a headache for the ISMC leadership—how to dispose of the weapons and other gear carried by the thousands of former Space Marines. There were no facilities on Terra Earth to store such a massive arsenal, but the Corps was loath to destroy it all.

The solution was simple. *Colossus* rendezvoused with the six other ISMC flagships and transferred their weapons and gear to *Colossus* for storage. Now that the transfers were complete, they planned to depressurize *Colossus* to prevent oxidation of the weapons and gear. The *Colossus* would join her sister ships in salvage orbit and await reactivation. It was Captain Kochav's sad duty to deliver the once-proud ship to her resting place.

Kochav dialed up the salvage order circuit at his console. "SOMO, this is *Colossus*."

"This is your SOMO agent calling from the transport Lorelei. We are fifty kilometers dead ahead of you, standing by to transfer you and your crew to Terra Earth."

The transmission puzzled Kochav. *Colossus* was still 30 hours from the approaches to Terra Earth and her scheduled rendezvous with SOMO.

"There must be some mistake," Kochav said. "We aren't due to transfer for almost a day and a half."

"My apologies, Captain, but the latest schedule from the salvage master shows us assuming control of Colossus *today to place her in deep orbit. With your permission, I will accompany my crew over on our shuttle, and we can discuss the matter face-to-face."*

"This is highly irregular. I need to contact Fleet Command."

"*As of this moment, you are no longer under Fleet Command,*" the voice insisted. "*Please be ready to receive our shuttle in one hour.*"

Like many long-serving senior officers, Kochav was accustomed to things being just so, and any deviation from procedures caused him some distress. The demobilization of Fleet and ISMC forces, unthinkable a year ago, created a great deal of angst and confusion Fleet-wide, and it seemed like all the rules and traditions that had guided him for many years were broken. He keyed his mic with numb fingers.

"This is *Colossus*, roger. We will be ready to receive your shuttle."

The communications and propulsion watch had turned around and witnessed the exchange, and she flashed him a big smile. The sooner they turned over *Colossus*, the sooner they returned home to Terra Earth.

A wave of sadness washed over Kochav as he contemplated his next steps. This was not what he imagined the end of his command tour would be like, but he understood the happiness of crewmembers like his watch stander. They had been away from home a long time and would be ecstatic to hear they would be relieved earlier than planned. He dialed up the ship's intercom.

"This is the captain speaking. We have just been contacted by SOMO. There has been a change to the schedule, and we will be turning over *Colossus* today. A SOMO crew will arrive via shuttle in one hour to begin the turnover procedure." He paused for a moment to give the crew time to react before he continued. "In thirty minutes, all department heads will muster with me in the control room and report the status of their departments. All hands are reminded to focus on the task at hand. *Colossus* is still our ship until the turnover process is complete, and we will operate her in a safe and orderly manner. That is all."

* * *

An hour later, Kochav and his leadership team stood in the passageway outside the shuttle bay and waited while the bay repressurized.

The shuttle hatch opened, and a familiar man dressed in battle armor emerged, followed by two dozen armor-clad individuals armed with pulse pistols who surrounded Kochav and his officers.

"What is the meaning of this?" Kochav demanded. The leader stepped forward and Kochav recognized him as a fellow Fleet captain. "Sam? What are you doing?"

"We're seizing your ship, my dear Ollie," said Sam Nicaro, using Kochav's nickname from their time together at Fleet Academy decades earlier.

"Seizing my ship? We're turning her over to SOMO."

Nicaro wagged a finger at Kochav. "You *were* turning her over to SOMO. Now you're turning her over to us."

A man with a severe crewcut that revealed a thick scar across his head motioned to the passageway with his pulse pistol. "All of you, go to your assigned stations. Control room, engineering control, and the armory. Disable exterior communications. If anyone resists, kill them. Collect all crew and secure them in Drop Ship Bay Six."

Kochav stepped toward Nicaro. "This is outrageous! You can't do this."

The scarred man leveled his pulse pistol at Kochav's face.

"We just did, Captain," he said with a hard edge in his voice. "It will go better for you and your crew if you cooperate."

"You're a Fleet officer, Sam," Kochav said as Nicaro and his men manhandled the *Colossus* officers toward the drop ship bays. "How can you engage in piracy?"

Nicaro pushed Kochav through the hatch into Drop Ship Bay Six.

"I *was* a Fleet officer, Ollie. The Peace Party decided to reap my career as a peace dividend, and I became a free agent. You call this piracy. I call it a reallocation of military resources."

For the next twenty minutes, Nicaro and his men searched for *Colossus* crewmembers and brought them to Drop Ship Bay Six. Zerec, the man with the scar, punched and kicked their captives as they arrived, and by the time the crew was rounded up, many had fresh bruises and split lips. Finally, Nicaro and a handful of his men returned to the bay and confronted Kochav and his crew.

"Is your entire crew accounted for, Captain?" he asked Kochav.

Kochav looked at the familiar faces surrounding him and shrugged. "It appears so."

"Wrong answer."

Two of Nicaro's men seized a chief petty officer and dragged him to the front. Zerec pressed his pulse pistol to the man's head.

"Is your entire crew accounted for?"

"Please. Give me a minute to get a full muster."

Kochav's crew fell into ranks and he took a headcount. One hundred and seventeen. "There are three missing," he said.

The hatch banged open, and pirates dragged two dead crewmen in by their heels. Behind them, the young female petty officer who had been the propulsion and communications watch in the control room stumbled in and collapsed into the arms of a female lieutenant. She had a fresh black eye and disheveled hair, and she sobbed uncontrollably.

Kochav gasped in shock and anger, and several of his crew crowded forward. Zerec leered at the group as if daring them to make their move.

"It seems everyone is accounted for now, Captain," Kochav said.

Nicaro, Zerec, and their men turned and exited the space without a word. The hatch slammed shut behind them.

The *Colossus* crew gathered around the injured woman.

"What are we going to do about this?" one of them demanded of Kochav.

"What can we do? We have no weapons, and they control the ship."

"We have to fight back!"

A warning klaxon sounded and amber warning lights began to flash. The motors that controlled the massive external doors whined to life.

"My God! They're de—"

His statement was cut off as the atmosphere inside the drop ship bay whooshed out through the open doors into the vacuum of space, along with Kochav and his crew.

* * *

Nicaro watched on a monitor in the control room as Kochav and his crew tumbled into space. The drop ship bay doors closed, and the warning lights went out.

"Inform *Lorelei* that we are setting a course for the Freedom Jump Gate," he ordered. He looked at Zerec, who stood next to him in the control room. "Who assaulted that woman?"

Zerec smiled, and Nicaro felt a twinge of fear.

"Who cares? She's gone now."

"We're not animals, Zerec." He turned to his second in command, a narrow-faced former Fleet major named Elean Dietz. "Who did it?"

"I don't know, sir," he said. "I was searching the engineering spaces. I didn't know anything had happened until they brought her to the drop ship bay."

Nicaro slammed his hand on his console. "Fucking find out!" He pointed a finger in Dietz's face. "I didn't select you as my exec because you make excuses, Elean. I chose you because you get results. So get them."

"Yes sir."

Zerec chuckled and walked away.

Thirty minutes later, Dietz returned to the control room with two men. They stood in front of Nicaro with nervous, downcast looks. He recognized one of them as a Fleet petty officer from his last command. The other was a former Space Marine.

Petty Officer Wicht.

"What do you have to say for yourselves?"

They shifted nervously as they stared at the deck in silence.

"Look at me!"

The pair looked up, wide-eyed. Wicht looked like he was on the verge of tears.

"Well?"

"Captain, sir, we found her hiding behind the consoles, and she fought when we dragged her out. One thing led to another, and…" Wicht's voice trailed away.

"And you raped her." Nicaro's accusation hung heavy in the air.

Wicht covered his face with his hands and sobbed, and he would have fallen to the deck if his companion hadn't supported him.

"We are on a great undertaking to make a better future for ourselves, not to show how savage we can be," Nicaro said. "I would have you flogged around the fleet if we were still serving." He glared at the two men for a long moment while his mind raced.

Nicaro was in a difficult position. He needed all his former Fleet hands to crew *Colossus* on the journey to the Free Sector, but he also needed to keep Zerec's former Space Marines under control. The good order and discipline of Fleet personnel and Space Marines were maintained by regulations and the consequences for violating them. Kochav had hit close to the truth when he accused Nicaro of piracy, and like pirates, the only thing that now kept the crew in line was fear of physical violence.

"This is the first and only warning to you and the rest of the crew. While you are on this ship, while you are under my command, you will not engage in such barbarism. If anything like this happens again, justice will be swift and severe. Do you understand?"

Wicht and his companion nodded.

"Exec, we have a long and perilous journey ahead of us. We can't afford any more screwups. Now, get them out of my sight."

Dietz escorted them out of the control room, and Nicaro stared at the navigation display, oblivious to the hypocrisy of his outrage at the rape while he himself had participated in the murder of over a hundred Fleet personnel.

"Are you finished with your show?" Zerec had observed the scene from across the control room and now walked over to Nicaro.

"What's wrong with you, Zerec? That wasn't a show. I can't maintain discipline aboard my ship if your men act like animals."

Zerec raised an eyebrow and smiled. "*Your* ship, Nicaro? This ship belongs to The Master."

"You know what I meant."

"Brother Nicaro, you are not in command of this mission. You are here to deliver this ship to The Master. You should keep that in mind."

Zerec's tone reverberated with malice that sent a shiver of fear down Nicaro's spine. Zerec's smile became a leer.

"Never fear, my dear Ollie. There will be no further rapes aboard this ship." Madness glinted in his eyes. "Unless you or your men volunteer."

* * * * *

Chapter Two

The United Nations of Terra (UNT) capitol complex in Lviv was built as a shining tribute to the triumph of humanity: soaring spires, elaborate architecture, and manicured gardens sprawled across two square kilometers of gently rolling hills west of the city center. All the government ministries had their own building, connected by a monorail that whisked government officials back and forth.

The Ministry of Defense (MoD) building squatted on the western edge of the complex. It was a plain structure except for an exotic antenna field that sprouted on the roof. Members of the government elite who worked in the complex quipped that the MoD building was distinguishable from the rest because it was so undistinguished.

Inside the MoD building, a rabbit warren of hallways with gleaming tile floors and low ceilings led to the various offices that kept the Ministry functioning. As one approached the center of power, the hallways widened, the ceilings got higher, and carpet and paneling replaced tile and paint.

The atmosphere inside the building was subdued. Even when the halls were filled with staffers, conversations were muted as people moved at a deliberate pace. The wheels of the ministry turned slowly, like the rest of the government.

A young staffer who clutched a folder to his chest as he fast-walked through the halls was such a rare and unexpected sight that people stopped and stared as he weaved his way to the inner complex of the General Staff. After a quick I.D. check with the Space Marines that guarded the area, the young man hurried directly to the office of Admiral Albert Schein, Chief of the General Staff, and entered without knocking. He rushed past the astonished receptionist and burst through the admiral's door.

"What's the meaning of this?" Schein demanded.

The staffer placed the folder on the desk in front of the admiral. "The watch officer told me to deliver this without delay. For your eyes only, sir."

Schein flipped open the folder and began to read.

The receptionist entered the office. "Admiral, I'm so sorry. I tried—"

The admiral held up his hand but didn't look up. "It's okay, Mrs. Adams. You can leave us, and close the door, please."

Mrs. Adams made a noise in her throat as she shot a displeased look at the young man before she retreated.

Schein finished reading. "Please tell me this is a joke."

"No-no sir. No joke."

The admiral re-read the report before he punched a button on his desktop communicator. "Mrs. Adams, call General Boudreaux and tell him to drop everything and get down here. Now."

Six minutes later, Mrs. Adams ushered General Boudreaux into Schein's office.

"What the hell's going on, Al? I was fixin' to go get in nine holes before the lunch crowd." He looked at the young man seated on the couch. "You get yourself a new assistant?"

"This is, uh, what's your name?" Schein said.

"Stockton, sir."

"This is Stockton, Ellis. He works on the watch floor. Have a seat and read this."

Boudreaux did as Schein directed. His eyes widened as he read.

"*Colossus* is missing?" He looked from Schein to Stockton and back. "Fucking *Colossus*?"

"Yes sir," Stockton said. "She stopped reporting her position approximately forty hours before her scheduled rendezvous with the SOMO crew, and there's been no confirmed locating data since."

"She's carrying—"

"General!" Schein cut off Boudreaux off. He looked at Stockton. "Thank you for bringing this directly to me, and pass my thanks on to the watch officer, too. I'll handle it from here. And remember, secrecy is critical."

"Yes sir. Thank you, sir."

After the door shut behind Stockton, the admiral leaned across his desk and lowered his voice. "The shit is about to hit the fan on this one, Ellis."

"What do you think happened?"

"Your guess is as good as mine." Schein closed the folder and stood up. "Right now, we need to go brief MBG."

"Why don't you go on ahead without me? Face time with the boss is important in your job. Besides, the last time I saw her, she chewed my ass."

"That's why I'm taking you with me. You've got experience. And she likes you."

"Fuck."

* * *

MBG was Minister of Defense Marjorie Brooks-Green, a prominent member of the Peace Party. She had been ambassador to Maltaan when diplomacy failed between the races and rose to MoD when the prior minister resigned. She was not a friend to the UNT military due to the dalliances of her ISMC colonel ex-husband, but Schein and Boudreaux knew she was more impartial than many other members of her party.

MBG's aide ushered the admiral and general into her office and stood by the door. She shook her head as they approached her desk.

"I was having a good day until you two showed up," she said with the faint trace of a smile. "Have a seat and tell me what's on your mind."

"Thank you, Minister," Schein said. He gestured to her aide. "This is close hold, ma'am. For your eyes only."

MBG waved her hand, and her aide flounced from the room. "I don't think Pietro likes you, Admiral."

Schein passed the folder to MBG. "*Colossus* is overdue, and it seems she has gone missing."

"What do you think happened to her?"

"At this point, we can't say for certain, Minister. She was on a routine transit to Terra Earth, so it's unlikely she encountered an unmapped space warp. There have been no reports of asteroids or other debris along her path, and we've received no reports of other vessels missing in the area, so a collision is also unlikely. It's possible she suffered an engineering casualty which caused her to deviate from her scheduled route, but her lack of communications is puzzling. That leaves the possibility that she intentionally deviated."

"Do you think she's been hijacked?"

The admiral nodded slowly. "That is the worst-case scenario, yes, ma'am."

"Let's assume she has been. For what reason?"

"Ma'am, there are seven ISMC divisions' worth of weapons and gear aboard *Colossus*. That's enough to cause a whole lot of trouble," Boudreaux said.

"That assumes that whoever took her has seven divisions worth of soldiers to wield those weapons and use that gear."

"That's a fair point, Minister. However, we have to consider that the Space Marine arsenal wasn't the primary target of a hijack. In addition to those weapons, *Colossus* also carried a Mark-654 High Yield Ground Penetrating Munition."

"A what?"

"A large weapon known as a 'planet killer,'" Schein said.

"Sounds ominous," MBG said. "What is it?"

"The planet killer was first developed as a ground-penetrating weapon to defeat subterranean bugs without the need to send Space Marines below ground. It was a good concept, but even the smaller versions caused too much indiscriminate damage on the surface to be practical. The production program was shelved.

"Our engineers developed a larger weapon and designated it the Mark-654. The Mark-654 weighs twenty metric tons and is dropped from orbit. Once launched, ramjet engines propel it downward at hypersonic speeds until it penetrates deep beneath the surface and detonates.

"The Mark-654 was tested on a lifeless plutoid near the Spagos Bellictum star formation. The plutoid was one-half the size of Terra Earth, and the explosion split the plutoid in half."

"Damn."

"The MoD at the time decided to deploy one planet killer on each ISMC flagship as a just-in-case weapon, but the presence of the weapon aboard the flagships was a closely guarded secret. Only three officers aboard each ship knew, and a select few at Fleet Headquarters. They stored the weapons in a special magazine where they were largely forgotten."

"Until now." The minister stood and began to pace, a sure sign that her mind was working in overdrive. "Where are the planet killers from the other six flagships? Are they also aboard *Colossus*?"

"No ma'am. They remained aboard the flagships, and we moved them to storage down here before Fleet turned the ships over to SOMO."

"That's a small mercy." MBG stopped pacing and looked at Schein. "Assuming she was hijacked, who took her?"

Schein sighed and shook his head. "We don't have any solid suspects yet."

"Was it an inside job?"

"I hate to admit it, Minister, but it's a possibility. Her role as the orbiting magazine wasn't a secret, nor was her expected arrival time at SOMO. Taking down a Fleet flagship would require capabilities we don't ascribe to an average pirate."

"Not to mention the balls it would take to attempt such a thing in this sector."

Schein and Boudreaux chuckled.

"Where do you think she's at, Admiral?"

"It's been forty hours since her last position report. I'm sorry to say, at this point, she could be anywhere."

MBG's legendary temper flashed in her eyes. "You don't know much, do you?"

"Madam Secretary, I received that report fifteen minutes ago and brought it straight to you. When we're finished, I intend to use every tool at my disposal to find *Colossus*."

"How do you propose to do that? We can't very well announce that we've lost a flagship full of weapons, including one that can destroy Terra Earth, and ask for the public's help finding it."

"We might have to do just that, Minister," Boudreaux said. Both MBG and Schein gave him shocked looks. "Not directly, of course. Civilian crews know what our flagships look like. We can't ask them directly, but we can go to the areas where they congregate and listen to the buzz, ask indirectly, and put money in the right hands."

"Do it."

"I'll have to bring another officer in on this," Boudreaux said. "General Anders, my deputy for Operations and Intelligence. He used to honcho the ISMC Intelligence, Surveillance, and Reconnaissance branch, so he knows how to run an intel gathering operation like this."

"I remember him from Maltaan. Bring in whomever you need but find that fucking bomb *now*." MBG consulted the time. "I need to go brief the president. Any other bad news?"

"That's it for today, ma'am."

* * *

Ten minutes later, Boudreaux's aide ushered General Anders into the inner office where Boudreaux was studying a holographic image of the Terra Earth sector.

"Nils, have a seat. We need to talk."

Anders went on alert. There was none of the usual aw shucks good ol' boy tone in Boudreaux's voice, which usually signaled trouble.

Boudreaux punched his keyboard and a yellow circle appeared on the holo.

"*Colossus* has gone missing. This is her last reported position, give or take."

"What happened, sir?"

"She was supposed to rendezvous with SOMO forty hours after this position report. She never made it."

"No reports from other ships in the area?"

"Nothing has been reported yet."

Anders examined the sector holo. "If she deviated from her route that long ago, she could be anywhere. She might have even jumped out of the sector."

"Affirmative."

"And she's the arsenal ship. We need to find her."

"The problem is bigger than you think, Nils. Have you ever heard of the Mark-654 HYGPM?"

"Hmm, no sir."

"The Mark-654 High Yield Ground Penetrating Munition. Hypersonic bomb that detonates underground," Boudreaux said. "It's a goddamn planet killer."

"I read something about that a long time ago. I thought they scrapped that idea. Too destructive."

"They stopped working on the smaller version, but some bright boys built a bigger one. They used it to destroy a whole fucking plutoid and then decided to put one on every flagship."

"There's a planet killer on *Colossus?*"

"Yes. Enough weapons and gear to equip forty thousand Space Marines and a bomb big enough to destroy a planet. We gotta find her, and fast."

"How to you want me to proceed, sir?"

"You're the master spook, Nils. Don't you have sources you can use or spy shit you can do? You led the ISR."

"The ISR branch folded when I deployed for the invasion, but I still have contact information for a lot of my old sources. I'll start there."

"There's a wrinkle we have to keep in mind. MBG asked if this was an inside job. Admiral Schein didn't say, but I believe it has to be. There's no pirate force out there capable of taking down a Fleet flagship without some help. Somebody is leaking information, accidentally or on purpose. Do you know Fleet Captain Oleg Kochav?"

"Not well. He was a couple years behind me at the Academy. How is he involved?"

"He just made captain, and they gave him command of *Colossus*. Caretaker command, anyway. He was to deliver her to SOMO when she disappeared."

"I'll have Major Rho deep dive into his background."

"Quietly, Nils. If word gets out that we've lost a ship full of weapons, there's no telling what the public reaction will be, and we don't want to tip our hand to the inside source, either."

* * * * *

Chapter Three

Twenty-four hours after Boudreaux tasked Anders with locating *Colossus*, they met in Boudreaux's office.

"I haven't found her yet, but I've gathered some intelligence on the situation," Anders said. "My sources report that *Colossus* was hijacked, probably by the Kuiper Knights."

"The Kuiper Knights? What the fuck are they doing in this sector?"

"The Knights have undergone a significant transformation since the drawdown, sir. Thousands of former Space Marines and Fleet personnel migrated to the Free Sector, and the Kuiper Knights recruited heavily among them. We even discovered Kuiper Knight recruiters operating in Kinshasa."

"What's that got to do with *Colossus* and our weapons?"

"We're still working on that, sir, but I have a theory. The Big Four don't have a military presence in the Free Sector, and there's no organized law enforcement, either. It's well known that the Kuiper Knights want to establish their own territory, ruled according to their faith. If they want to assert control over the sector, they need two things. Men—"

"And weapons." Boudreaux rubbed his hands together. "Dammit, Nils, why do you always dream up this nightmare scenario shit?"

"It's just a theory. I could be wrong."

"What are we doing to test your theory? More importantly, what are we doing to find *Colossus?*"

"I put feelers out to the civilian space fleet, and the word I'm getting back is that a ship with a sizable force of Kuiper Knights entered this sector a week to ten days ago. I also received two reports of a large vessel, possibly a flagship, in the vicinity of the Freedom Jump Gate within the last day. Unfortunately, we don't have any assets near the jump gate to confirm it, but it fits."

"If *Colossus* is through the gate, we'll never find her. The Big Four aren't going to allow us to operate in the Free Sector."

"It would be difficult, but not impossible, General."

"Huh. Maybe. Any progress on our internal situation?"

"Nothing yet. Major Rho didn't find anything during her background research on Captain Kochav. He commanded a Fleet destroyer before his promotion to captain, and he took command of *Colossus* before she became the arsenal ship. He has a wife and two children in Vladivostok, and I confirmed they still live there. There's nothing remarkable in his background or personal life to suggest he's involved in this.

"There's been grumbling in the ranks since the drawdown started, but the Security Service hasn't detected anything specific to *Colossus* or the weapons. If there's a leak, we'll find it."

"All right then, keep me posted."

"Sir, there's one more thing, a sensitive matter. I tasked one of my sources to insinuate himself with the Kuiper Knights to find out what he can from the inside. It's a long shot, but if he gets recruited and sent to the Free Sector, we could have our answer."

* * *

Captain Abner Fortis took a final look around at the vivid green Maltaan landscape before he climbed aboard the shuttle with Gunnery Sergeant Petr Ystremski right behind him. They sank into two empty seats and buckled in for the ride to the Fleet contract transport *Long Horizon* and the journey back to Terra Earth.

Home.

Six months earlier, Fortis and Ystremski had deployed with a company of Space Marines to Maltaan to gather intelligence on the apparent invasion by the Badaax, a previously unknown race of aliens from beyond an unmapped space warp located inside an asteroid belt. The Badaax had destroyed two Terran fleets and killed or captured nearly all the Terran civilians and Space Marines stationed on Maltaan.

The United Nations of Terra (UNT) Grand Council had ordered their forces to disengage with the Badaax, but Fortis had disobeyed that order and led India Company in an attack to rescue the human captives. The captives died in the attempt, and the Badaax fled back through the unmapped warp which was then fouled by orbiting asteroids.

The UNT ordered a full inquiry into what became known as the "Maltaan Incident." Investigators interviewed Fortis and his men and collected the Badaax technology and bodies the invaders left behind.

The result of the investigation was inconclusive. The responsibility for the UNT defeat was laid at the feet of the local commanders who died in the fighting and were therefore unable to defend themselves. After six long months of investigation, Fortis and his men were permitted to return to Terra Earth. "Have I told you how much I hate this fucking place?" Fortis asked Ystremski.

The gunny groaned. "Only every day for the last six months, sir. Someday, you're going to miss Maltaan."

Fortis snorted. "Fat chance."

"At lease we got out before the rainy season started."

The shuttle docked with *Long Horizon* and the Space Marines transferred to the transport. A bald crewman with a pudgy, moon-shaped face handed each of them a folder.

"Welcome aboard *Long Horizon*. I'm Third Mate Chael Belmo. Everything you need for our trip to Terra Earth is in your folder, including your bunk assignments and meal hours. That hatch leads to the main passageway that will take you to the berthing compartments.

"My communicator number is in there in case you have any questions. You're all experienced travelers, so I won't bore you with the details. Feel free to explore the ship, but we ask that you steer clear of engineering spaces, for your safety."

Fortis and First Lieutenant Dean Young were assigned to share a stateroom. Next door were Ystremski and Sergeant Mitch Udoh. The quarters were spartan but a big step up from the open barracks they'd been living in on Maltaan.

"Do you want the top or bottom bunk?" Young asked.

"I'll sleep on the deck if I have to," Fortis said.

Young tossed his duffel on the top bunk while Fortis consulted his folder.

"Fifteen minutes to chow. Let's grab Ystremski and Udoh and find the mess decks."

The food was bland compared to the native Maltaani food the Space Marines had eaten for the past six months, but they welcomed it as more proof that they were indeed heading home.

After they ate, Fortis invited the group to binge-watch the holographic news broadcasts they had missed during their sequestration on Maltaan.

"Thanks, but I've got several weeks of holos from Tanya to catch up on," Ystremski said. Udoh also declined, so Fortis and Young returned to their stateroom.

After the first several holos, the two officers paused to discuss what they'd seen.

"Am I hearing this right?" Young asked. "In response to our defeat, the Peace Party mothballed most of the fleet and deactivated seven Space Marine divisions?"

"That's what it looks like," Fortis said. "They've declared the budgetary savings 'peace dividends,' and they're reaping them to fund other things on their political agenda."

"That makes a lot of sense. We lost, so we might as well disarm. What's going to happen to us?"

"According to the latest message I received from General Anders, we'll go through the process like every other Space Marine and see what happens."

ISMC Manpower had been tasked with reviewing the records of all Space Marines not assigned to one of the seven deactivated divisions. Manpower evaluated their service and disciplinary records and medical history before making a retention or termination decision. Personnel discharged by deactivation or the review process referred to themselves as "divvies."

In a private communication Fortis hadn't shared with his fellow Space Marines, Anders had assured Fortis that the Space Marines of India Company would be assigned to one of the two remaining ISMC divisions instead of being separated.

"It's like the whole world has changed since we left," Young said when the next segment started. "Look at this."

The holo talking head described how Taiwan had recently exited the United Nations of Terra and joined the Big Three, the three major economies that were not part of the UNT —Japan, Unified Korea, and New Zealand. The new bloc had become known as the Big Four.

"I guess the Big Four are pissed off about the helenium in the Maduro Sector?"

"Wouldn't you be?" Fortis asked. "The whole asteroid belt is helenium. The UNT declared the Maduro Sector off limits so the Big Four can't get to it, which means their economy is in big trouble. Then the UNT gave the Galactic Resource Conglomeration special dispensation to mine the belt. I'm not a politician or historian, but this seems like the kind of thing wars are fought over."

"Fuck it." Young rolled over and punched his pillow into shape. "I just hope I have a job when we get back home."

* * *

The following day, Fortis caught up with Ystremski in the crew's mess. The gunny's mood was subdued as if he had something on his mind, and Fortis knew it was better to wait and let him speak in his own time than ask questions.

"Did you get caught up on the news?" Ystremski asked.

"Yeah, I did."

"Any of it good?"

"Is it ever?"

The pair shared a chuckle.

"I'm glad I missed it. Before you ask, Tanya and the kids are fine."

"That's good news."

Ystremski's expression became thoughtful. "You know, I lied about my age to join the Corps."

Although Fortis and Ystremski were close friends, Ystremski had never said much about his life before the ISMC.

"Oh, yeah? How old were you?"

"Sixteen. My mother wouldn't sign the form to let me join, so I told 'em I was eighteen."

"Sixteen? Geez. So young."

Ystremski nodded. "My old man was a mean bastard when he was sober and worse when he drank. Same story told a million times before, right? I knew if I didn't get out of there, I'd kill him, so I left. Didn't say a word to anybody."

"Damn. I'm sorry to hear it."

"Nah, don't be. They gave us a week's leave after boot camp, so I went home dressed in my blues, thinking I would surprise him. The sonofabitch died while I was in training."

Ystremski chuckled, and Fortis couldn't keep a straight face. They laughed together for a minute, then Ystremski's face grew somber again.

"The day Petr Junior was born, I promised Tanya I would get out of the Corps. Here I am, six kids and twenty-one years later, still humping."

"DINLI."

"Yeah, but for how much longer? This peace dividend bullshit has me worried, especially for Junior. He's supposed to graduate from Fleet Academy soon, and the rumor is that a lot of the cadets will be going home after graduation instead of into the service."

"Wow. No commission?"

"No nothing. No commission, no flight school, nothing. At least they're not forcing the cadets to pay back their tuition. Not yet anyway."

"Hmm. I guess we'll have to wait and see how it plays out," Fortis said. "They can't get rid of everybody in the training pipeline. *Imperio* should have taught them that."

Imperio was an Academy training vessel captured by slavers with the entire junior and senior classes of cadets aboard. It had taken years for the Fleet and ISMC officer personnel communities to recover, and the incident was the catalyst that led to Fortis joining the ISMC.

"Because they're capable of learning from their mistakes?"

Fortis and Ystremski laughed again.

"At least he'll have a university degree instead of being a dumbass grunt like his old man," Ystremski said.

Fortis feigned indignation. "Hey, wait a minute. I have a university degree, and I'm a dumbass grunt like Junior's old man."

Ystremski thumped him on the shoulder. "You're a special case, sir."

"Maybe not for much longer." The words were out before Fortis could stop them.

"You think you'll get divvied?"

"From what I've read, I check most of their boxes to get separated," Fortis said. "Disciplinary record and injury history. I'm tailor-made."

"Not a chance. You're a fuckin' hero. You were the poster boy for the Maltaan war bond drive. They'll look like complete assholes if they cut you."

"The Maltaan war isn't big with the Peace Party. They might do it out of spite."

"Ah, don't worry about it. What happens will happen, and fuck 'em. DINLI."

"DINLI, indeed." Fortis looked at Ystremski. "I think I'm going to get out of the Corps."

"What? Bullshit."

"No, I'm serious. I did my required service, and they paid off my student loans while we were on Maltaan. I don't owe them anything, and they don't owe me anything."

"What are you going to do, go work for your dad building biodomes?"

"I don't know. A lot of divvies are moving to the Free Sector. Maybe there are opportunities out there."

Ystremski laughed and clapped Fortis on the shoulder. "You're not going anywhere, young Captain Fortis. I have the feeling you're going to get a cushy staff job with a pretty secretary and long lunches. Just wait and see."

* * *

Anders called Boudreaux two days later with some bad news.

"Two things, sir. I confirmed that *Colossus* jumped through the Freedom Gate five days ago. Her whereabouts in the Free Sector are unknown."

"Huh. We knew that was probably going to happen. What's the other one?"

"Police discovered the body of my source near the space port early this morning. Someone beat him to death and dumped him in the bushes."

"Was it the Kuiper Knights?"

"They don't have any suspects yet. They think it was a mugging or street fight gone wrong."

"It doesn't sound like you agree."

"He had made some progress infiltrating the Kuiper Knights over the past two days. In fact, he reported he was supposed to meet them for an induction ceremony last night. Then he turned up dead."

"Quite a coincidence."

"From what he told me, the recruiters seemed disappointed that he didn't have any military experience. I think I'm going to try again, with a divvie this time. It's a little short notice, but I think it will work."

* * * * *

Chapter Four

The shuttle from *Long Horizon* touched down at the Kinshasa space port four hours after dark. The Space Marines almost ran down the ramp to board the buses waiting to take them to the ISMC base. Ystremski and Fortis were the last two down, and when their boots hit the tarmac, a van rolled to a stop next to them. The driver, a staff sergeant, climbed out.

"Captain Fortis, Gunny Ystremski. The general is waiting," he said as he opened the door.

"Oh, shit," Ystremski said under his breath.

"Welcome home boys," Anders called from inside the van. "Climb in, I'll give you a ride."

Fortis and Ystremski traded looks as they dumped their duffels inside and climbed in behind them. Anders greeted them with a smile and handshakes.

"It's good to see you home safe and sound."

"Thank you, sir," Fortis said. "It's good to be back."

General Anders had led the Maltaan reconnaissance mission aboard the *Eclipse Wonder* and was the nominal commander of Fortis and India Company. He tried to take responsibility for their deployment, but there was no getting around Fortis' disregard for his orders. Anders had returned to Terra Earth five months earlier and resumed his duties as Deputy Director for Operations and Intelligence on the UNT General Staff.

"Sergeant, let's drop Captain Fortis off at the ISR building first," Anders told the driver. He looked at Fortis. "Your old room is waiting. I hope you don't mind."

"Thank you, sir. Much better than the hotel I expected to sleep in tonight."

The Intelligence, Surveillance, and Reconnaissance (ISR) branch had been an operational unit of ISMC intelligence led by then-colonel Anders. Fortis had been a member of the ISR branch until his transfer to a reconnaissance company just before the invasion of Maltaan, and the unit disbanded.

"You're all set with Manpower tomorrow at 0800 hours," Anders told them. "It should be a quick and painless process. Each man will receive new orders and two weeks of leave before they have to report to their new companies."

"For the guys who are retained," Ystremski said.

"Like I told the captain, I've arranged for all of India Company to be retained."

Ystremski looked at Fortis, who shrugged as if to say, *Sorry*.

Before the gunny could respond, the van braked to a stop in front of the ISR building.

"Go on in, Captain. The desk watch is expecting you."

"Thank you, General," Fortis said as he climbed out of the van. "See you in the morning, Gunny."

"Good night, sir."

The van pulled away and turned onto the perimeter road that ran down toward the ISMC training grounds.

"Where are we going?" Ystremski asked. "My base quarters aren't this way."

"Stop here, Sergeant. Hop out so we can speak in private."

The driver did as Anders instructed and walked several meters from the van. Ystremski's curiosity roused, but he knew he wouldn't get anything from Anders until the general was ready to talk.

"This is a dangerous time, Petr," the general said.

Petr? Uh-oh.

"We've drawn down our military to the lowest levels in UNT history. Thousands of lives have been thrown into chaos and perhaps even ruined, and there's a lot of anger out there. Righteous anger."

"We heard some of that, sir, but we didn't get a lot of current news on Maltaan. They kept us in the dark because of the investigation."

"Forty thousand Space Marines and half as many Fleet personnel were discharged in ninety days. Seven divisions and all their ships, simply gone. How does that make you feel?"

Ystremski thought for a second. He could almost hear alarm bells ringing in his head. "It makes me angry, of course. A lot of good people got screwed. Still, from a bean counter point of view, it makes sense. The Maltaani are no threat, and they say the Badaax won't be back until the warp opens in eighty years or so. I read that the global economy is in the crapper, and there's a drought brewing in South America. I guess it's more important to reduce military spending and direct the money elsewhere. It still sucks." He paused. "What's this all about, General?"

"When I said I arranged for all of India Company to be retained, that wasn't entirely accurate. All of India Company will be retained, except you. You will be divvied."

Anders' words shocked Ystremski, and his face flushed. "What? I'm being divvied? Why?"

"You're worth more to me as a divvie than a gunny."

"General, with all due respect, what the fuck are you saying?"

"Approximately thirty thousand divvies have relocated to the Free Sector since the drawdown began. This massive influx of people has created a lot of problems in the sector and added to the tension between the Big Four and the UNT back here. The Big Four blame the UNT for the sudden spike in piracy and other violent crimes against the citizens of the Free Sector."

"What's that got to do with me?"

"Nine days ago, someone hijacked *Colossus*, the flagship we used as an orbiting arsenal for the weapons from the seven deactivated divisions. Five days ago, we received a report that *Colossus* had passed through the Freedom Gate enroute to an unidentified destination in the Free Sector. I have uncorroborated reports that some of the divvies have organized in the Free Sector under the banner of the Kuiper Knights. The logical assumption is that those weapons are intended for them."

"Thirty thousand trained divvies, organized, armed, and pissed off. Sounds like a big problem."

"It is, and it's exacerbated by the fact that the UNT military cannot legally operate in the Free Sector. That's where you come in."

Ystremski chuckled. "I'm good, General, but I'm not that good. Thirty thousand to one are pretty steep odds."

"I don't want you to fight them, I want you to join them, travel to the Free Sector, and locate the weapons. I'll take care of the rest."

"Why me, General? I'm not one of your ISR spooks. What about Captain Fortis?"

"You're perfect for the mission. You enjoy a good reputation among your fellow Space Marines. You've served for a long time, but you have no record of service with ISR. You've had some discipline issues, and your medical history alone should probably land you on the termination list. In short, you've got the perfect profile for a disgruntled divvie. I couldn't have scripted it better if I tried."

"So, I'm supposed to get kicked out of the Corps and somehow go to the Free Sector without raising any suspicions?"

"No. The Knights have an organization here, in Kinshasa, that has been recruiting select divvies and arranging transportation for them to the Free Sector. You'll contact them and allow yourself to be recruited."

"What if they don't bite, or they sniff me out?"

"I'll arrange to bring you back on active duty with full pay and allowances and come up with another plan."

Ystremski thought for a second.

"What do I tell Tanya? I haven't even made it home from the last six-month deployment, and you want me to leave again?"

"I'm sorry, Petr. I know I'm asking a lot, but this situation is quickly becoming a major crisis. Tell Tanya as much as you have to, but as little as possible. It's better for you and her."

"Hold on a second. I'll take all kinds of risks myself, but I won't put my family in danger. The Kuiper Knights are lunatics."

"I totally understand, and I will take measures to protect them. My advice would be for her and the kids to live with her family in North America until your mission is complete."

"How long do you think the mission will last?"

"Open-ended. However long it takes you to go to the Free Sector and locate the weapons. We'll do the rest. Despite our agreement not to send military forces into the Free Sector, I think the Big Four will look the other way when we send someone in to deal with the Kuiper Knights."

"Can I think about it?"

"You have until 0800 hours tomorrow. If you don't accept the mission, I'll arrange for your retention and transfer to one of the active ISMC companies. If you accept, your mission begins immediately after you're divvied." He put a hand on Ystremski's arm. "Whatever you decide, you need to know that you cannot trust anybody. *Anybody*. The drawdown has created hard feelings outside and inside the Corps. Your mission is known by three people: General Boudreaux, me, and you."

"Roger that, sir. I won't say a word to anyone."

"Good. If you accept the mission, I'll be in touch with more details and tasking. For now, your first mission objective is to pick a fight with Fortis after you're divvied."

"Pick a fight with Fortis?"

"Your friendship with him is well known. If you have a public confrontation with him, it will help establish your cover." Anders opened the door and called the driver. "Sergeant, we're ready to go."

The ride to Ystremski's base quarters was quiet. Ystremski was afraid to say anything in front of the driver, so he stared out at the dark base in silence. When they arrived, he opened the door and grabbed his duffel.

"Thanks for the ride, General," he said as he slid the door shut. The van accelerated away just as his front door slammed open, and his family poured outside.

"Daddy!"

* * *

Three hours later, Tanya Ystremski slumped onto the couch in her living room. The excitement level among their four small children at Petr's return had gone into the stratosphere, and it was all she could do to keep them under control while they paraded six months' worth of art projects, schoolwork, and a random collection of rocks the boys had dug up in the back yard before him. Petr laughed through it all and let the kids run wild, and his strategy worked. After all their frenzied exhilaration burned off, Tanya took over and announced bedtime. Ten minutes later, they were all tucked in, and Tanya got her own time with Petr.

"C'mon," Petr said and held out his hand. "Let's go outside."

"I'm exhausted."

"Nah, c'mon. The moon is beautiful tonight."

They stepped out into the backyard, and Petr took her into his arms.

"It's been a long time since we danced in the moonlight," he said. They moved easily together as Tanya hummed a few bars of a favorite song. After a few minutes, she stopped and held Petr at arm's length.

"What is it?" she asked.

"What's what?"

"Petr Ystremski, we've been married too long for me to fall for the 'let's dance in the moonlight' routine. What is it?"

"That hurts, Tanya," Petr said in a teasing tone. "Maybe I became a hopeless romantic while I was away."

She chuckled and held him tight. He put his lips to her ear.

"Anders wants me to go on a mission for him."

"When?"

"It starts tomorrow."

Her body tensed and then relaxed.

"When will you be back?"

"I don't even know if I'll be leaving."

They continued to dance as they traded whispers.

"Typical. Do you have to accept it?"

"No."

"What are you going to do?"

"It's an important mission, Tanya. Critical, even. If I'm successful, it might prevent a war."

"Do your duty, Space Marine," she said as her voice caught in her throat. "Just don't forget your duty to us."

"I won't be a Space Marine much longer."

Tanya stopped moving. "What?"

"It's part of the mission. I'm going to get divvied tomorrow."

"What about us?"

"Anders recommended that you take the kids and stay with your folks in North America until I get back. We can't stay in base housing if I'm not in the Corps."

"And when is this supposed to happen?"

Petr shrugged. "I don't know. Soon, I guess."

"How could you agree to that without talking to me?" Tanya pulled away, and her voice seemed loud in the darkness.

"Keep your voice down," Petr said. "I haven't agreed to anything yet, and I'm talking to you right now. If you tell me no, I'll refuse the mission."

Tanya's shoulders slumped. "I'm not telling you no. It's just a lot to process. It makes sense that we can't stay on base, but *North America*? Where will you be?"

"Here in Kinshasa, I suppose."

"Will we get a chance to say goodbye to Abner? The kids are looking forward to seeing him."

"I don't think so. We're going to fight tomorrow."

* * * * *

Chapter Five

Gunny Ystremski was the first to arrive at the parade ground in front of the ISMC headquarters building. It was early morning in Kinshasa, but after six months on Maltaan, the African humidity was already stifling.

He greeted the Space Marines of India Company as they arrived and fell into formation. Captain Fortis approached, and they exchanged salutes.

"Good morning, Gunny. How's it feel to be home?"

"Sweaty, sir."

"How are Tanya and the kids? Good?"

"They're all great. We stayed up half the night trying to get the kids to bed, but it's great to be home."

1LT Young approached and saluted Fortis. "Good morning, sir. All present."

"Outstanding. March them over to headquarters and let's get this started."

"Aye aye, sir."

Fortis and Ystremski stood by and watched the Space Marines file into the building.

"Any idea which division they're going to?" Ystremski asked.

"No idea. Anders didn't say." He gave Ystremski a sheepish grin. "I didn't say anything when he told me we would be retained. This whole situation has been such a clusterfuck that I didn't want to get anyone's hopes up."

"You still getting out?"

"I dunno. I guess so."

"Well, wait and see what they offer before you do anything stupid. You never know, you might get assigned to be the lifeguard at a women-only nude beach."

Fortis rolled his eyes. "I'm sure that's exactly what it will be."

The Manpower Branch personnel had a well-organized system set up to process the Space Marines in a timely manner. They called the junior Space Marines into their offices first, and it gratified Fortis to see them emerge with broad smiles as they received their new assignments. The sixth-month investigation sequestration on Maltaan had been stressful on everyone, and the uncertainty of the drawdown only made it worse.

It was finally Ystremski's turn, and as he headed for the office, he saw Fortis wink and smile at him.

I guess he's staying.

He was ushered into an office by a pleasant-looking civilian with white hair and bifocals hanging on a chain around her neck. A nameplate on the desk identified her as Mrs. Alsop.

"Gunnery Sergeant Petr Ystremski," she said as she flipped through his file.

"Yes, ma'am."

Mrs. Alsop stopped paging. "Hmm." She skimmed through another section before she stopped again. "Hmm."

Ystremski counted five "Hmms" before she reached the back of file and closed it. She picked up a red file folder from her desk and passed it across to him.

"I hate to be the bearer of bad news, but you've been selected for separation."

Even though Ystremski expected it, the news hit him like a slap across the face, and he blinked in surprise.

"What? Why?"

"Your service has been exemplary, but your disciplinary record is problematic. You've been court martialed, and you've had other, lesser issues as well. Then there's your medical history. It's extensive, to put it mildly. In my opinion, you're lucky you weren't medically retired already."

Ystremski opened the file and read the top sheet.

"Pursuant to the Budgetary Realignment Act (BRA), you are hereby discharged from active service in the International Space Marine Corps, effective immediately. The United Nations of Terra gratefully acknowledges your service and wishes you all the best in the future."

It was followed by several paragraphs of officialese, ending with instructions for appealing the decision.

"Everything you need to know about vacating housing and closing out your accounts is in there."

"This is nuts. I have four kids at home. How am I supposed to feed them?" Ystremski felt the blood rush to his face as he stood and leaned across the desk. "I almost fucking *died* for you people, and this is how you treat me?" he shouted.

"Take it easy, Gunny." Mrs. Alsop held up her open hands as she rolled her chair away from the desk. "I don't make the decisions; I just deliver the news. Frankly speaking, with your disciplinary record, I'm surprised they didn't discharge you sooner."

Before Ystremski could respond, two burly military policemen appeared in the door. "Is there a problem, ma'am?"

Mrs. Alsop looked at Ystremski, and the gunny let the tension drain from his body.

"No. No problem, boys." Ystremski picked up the pen and signed the discharge papers with a flourish. "Just an old Space Marine getting dry-fucked by bean counters who don't know the first thing about honor or loyalty." He dropped the pen on the desk. "Is there anything else, Mrs. Alsop?"

She shook her head and offered her hand. "I'm sorry, Gunny."

"Yeah, me too." He looked at her hand for a moment before he turned away.

The raised voices had drawn the attention of the Space Marines in the waiting room, and Ystremski felt their eyes on him as he headed for the door.

"Hey, Gunny."

He heard Fortis behind him, but he kept walking.

"Gunny!"

Here we go.

When he turned around, he saw Fortis waving a sheaf of papers. The second thing he saw was the gold leaf of a major on Fortis' utilities.

What the fuck?

"Hey, what's going on?" Fortis asked.

"You're a major."

Fortis touched the insignia and chuckled. "Yeah. Can you believe that? They promoted me when we were on Maltaan." He searched Ystremski's face. "What's wrong?"

"I've been divvied."

"You're joking!"

"The joke's on me, *Major.*" Ystremski spat out the last word, and Fortis gave him a confused look. "And I'm not laughing."

"Hey, Gunny, let me talk to the general. Maybe—"

"It's too late for that. I'm not a gunny anymore. As of ten minutes ago, I'm nothing."

Ystremski turned for the door, and Fortis put a hand on his shoulder. Ystremski whirled and threw a straight left punch that hit Fortis square in the face. The major stumbled backward and landed on his backside as blood spurted from his nose.

"Don't fucking touch me!" Ystremski shouted. He looked at the stunned faces of the Space Marines gathered around him. "Don't any of you touch me." He turned on his heel and stormed outside.

The whole way home he expected MPs to arrest him, but he made it home unmolested. When he got there, Tanya met him at the front door.

"Are you okay?"

"I am now," Ystremski said as he followed her inside and gathered her into his arms. "How are the kids?"

"The twins are at school, and the boys are out back digging up the yard with Mongo."

He held up the folder. "It's official. I've been divvied."

Her face fell. "Now what?"

"I'm a little fuzzy on that. I guess you leave me and take the kids with you." He gave her a playful poke on the shoulder. "Wanna fight?"

She poked him back. "Do we get to have make-up sex?"

There was a loud shriek from the back of the house and the unmistakable sound of fraternal strife.

"Maybe next time."

* * *

Fortis groaned and sat up when Anders entered the medical center treatment room.

"How's your nose, Major?"

"Feels great, sir. The doc says he'll have it straightened out and looking better than new in a couple weeks."

"Good." Anders leaned in close. "Petr said he's sorry."

"You talked to him?"

"Not exactly."

"I don't get it. He just lost it."

"We'll talk more when you get out of here," the general said as he straightened up. "When you're through, report to the ISR building, and I'll fill you in."

Two hours later, Fortis trudged up the steps of the ISR building. The desk watch waved him to the passageway that led to Anders' former office.

Fortis knocked and entered. He found General Anders stretched out on the sofa.

"Sit down, Abner," the general said. "I apologize for the casual greeting, but I strained a muscle in my back a couple months ago. It helps to rest it throughout the day."

"Sorry to hear it, sir." He sat in one of the plush chairs close to the couch. "What's all this about Gunny Ystremski?"

"Petr Ystremski is no longer a Space Marine. He's on a classified mission for the General Staff, and you are not to attempt to contact him or his family, directly or indirectly."

"Yes sir." Fortis' confusion must have been evident on his face.

"I mean it, Abner. Sometimes you do things your own way, but not this time. Don't do it."

"Yes sir." Fortis stood. "Is there anything else, General?"

Anders swung his feet off the couch and sat up.

"Take it easy, Abner. It's nothing personal. It's for his protection, and yours. Now, let's talk about your new job as the ISR branch head."

"New job?" It suddenly occurred to Fortis that he'd been so surprised by his promotion that he'd forgotten to ask about his new assignment.

"You're now assigned to the General Staff. General Boudreaux and I want you to run the ISR branch."

"I thought that was a colonel's billet?"

"It was, before they shut it down. Now that we're bringing it back and there's a shortage of colonels, it is a talented major's billet."

Fortis didn't respond right away.

"You're not disappointed, are you, Abner? I can have your orders changed and find someone else for the job."

"No sir, I'm not disappointed. Not at all. I'm grateful for the opportunity and your confidence in me. I've just had a lot to process this morning." He touched the bandages on his nose. "And a pounding headache."

"I can't do much for you there."

"What's the plan, sir? Is it operational, or will I be driving a desk?"

"Before you take over ISR, you have to undergo a mandatory psych eval with a civilian doctor."

"I'm not crazy."

"Nobody said you are. It's an ISMC requirement for prospective commanding officers. You won't be a commanding officer per se, but you'll operate autonomously because I'll be in Lviv. It's a formality. Unless you confess to the doctor that you're a serial killer, you'll be fine. I'll send you the date and time for your appointment.

"Your first task will be to make a complete assessment of the building and all the facilities inside. When the ISR folded, the base facilities manager took over this building. I don't know what they took, what they left behind, or whether anything was damaged. You were here with ISR long enough to know what used to be here, so you'll know best what's not right."

"I'm just a caretaker."

"Of course not. We can't rebuild the ISR branch without knowing what we have to work with."

"Will there be other personnel assigned?"

"That's a bit more complicated. The drawdown has created plenty of hard feelings among the divvies, and a lot of active duty Space Marines, too. I'm reluctant to start adding people until I know for sure where they stand."

"Do you think there are disloyal Space Marines in the Corps?"

Anders hesitated, and Fortis realized he had struck a nerve.

The general cleared his throat. "It is certainly a possibility, but we have no evidence that it has occurred."

He's lying.

"When you're finished with the survey, we'll submit a budget request to General Boudreaux's office. While he's shouting at me in Lviv, you'll be safe in Kinshasa."

* * *

It took all Ystremski's self-control to help Tanya load the kids into the transporter headed for the space port. His six-year-old twin girls, Abby and Gabby, were inconsolable, and their younger brothers took that as their cue to act out as well. As the day wore on and their departure got closer, Tanya's anger at Petr seemed genuine. He hadn't detected a hint of understanding during the few times he had been able to make eye contact with her.

Mongo sat on the curb next to him and whined as the transporter pulled away. Ystremski waved until they were out of sight and then walked to the front door.

"C'mon, buddy. Let's get this over with."

He spent the next six hours packing their personal property into boxes destined for storage. His quarters had come with basic furnishings, and he and Tanya had decided early on that it would be cheaper and easier to replace the furniture damaged by six kids and a dog when they moved out than buy their own.

By the time he taped up the eighth box, it shocked him to see the sun had set. Mongo sat next to his food bowl with an expectant expression on his face, and Petr's stomach announced that breakfast had been many hours earlier. Mongo got two scoops of his usual food, and Ystremski ate some cold leftover casserole with his fingers because he had already packed the silverware.

He dumped his dirty dish in the sink and decided to turn in. The day-long emotional rollercoaster had left him exhausted, and the house was painfully quiet without the thunder of little feet and the laughter of children. Years of service in the ISMC had conditioned Ystremski to grab sleep whenever he could, and he fell into a deep slumber.

A few hours later he opened his eyes, wide awake in the darkness. Mongo snored from the foot of the bed, and Ystremski almost rolled over to go back to sleep when he heard a strange noise.

There's someone in the backyard.

He rolled off the bed and grabbed his kukri from the nightstand next to him and then peeked out the window. There was someone, a man judging by the size, standing in the back yard. He decided to sneak out the front door to see if he could get the drop on him.

He padded through the darkened house, heedless of his bare feet and boxers, and closed the front door with a soft *click*.

Ystremski ignored the rocks and sticks that stabbed at his feet as he crept around the house. All his senses were focused on the backyard, and when he got to the corner, he paused to take in the sights and sounds of the darkness.

When he was satisfied the man was alone, he tensed, ready to leap out and confront him. He took two careful steps across the yard and froze.

"Petr?"

All the tension drained from Ystremski's body when he heard Anders' whisper in the dark. The shadow waved to him.

"Petr, is that you?"

"What the fuck, General?" Ystremski asked as he walked across the yard. "Why are you creeping around my house in the middle of the night?" He brandished the kukri. "It can be dangerous."

A red laser dot blinked on his chest and went out.

"Yeah, it can."

An unseen shooter emerged from the bushes on the other side of the yard and joined Anders and Ystremski.

"Congratulations. You snuck up on a guy who was just sound asleep," Ystremski told the shooter. He looked at Anders. "What's up, General?"

"That was quite a scene at Manpower this morning."

"I got a little carried away at the end."

"I saw Major Fortis at the hospital after."

"Is he okay?"

"Nothing some time can't heal. He's a little confused, but he'll be fine. I hurt his feelings when I told him he was forbidden to contact you or Tanya. Speaking of Tanya, how is she? She looked angry when they left this afternoon."

"You were watching?"

"We've been watching you since last night. Two of my agents sat on the flight right behind her, and we'll maintain surveillance of her and the kids until your mission is over."

"Is that really necessary, General? I feel like you're not telling me the whole story about this mission."

"I don't think it's necessary, Petr, but I don't believe in taking chances. If anybody asks, it's exactly what it looks like. You got divvied and argued with her, and she decided to take the kids to stay with her family for a while."

Ystremski thought for a moment. "What's the next step?"

"You're a former Space Marine who's about to get kicked out of his house. Move your belongings into storage, find a place to live, and visit the employment bureau." He handed Ystremski a slip of paper. "There's a couple places you should look at for apartments. They're cheap. When you get done with all that, go to a bar called Delphine's. It's right down the street from those apartments. Many divvies have passed through Delphine's on their way to the Free Sector, and we believe there is a recruiting organization operating there. Take it slow and let them come to you."

"Do you have someone inside the bar?"

"No, but there will be someone watching from outside."

"Okay, General. Anything else?"

"There's a number on the bottom of that paper. It's a pet foster operation. They'll take good care of Mongo while you're gone."

"It seems like you've thought of everything."

"One more thing. Your code name is Graham. If it becomes necessary to reveal your existence to anyone, you will only be referred to your code name. That's all I have for now. Good job today, and good luck tomorrow."

Ystremski snuck back inside and put his kukri back on the nightstand before he slipped between the sheets. Mongo never stirred.

* * * * *

Chapter Six

The next morning, the moving and storage company arrived at Ystremski's quarters on time. It was obvious from the way they worked that they had plenty of recent experience moving personal property from base housing into storage. When they were finished, Ystremski tried to tip them a few credits for a job well done, but the crew leader refused.

"Thanks, but keep it," he said. "You guys got screwed, and it doesn't seem right to take your money."

Ystremski chuckled at the next item on his mental checklist. Mongo was the least personable dog he'd ever seen, and he wasn't sure what to expect when the van pulled up in front of the house. A diminutive woman climbed out, and Mongo barked like he always did at strangers.

Without hesitation, the woman walked toward him and stopped a few feet away. Mongo's barking went from a warning to confusion to a quiet whimper as she waited for him to finish. Finally, she pulled a treat out of her pocket and held it out. Mongo sniffed the air and turned to look at Ystremski, who was watching from the steps.

"Go ahead," he told the dog.

With his ears down and tail wagging, Mongo accepted the treat and sat down on the sidewalk.

"I'm Elaine Welch," the woman told Ystremski.

"Petr Ystremski. This is our vicious guard dog Mongo."

"He looks vicious," she said as she pulled out another treat. Mongo took it, only this time, he allowed Elaine to scratch his head and ears. "Absolutely terrifying."

After several more minutes of trading treats for scratches, Elaine walked to her van and opened the door. "Come on, Mongo. Let's go meet all the other dogs at the ranch."

Mongo climbed right into the van and perched on the passenger seat as though he'd done it a thousand times.

"Give us a call when you get settled and have a new home for Mongo," Elaine told Ystremski. "He'll be just fine with us."

Ystremski waved as the van pulled away, and Mongo gave him a sad look in return.

Traitor.

Ystremski gathered his duffel bag and suitcase, tossed the keys onto the floor in the now-empty foyer, and pulled the door shut behind him. After a quick cab ride, he arrived at the first address on Anders' list. It was run-down but clean, so he agreed to pay bi-weekly rent and collected keys from the landlord.

The apartment was right around the corner from the government employment bureau, so he headed there to look for a job. It surprised him to see Delphine's right across the street from the office. He almost went there instead but decided that finding a job was more important than having a beer, at least before five o'clock.

Ystremski filled out a mountain of job and skills surveys designed to discover what sort of work he was best suited for and then waited for almost an hour as the system analyzed his responses. Finally, he was summoned in to meet with a job counselor.

"You're well qualified for any position in the physical security field," she said. "There are a few positions open here on Terra Earth, but there's always a need for security officers in the mining colonies."

Ystremski shook his head. "No security work, I'll go crazy."

"Then I'm afraid there's nothing we can do for you right now." She stamped a form and passed it across to him. "Here's your proof of registration with this office. Check back with us once a week to see if anything has opened up, okay?"

"Sure."

Ystremski glanced over the form as he walked outside. "Refused employment offer" was circled. While technically true, it infuriated him, and he wadded up the form and threw it away. He wasn't acting when he scowled as he pushed his way through the heavy door into Delphine's.

* * *

Fortis procrastinated as long as his conscience and morning coffee allowed before he started to survey the ISR building. He began in the team quarters wing where he was staying. The rooms and heads were dusty but otherwise untouched. The galley was in the same condition, so he moved on.

The briefing theater was empty. Someone had removed the holo projectors and white boards. The only things they left behind were the rows of seats bolted to the deck.

The cavernous hangar was as empty as he remembered, but he discovered a storage room next door that he hadn't noticed before. Inside, he found a variety of equipment someone had developed for long-forgotten ISR missions. He opened a trunk and saw it was full of miniature reconnaissance drones, some no larger than a small insect.

There were no controllers or display equipment, but it was interesting to see what ISR engineers had developed. He saw two full sets of autoflage armor and enough components to assemble an early prototype of the Integrated Exoskeletal Battle System, or IEBS, which he'd been testing prior to his most recent deployment to Maltaan.

By then, it was lunch time, so he headed for the chow hall. The massive building had served thousands of Space Marines every day before the drawdown, but like many of the other base facilities, it was functioning far below capacity. The dining areas for enlisted and officers were still separate, but Fortis noted that the officer dining room was partitioned into a much smaller footprint. The tacit pecking order remained: captains and lieutenants on one end, majors in the middle, and colonels clustered at the other, nearest the door that led to the private dining area for generals and admirals.

He got his food and nodded to a couple familiar faces among the captains and lieutenants as he wound his way to the middle of the room. He felt a lot of eyes on him, which he attributed to the bandage on his nose.

Just as Fortis was about to sit at an empty table, a female major waved to him from nearby. When she had his attention, she gestured to an empty seat and smiled.

"Thank you, ma'am," Fortis said as he set his tray down and slid into the chair.

"You don't have to call me ma'am." She touched the gold oak leaf on her chest and extended her hand. "Holly Markovsky."

"Abner Fortis."

Her hand was warm and soft, and Fortis held it for a beat too long. His face blushed, and he chuckled self-consciously.

"Sorry. I'm not used to being a major."

"It's been a whole day."

Fortis didn't know how to respond.

"I handled your file," Markovsky said by way of explanation. "I work in Manpower."

"Ah, I see. Tough place to work these days."

"It's a lot easier now. I was trying to get back to a mech battalion when the drawdown started. That sucked."

A knot of generals emerged from the private dining area. One of them made a loud remark, and her comrades laughed as they exited the facility. The entire room had fallen silent until they were gone.

"We divvied seven active divisions. Over forty-thousand Space Marines. Do you know how many generals we cut?" Markovsky asked.

Fortis shrugged. "I don't know. Ten?"

"Two." She held up two fingers and ticked them off. "One of them was under investigation for financial irregularities, and the other was about to be fired anyway. Can you believe that?" As she spoke, her face had darkened.

"They kept me, and I'm missing a leg, and I've been court martialed. Anything is possible." Fortis tried to keep his comment light.

"They're hogs. They feed at the government trough until they're nice and fat, and then they waddle off to high-paying jobs while the average Space Marine gets screwed."

Fortis nodded but said nothing.

Markovsky smiled, and her entire expression changed. "I'm sorry. I shouldn't have gotten started, but it makes me so damned mad sometimes. How has your first day on the General Staff been so far?"

Now it was Fortis' turn to smile. "Supercharged with excitement. I've been tasked with surveying a vacant building and inventorying the contents. A thrill a minute. It beats not having a job, I guess."

"DINLI."

"DINLI, indeed."

* * *

Ystremski saw a knot of men at the end of the bar and others grouped in ones and twos at small tables around the room. Nobody seemed to notice Ystremski, so he slid onto an empty bar stool and dug out some credits.

"Beer, please. Whatever is on tap," he told the bartender. "Make it a short one."

"You look like you've had a tough day," the bartender said as he put a half-pint glass in front of Ystremski.

"Yeah. I got divvied yesterday, and things aren't going so well."

"Oh, well, in that case." The bartender turned around and rang a brass bell mounted on the wall behind the bar. "We've got another divvie, gents."

The men at the end of the bar surrounded Ystremski, smiling and jostling each other.

"Welcome to the club," the largest man said. "My name is Gilliam. Miles Gilliam."

"Petr Ystremski."

The two men shook hands, and the rest of the group introduced themselves.

"What brings you to Delphine's, Petr?"

"Like I told the bartender, I got divvied yesterday. I spent the rest of the day fighting with my wife, and then she left with the kids. I went down to the employment bureau, and they told me I could be a guard at a mine."

Gilliam gave him a sympathetic smile. "Well, you're among friends here, Petr. We're all divvies of one flavor or another. Where did you serve?"

"I've been stuck on Maltaan for the last six months while they tried to figure out who to pin that clusterfuck on. Before that, I was with Second Division. Spent a bunch of time in the Fleet hospital fighting the Maltaani mushrooms."

"You get wounded during the invasion?"

"Yeah, I got radiation sickness when a nuke went off at the space port. I got the mushrooms when a Maltaani fucker stuck me with a sword before I aerated his skull with my kukri."

Gilliam laughed. "Well, hot damn! Hey, you guys, Petr is a twice-wounded combat vet and earned his crimson cord, and the Corps still divvied him."

The group jeered and groaned.

"The peace dividend fucked over a lot of good Space Marines," Gilliam said. He waved to the bartender. "Hey Steve, get my friend Petr a shot of that DINLI you're hiding back there."

Ystremski shook his head. "Miles, I appreciate the offer, but I'm not much of a drinker."

"Nah, it'll be okay. Just one."

Steve the bartender slid two shots in front of the men. Gilliam raised his in a toast to Ystremski.

"DINLI, and fuck 'em."

"DINLI, and fuck 'em," the group responded. Ystremski threw down the shot.

Conversations swirled among the group, and it didn't take Ystremski long to figure out what they were up to.

The men approached in turn, smiled, and tapped glasses or raised theirs in toast, expecting him to follow suit. Had he kept their pace, he would have become quite drunk before they peppered him with questions about his service. Where had he been? Did he know Sergeant So-and-so? What did he think of this bar or that bar? Ystremski answered their questions and tried to work in a few of his own, but they were skilled at deflecting the attention back to him. They were definitely feeling him out and collecting information.

Gilliam approached and stuck out his hand. "Petr, it was a pleasure to meet you. Unfortunately, tomorrow comes too early, and I need to get to bed. I'll leave your care and feeding to these heathens."

"Yeah, I think I'll go—oh," Ystremski said as a full drink was pushed into his hand. "I guess I'm staying for one more."

The group laughed and went back to plying Ystremski with alcohol and prying into his past. He finished his drink and waved off another.

"Thanks for the offer, but I have to go, seriously. I need to get up early and continue the job hunt." He managed to disengage from the group with promises to come back again soon and stepped outside.

It wasn't much cooler on the street, but Ystremski was grateful to be out of the stuffy bar. He sighed and started down the broken sidewalk toward his empty apartment.

* * * * *

Chapter Seven

Mindful of the need to look like any other unemployed divvie, Ystremski returned to the employment bureau first thing in the morning. He filled out some more questionnaires and waited. Finally, he was called to the window.

"Mr. Ystremski, it says here you refused an offer of employment," the pinch-faced man behind the glass said.

"Not exactly," Ystremski said. "They offered me a security position at a mining colony somewhere, and I asked for anything besides security."

"Hmm. Well, office policy is that once you refuse an offer, we adjust your case priority. I'm afraid the earliest I can offer you a new position is three days from now."

Ystremski's face flushed and he fought the urge to yank the man through the little hole in the glass. Even though he didn't truly need the job, the man's callous adherence to policy infuriated him.

"I'll be back."

Ystremski stalked out of the building and checked the time. Although it was early, he decided to stop in Delphine's for a quick beer.

The bar was empty except for Steve the bartender, who didn't look like he'd moved from the spot he'd been standing in when Ystremski first saw him the night before.

"Hiya, Petr," the bartender greeted him. "The usual?"

"Uh, yeah. If you mean a short beer, then yes."

"Still drinking those diet beers." Steve smiled as he gave Ystremski a glass. "You know it doesn't count if you order short ones and drink twice as many."

"One is usually my limit," Ystremski said. "Last night was an exception."

Steve shook his head as he dried his hands on his apron. "You were entitled, after the day you had. How's it going today?"

"Steve, do you have any idea where I can get some work? I just left the employment bureau, and they won't even talk to me for another three days because I didn't accept their offer of a security guard job in some far-flung asshole of the galaxy. I know I was just an infantry gunny, but that's got to count for something more than walking around with a flashlight and a clipboard, doesn't it?"

"I'd love to help you, Petr. I really would, but I'm lucky to have this job. You guys are getting screwed, that's for sure."

"Ah, fuck it. I'm gonna go home." Ystremski drained his glass and stood up. He dug in his pocket for some credits, but Steve waved him off.

"First one is on the house."

"I appreciate it, Steve. Maybe I'll see you later."

The bartender smiled. "I'm always here."

* * *

When Ystremski got back to his apartment, he found a small package by the front door. After a quick examination, he decided it wasn't a bomb, so he unwrapped it. It was an unmarked communicator, the kind people used when they wanted to remain anonymous. He suspected it was from

Anders, and his suspicion was confirmed when it rang, and he recognized Anders' voice.

"No names," Anders said. "How's it going?"

"Good. I struck out at the employment bureau and made a couple new friends."

"Any leads?"

"None yet, but I planted some seeds. Maybe they'll sprout."

"Okay. Save this number as 'Uncle Ivan,' your mother's brother, except spell his name with a capital I and a capital V. The communicator will ring me around the clock, and I will answer as your uncle. If you're free to talk, say, 'Uncle Ivan, it's your nephew, Petr.' If you say anything else, I will assume someone is listening."

"Uncle Ivan, it's your nephew, Petr."

"Perfect. The communicator has a locator beacon inside. If you leave it on, we can track you to within five meters anywhere on Terra Earth."

"What about off-planet? You're still expecting me to go down range, right?"

"It will work anywhere we have coverage. It just depends on where you go."

"How long will the battery last?"

"Ten Terra days without recharge. It will contact charge anywhere you can find some stray voltage."

"Roger that. Any other instructions?"

"Not right now. Keep doing what you're doing, and we'll see where it leads."

* * *

After a couple hours alternating between pacing and staring out the window, Ystremski decided to return to Delphine's. He was mindful of Anders' advice to go slow and let the recruiters come to him, but he wanted to get the mission moving. If the general was wrong, and there was no recruiting going on at the bar, or they decided to take a pass on Ystremski, he wanted to find out sooner rather than later.

When Ystremski pushed his way through the door into Delphine's, he saw Gilliam and the others gathered at the end of the bar. They called a greeting and waved for him to join them. After introductions to a couple unfamiliar faces, he sensed something had changed. The group seemed more at ease around him, and the round-robin interrogation was replaced by the kind of crude, profane, and sometimes pornographic banter one would expect in a bar full of combat veterans.

"Steve said you're looking for work," Gilliam said after he and Ystremski drifted away from the main group.

"I went to the employment bureau today, if you want to call that looking for work."

"How did you make out?"

Ystremski looked at Gilliam and scoffed. "How do you think I did? I'm an unemployed trigger puller, just like thirty thousand other unemployed trigger pullers. The counselor suggested I think about becoming a security officer at a mining colony, and when I told her no thanks, she noted that I refused an employment offer. Now they won't talk to me for three days. What the fuck kind of system is that?"

Gilliam put a hand on his shoulder. "I know how you feel. We've all been through it."

Ystremski didn't respond. It felt like Gilliam had more to say, but instead, the two men stood in silence and drank their beers. By then, the group had migrated in their direction, and Ystremski found himself swapping jokes and stories.

"I gotta go, guys," Gilliam announced. "Early day tomorrow."

After Gilliam was gone and the razzing subsided, Ystremski decided to leave as well. None of the other men seemed interested in anything other than drinking themselves stupid, and Ystremski felt his patience wearing thin.

He was halfway down the block when a voice called his name. A dark figure detached from the shadows across the street.

"Petr Ystremski."

Ystremski turned and braced for an attack. The figure got closer, and he was joined by another who stood close behind.

"Who the fuck are you?"

The pair stopped three meters away.

"My name is Arthur Booth. You've met my associate, Miles Gilliam."

Gilliam gave a half-wave.

"What do you want?"

"I have a proposal for you."

Booth and Gilliam led Ystremski to a small house set back off the main street across from Delphine's. They didn't turn the lights on until the door was shut, and when they did, Ystremski saw heavy blackout curtains over the windows. Booth motioned to the only furniture visible on the first floor, a table and chairs in the middle of the room. Ystremski slid a chair around so he could see the front door and the doorway that led deeper into the house.

"Drink?" Booth offered. He was dressed in a neat black suit with a white shirt and deep red tie, and his blue eyes glittered under curly greyish bangs.

"No thanks."

"Good. We view temperance as something worth striving for."

"Do you want to tell me what this is all about?" Ystremski demanded. He was mildly annoyed by Booth's slick attitude, and he let some of his annoyance creep into his voice. "I view getting home and getting a good night's sleep as something worth striving for."

Gilliam stifled a laugh, and Booth smiled. "Plain-spoken and direct. I like it." Booth took a chair opposite Ystremski. "Petr, what do you know about the Kuiper Knights?"

Ystremski thought for a second. "Religious fanatics. My platoon killed a few of them on Eros-28 and blew up their drug lab. Why?"

Booth and Gilliam traded looks. "We are Kuiper Knights," Booth said.

"You don't look like Kuiper Knights." Ystremski touched his cheek. "Where are your scars?"

"Things have changed in the Knighthood, Petr. We no longer require dueling for advancement. And yes, we are devout in our beliefs, but we're hardly fanatics. I'm familiar with the Knights you fought on Eros-28. It was an unfortunate situation. All I can say is that Mikel Chive and his followers allowed personal greed and ambition to blind them, and it cost them."

Ystremski snorted at the memory of Fortis gutting Chive with his kukri. "I'll say." He shrugged. "What's this got to do with me?"

"Like I said, the Knighthood has changed. Since the Budgetary Realignment Act, we've become more involved in mutual aid for our brothers and sisters who the UNT treated so poorly. A lot of people are hurting, financially and emotionally, and we want to help. Join our order, and we can provide you with meaningful work more suited to your skills and experience than a mere watchman in a remote mining colony."

"What kind of work?"

Booth spread his hands. "I can't get into specifics without some kind of commitment from you, but I promise your leadership and operational experience won't go to waste in the Kuiper Knighthood. Nobody is going to help us build our future, so we're helping ourselves."

Ystremski considered Booth and Gilliam for a long moment.

"I have a family. Well, I *had* a family. I'm not sure what I have, now."

"You would have to leave them here on Terra Earth, at first, anyway. Eventually, our brothers will be allowed to send for their families."

"And where is this again?"

Booth smiled. "That's one of the specifics I can't go into right now." He slid his chair back and stood. "Give it some thought, Petr. This is an opportunity to get your life back on track." He offered his hand, and they shook. "I'm going to leave you and Miles to talk. He might be able to better describe what the Kuiper Knighthood can do for you, since he was in your exact situation a few months ago."

After Booth was gone, Ystremski turned to Gilliam.

"Is he for real?"

Gilliam's eyes gleamed with excitement.

"Petr, every word of it is true. The Knighthood is real, and we're looking out for ourselves and forging our future. After Fleet divvied me, I was in your exact situation—unemployed, wife and kids, no real future. I had almost given in to the demons in my head when I met Booth, then everything changed. The Knighthood has given me purpose and a reason to get out of bed every day—"

"And a paycheck?" Ystremski interjected.

Gilliam nodded. "And a paycheck. It's not much right now, but I can see the potential. Plus, I get to help guys like you. Guys like us."

"You want me to be a recruiter?"

"No, not a recruiter. Like Booth said, your knowledge and experience won't go to waste." He lowered his voice to a conspiratorial tone and looked around the empty room. "Just between us, I wasn't a trigger puller. I was a Fleet Logistics Specialist aboard the flagship *Giant*. When the ISMC retired Seventh Division, *Giant* went into salvage orbit with the rest of her fleet, and they divvied the crew. The employment bureau offered me a job as a clerk on a deep space resupply vessel preparing to make a three-year lap around the galaxy."

"Fuck that."

"Damn right, fuck that. I went from moving millions of credits worth of parts and equipment around the fleet to wondering where my next meal was going to come from. I had stopped at Delphine's to drink enough courage to end it all when Booth found me."

"Huh. That was close."

"Two days after we talked, the Kuiper Knights inducted me and assigned me to recruiting duties." Gilliam chuckled. "It's not logistics, but I get to hang around in bars all the time, so it's not all bad."

"Can I think about it? It's a big decision."

"Sure thing, Petr. Take a couple days, talk it over with Tanya, and see if it sounds like something you'd be interested in."

Ystremski and Gilliam left the vacant house and went their separate ways. As Ystremski walked toward his apartment, one thought tumbled in his mind.

How did he know Tanya's name?

* * * * *

Chapter Eight

Fortis' psyche eval appointment was on the twenty-second floor of the Kinshasa Professional Building, the second-tallest building in the city. He was drawn to the window of the waiting area and surveyed the sprawling city while he waited to be called.

When he was shown into the doctor's office, it surprised him to be greeted by a pleasant looking woman in a neat pantsuit seated behind a desk. He had expected someone much older, with a thick accent and a tweed jacket with patches on the elbow.

"Please sit down, Mr. Fortis." The doctor reached across the desk and they shook hands. "I'm Doctor Branson."

Doctor Branson referred to the file opened on the desk in front of her. "Have there been any changes to your physical condition since you were last assessed aboard the hospital ship *Solicitude*?"

Fortis touched the bandage on his nose. "Broken nose, but that's it."

"How did that happen?"

"A friend of mine got some bad news and didn't take it well."

"Hmm." She closed the folder. "You're here for a pre-command psychological assessment?"

"Yes ma'am."

"Why don't you tell me a little about yourself?"

Fortis told the doctor about his upbringing, his university experience, and his impulsive decision to join the ISMC. She listened carefully but didn't interrupt except to ask an occasional question. Fortis was usually reticent to discuss his personal affairs, but Branson had an interviewing style that made her easy to talk to.

He talked about his experiences in the Corps, from his cherry drop on Pada-Pada to the sequestration on Maltaan during the investigation. With gentle prompting, Fortis told her about the heroics of the Space Marines he had served with and his feelings about their sacrifices.

"You think their service was in vain?"

Fortis shook his head. "No. I mean, in the grand scheme of things, nothing was changed by their deaths, so in that sense, yes, they died in vain. Still, they died to save other Marines, sometimes me, so they didn't die in vain, if me and the other survivors carry on and give their sacrifices meaning."

They delved into his feelings about the ISMC bureaucracy that often seemed to work against the Space Marines in the field, and he became animated, almost angry, as he described the situation surrounding his osseointegrated leg and his desire to return to the infantry.

"If it wasn't for General Anders, I would have separated long ago," he said. "I'm not going to stay in the Corps and drive a desk for a living. That's the life for office drones, not me."

She raised her eyebrows and smiled as she placed her hand on the desk, and Fortis broke into self-conscious laughter.

"That's not what I meant," he said as his face flushed.

"I know, Abner. I chose this work because I enjoy it, but it's not for everyone."

When she brought the interview to an end, it shocked him to see that three hours had passed since they started.

"So, am I crazy?"

Doctor Branson laughed. "You are definitely not crazy. I would say that you're well-adjusted considering your operational tempo and the situations you've encountered. In my professional opinion, you are prepared for the challenges of command. That said, I encourage you to find a therapist that you can trust to periodically discuss some of the things we talked about today. It can be helpful to unburden oneself instead of bottling all those emotions inside."

Fortis left her office and waited for the elevator with several other people, including a tall, thin man with grey hair in a cheap sports coat who smelled faintly of pipe tobacco. He laughed inside as he followed the group into the elevator.

"Doctor?"

A young man in a red shirt stuck his hand in the door. "I need to talk to you, Doctor," he said to the grey-haired man.

"Mr. Zeiler, we've already spoken."

"But I need to talk to you." A vein stood out on the neck of the man in red, and sweat beads broke out on his forehead.

"Take your hand off the door, Adam. Your appointment is over, and you're holding everyone up."

Zeiler drew a ballistic pistol from under his shirt, pointed it at the doctor's face, and squeezed the trigger.

Boom!

The sound of the shot in the confines of the elevator momentarily deafened Fortis, and he flinched as blood and gore spattered him. The other people in the elevator screamed and ducked as the doctor went down, half in and half out of the elevator. The bullet had punched a hole in his face and left a crater where the back of his head used to be. By the time Fortis could react, the man in red was gone.

"Call a doctor!" someone shouted.

"Too late for that," Fortis said as he exited the elevator. "Which way did he go?"

A terrified woman pointed to the emergency stairwell, and Fortis followed. He heard noise above him and sunlight flooded the stairwell as a door at the top banged open.

Fortis stepped through the door that led to the roof and stopped. A dense haze squatted over the city and blocked the punishing afternoon sun, but it trapped the stifling sub-Saharan humidity. His neck blossomed with sweat as he looked around until he spotted the man in the red shirt. The man sat on the wall that bordered the edge of the roof with his back to the door, and he didn't move when Fortis allowed the door to slam shut.

"Hey," Fortis called.

The man in red didn't react.

"Hey, can you help me out?"

The man looked over his shoulder. When he saw Fortis, he swiveled around and straddled the wall. Fortis caught sight of the pistol the man cradled in his lap and stopped with his hands held out by his sides.

"What do you want?"

"I'm hoping you can help me understand what's going on."

The man shook his head. "There's nothing to understand."

"Sure, there is." Fortis took a couple steps forward but stopped when the pistol came up. He knew without being told that the man was a fellow Space Marine. "Brother, I'm not looking for trouble."

"If you keep coming at me, you're going to find it."

"Hey, look. My name is Abner. What's yours?"

"I know who you are. Everyone knows who you are."

Fortis shrugged. "I don't know. I guess. I still don't know who you are."

The man considered Fortis for a long second. "Zeiler. Adam Zeiler."

"Good to meet you, Adam. Where did you serve?"

"Ha'aka Ro, Demouli-4." Zeiler scowled. "Maltaan, of course."

"I haven't been to Ha'aka Ro or Demouli-4. Bug hunts?"

"What else?"

Fortis heard the wail of distant sirens, and he knew he was running out of time.

"I've spent enough time on Maltaan to last me a lifetime," Fortis said.

"You and me both, bro."

"DINLI."

Zeiler nodded but said nothing.

Fortis gestured to the wall next to Zeiler. "You mind if I sit down?" He patted his right leg. "Fake leg."

Zeiler tilted his chin further down the wall. "You can sit over there. Not too close."

Fortis sat down facing Zeiler and looked out over the city. The sirens had grown louder, and he could see flashing lights several blocks away.

"Adam, what was all that about back there? In the elevator, I mean."

Zeiler shook his head and looked at the pistol in his lap. "I dunno. Fuckin' doctor... I just... had enough, I guess."

"I know how that feels. Still—"

"What the fuck do you know?" Zeiler demanded. "You don't know shit. Fuckin' war hero has everyone kissing your ass, and you think you know how I feel?" Zeiler's face darkened, and he brandished his weapon. "What are you doing up here, anyway? Leave me alone and let the tac squad deal with me."

"That's not the way, and you know it," Fortis said. "I can't leave."

Zeiler scoffed. "It's your funeral."

The sirens echoed through the canyons created by the tall buildings of downtown Kinshasa, and Fortis saw several tac squad cars stop in front of the Kinshasa Professional Building.

"Tell me what this is about, and maybe I can help," Fortis urged. "It's not too late to stop it."

"You can't help me. Nobody can." Zeiler's chin sank to his chest, and he gave a ragged sob.

In Fortis' mind, he saw heavily armed tac officers race into the building and begin the search for the shooter.

There's still time.

"They're coming, Adam. Let me help you."

Zeiler jumped to his feet, and Fortis got a sudden rush of fear when he thought the distraught man was going to jump. Instead, Zeiler balanced atop the wall and looked at the city around them.

"Are you going to bring my wife and kids back?" he demanded. "Are you gonna go to Manitoba and put them on a plane?" Zeiler began to pace. "Are you going to give me a fucking job?"

"I don't know," Fortis said. "Maybe. I know that none of that can happen if you don't stop what you're doing right now."

Fortis knew it wouldn't take the tac squad long to zero in on their location, and even if they cleared each floor on the way up, they would appear on the roof in a few minutes.

Zeiler jumped down and sat on the wall next to Fortis. "How about some fucking sleep?" Tears leaked down his cheeks, and Fortis saw the dark circles and heavy bags under his eyes. "These doctors. They gave me pills, but they don't do shit about the dreams. My guys…" He blinked. "You don't know what it's like."

"I know what it's like. They come to me every night," Fortis said. His throat was dry and tight, and his voice came out in a croak. He cleared his throat. "Every fucking night."

Zeiler looked puzzled, and Fortis nodded.

"Yeah. That's right. What do you think I'm doing here? My shrink is on the twenty-second floor, just like yours. Every night, dead Space Marines come to me. Hundreds of them. That's why I'm here."

"You? You're Abner Fortis. Why would *you* need a shrink?"

"I'm not special."

Fortis felt raw from his marathon session with Doctor Branson, and a sudden rush of tears threatened to spill down his cheeks. Fortis blinked them away, snorted, and spat over the edge.

"I thought I had everything under control," he admitted to Zeiler. "I pushed it all away for so long that I thought nothing could touch me. Then Petr… ah fuck." He took a deep breath and wiped his eyes. "My best friend. Stabbed through the guts by a fucking Maltaani." Fortis shook his head. "I thought he was dead. It's been a year and a half, and sometimes it seems like yesterday."

"Hey man, it's okay." Zeiler approached and put a sympathetic hand on Fortis' shoulder. "I'm sorry your friend died."

Fortis wiped his eyes again. "He's not dead. That old bastard is too tough to die." He chuckled, and Zeiler joined him.

"Geez. I thought he died," Zeiler said.

The two Space Marines sat in silence for a moment.

"Do you think the therapy helped?" Zeiler asked.

Fortis nodded. "Yeah. Yeah, it did. We can't change the past, but unloading it helps."

"A grunt can take anything life throws at him. DINLI."

"Listen to you, dispensing advice," Fortis said with a smile. He nodded toward the stairwell. "The police are going to bust through that door any second now. Do you really want to greet them with a pistol?"

"You were on the elevator. Will it make a difference?"

Fortis flashed back to the grisly scene in the elevator. He nodded.

"Yeah, I was on the elevator, and yeah, I think it'll make a difference. You want to go out like this?"

"There are worse ways." Zeiler stood up.

"Adam, seriously, don't do this." Fortis also stood and took two steps back. If the tac squad came through the door and Zeiler started shooting, he wanted some separation. "Is this how you want people to remember you?"

Zeiler nodded. "I blew that doctor's brains out. How else do you think they'll remember me?" He stared at the pistol in his hand. "This is all I have left."

The stairwell door slammed open. A team of tacs clad in body armor with automatic pulse rifles at the ready poured onto the roof. A hundred voices shouted commands at Zeiler.

"Drop it!"

"Hands! Let me see your hands!"

"Get down!"

"Do it now!"

Zeiler looked at Fortis, and Fortis saw his fear and confusion. Something else flashed across his face.

Betrayal.

"No!" Fortis shouted.

Blue-white energy bolts punched into Zeiler's body, and he staggered backward toward the edge of the roof. His heels hit the wall, and momentum carried him over the edge and out of sight.

Fortis found himself staring at the business ends of a dozen pulse rifles, and he froze. He raised his hands high overhead and sank to his knees as the tacs swarmed him.

* * *

"And that's when your guys showed up and gave me this," Fortis said through the bloody towel he had pressed to his new fat lip.

The chief inspector, who had taken Fortis' statement four times in the last five hours, examined his notes as if the answer to an ancient riddle were written there.

"You didn't know Zeiler?" It was an accusation disguised as a question.

"I never met him before."

"And he didn't tell you why he murdered the victim in the elevator?"

"No. Like I told you, Zeiler said he had just had enough. He didn't explain."

The inspector put his notebook down. "Why did you follow him to the roof? I know you Space Marines are supposed to be tough, but it's kind of foolish to chase a homicidal maniac armed with a gun, when you didn't even have a pen knife."

Fortis thought for a second. The simple truth was that Space Marines didn't leave anyone behind, but he knew the tac squad would never understand that. The inspector had said Fortis could have secured the door and waited for them to arrive, and the result would have been the same. It was true, but it wasn't right.

"I don't know," Fortis said. "I guess I was looking for an opening to try and stop him before he hurt anyone else."

"Okay, Mr. Fortis." The chief inspector hauled himself to his feet. "That's all I have for you right now. In the future, leave law enforcement to the professionals, okay?"

* * *

Fortis debated calling Anders that night or waiting until the following morning, but the buzz of his communicator made the decision for him.

"What the hell happened on that roof?" Anders demanded.

Fortis recounted his attempt to help Adam Zeiler. He choked up when he got to the part where he described Zeiler going off the roof. "They didn't have to kill him."

"It wasn't going to end any other way, Abner. I read the report. He murdered a doctor and was intent on killing himself."

"You read the report already?"

"Word gets around fast when a member of the General Staff is involved in something like this. You might want to keep that in mind."

"Yes sir. I don't know what the report says, but I think he would have surrendered if the tacs had given him a chance."

"We'll never know. It's not your job to rescue every fucked up divvie, Abner. Your job is a helluva lot more important than one man."

Fortis felt his face flush, but he fought back the urge to respond.

"How did your assessment with Dr. Branson go?"

"You haven't read the report yet?" The words were out before Fortis could stop them.

"Actually, I have, but I wanted to hear how you thought it went."

"I thought it went okay. I would never have considered talking to someone like her before, but now that I have, I'm glad I did."

"Good. She reported that you are ready for the responsibilities of command. I already knew that, but the assessment is a wicket we all have to pass through. I'll caution you to remember that you're on the big stage now. It's one thing to make it up as you go along as a platoon leader on Pada-Pada, but quite another while you're on the General Staff here on Terra Earth."

"Understood, sir."

"Now that that's out of the way, how's your survey coming?"

Fortis updated Anders on the progress he'd made in the ISR building. The general chuckled when he described the trunk load of reconnaissance drones.

"We had some fun with those before the invasion," he said. "I don't think you got a chance to use them. Someday, maybe."

A twinge of guilt tugged at Fortis as he considered his next words. "General, there's something else I'd like to talk about. We briefly touched on the idea that there may be some within the ISMC who aren't one hundred percent loyal. Do you have any more thoughts on that?"

"I have my suspicions. News reports containing information that is only available within the Corps, that sort of thing. Why?"

"At lunch yesterday, I met an officer from Manpower. Major Holly Markovsky. She has some strong opinions about the drawdown that she wasn't afraid to share." He described the scene with the generals in the mess hall. "I'm not making any accusations, but if her opinions are prevalent in the ranks, I'd say your suspicions are accurate."

"The name doesn't ring any bells, but I'll have her checked out. Thanks for the tip."

* * * * *

Chapter Nine

Ystremski was up early the following morning. After a quick shower, he crossed the street to a little deli squeezed between two retail stores. He ordered coffee and a breakfast sandwich and watched people and traffic go by while he ate.

A stranger slid into the seat across from him. "Hi, Cousin Graham. Uncle Ivan says hello."

Ystremski scanned the street but didn't see anything that looked out of place. Nobody loitered in a reflective storefront or a vehicle stopped at the curb.

"Who are you?"

"I'm a friend of Uncle Ivan. He couldn't come in person, but he wanted to know how things went last night after Delphine's."

"Miles Gilliam and a guy named Arthur Booth approached me and pulled me into a little place over by the bar. They tried to recruit me into the Kuiper Knights. Are they part of all this?"

"That's not for me to say. Maybe Uncle Ivan can confirm that."

"Yeah, sure. Anyway, they gave me a soft sell about the Kuiper Knights. The Knights are all about mutual aid and taking care of their own these days. They said if I joined the Knighthood, they'll give me a job suited to my knowledge and experience."

"What kind of job?"

"Booth wouldn't say. He said he couldn't get into specifics until I commit to the Knighthood, but it's off-Terra, and it sounds operational."

"What did you tell them?"

"I said I had to think about it and talk to my wife. Which reminds me—that Gilliam guy pretty much confirmed they've got somebody inside looking at personnel files. They questioned me closely the first night, but I never told them my wife's name. Last night, he told me to take some time with my decision and talk it over with Tanya."

"Okay, well, do what they say. Take some time to think about it before you accept their offer."

"Should I call Uncle Ivan?" Ystremski asked.

"Not necessary, unless you want to. He's up north handling some other details, but he wanted me to check in with you and see what's new." The man stood up. "It's been great catching up, Cousin Graham, but I have to get going. Be safe out there, and I'll see you again real soon."

Before Ystremski could respond, the man vanished into the crowd of people walking on the sidewalk. He shook his head.

Fuckin' spooks.

* * *

Ystremski avoided Delphine's and canvassed the city around his apartment for jobs and familiar faces. He stopped at a bar that he knew Space Marines frequented back in the day, but the door was locked, and a hand-lettered sign announced it was closed until further notice. As he walked, he took note of the many businesses that catered to Space Marines which had gone out of business. It wasn't just bars and whorehouses; he saw tattoo parlors, tailor shops, laundries, and fast-food joints shut down, too. Kinshasa had been home away from home for thousands of Space Marines through the years, and now this section of the city was fading away just like the Corps had.

A wave of sadness washed over him as he stopped and stared at a faded sign that read, "Gunny Pete's" hanging over a boarded-up storefront. Gunny Pete's had been a place where a down-on-his-luck Space Marine could get a cheap meal and a bunk with clean sheets between paydays for over one hundred years. The original Gunny Pete had willed the place to another retired Space Marine before he died, and ownership had been handed down from generation to generation. In the twenty years Ystremski had served, it had never changed.

"It's a goddamn shame, innit?"

He turned and saw an elderly man leaning on a cane next to him. The man had wrinkled skin and a bulbous nose covered in broken veins, and his clothes were wrinkled and worn.

"I had my first taste of DINLI as a buck private in that place," the old man continued. "My first woman, too."

Ystremski nodded. "It's a shame, all right. This whole part of the city is dying."

"Me, too." The old man held out his hand. "Sam Hart. Sergeant, retired."

"Petr Ystremski. Gunnery sergeant, divvied."

The strength in Sam's grip surprised Ystremski, and the old man grinned at the look on his face.

"None of this strength enhancement shit in my day, Petr. We earned it the hard way."

Ystremski laughed, and he felt a rush of affection for the old timer. He looked up and down the street.

"I was going to get something to eat. Care to join me, Sam? I could use the company. It's on me until my paycheck runs out."

"Ah, I'm not hungry, but if you offer me a drink, I wouldn't say no."

"Okay, then, let's find somewhere we can get both. Any suggestions?"

Hart led the way to a small place crouched next to a boarded-up jeweler.

"Does this place have a name?" Ystremski asked as he followed Hart inside.

"It used to be Molly's, but Molly died. I don't know what they call it now," Hart said as he bellied up to the bar.

Ystremski looked around as he slid onto the next barstool. Someone had painted the walls and ceiling black, and the rays of sunlight that peeked through the window shades died before they made it too far into the place. The bar top was scarred with burn marks, and the place smelled like stale beer, vomit, and desperation.

"I gotta take a leak." Hart slipped off his barstool and disappeared into the back.

"Why the fuck did you bring that old freeloader here?" The bartender stood behind the bar and polished a glass with a filthy rag.

"We're just looking for a beer and something to eat. I'm paying."

The bartender scoffed. "He suckered you, my friend," he said as he put two beers on the bar in front of Ystremski. "He owes me so much that I shouldn't even let him drink in here on your dime."

"How much does he owe?"

The bartender pulled out a small notebook and opened it on the bar. "Two hundred and eight credits." He spun the ledger around and stabbed at it with a dirty fingernail. "It's right there."

Ystremski shrugged. Two hundred and eight credits would put a serious dent in his funds, but he was in a nostalgic mood. He pulled out his card.

"Take it off of this," he said. "Sam said you serve food here. What's on the menu?"

Ystremski ordered four hotdogs and sipped his beer. Hart returned and sat next to him. He picked up his beer and held it up in salute.

"Here's to you, Petr."

"Here's to you, Sam."

They clinked their bottles and took deep drinks. By the time they finished, the bartender had returned with Ystremski's card and a tray of steaming hotdogs.

"Here you go, sucker," he said before he walked away.

"What the fuck's his problem?" Hart asked through a mouthful of hotdog.

"I don't know." Ystremski stuck his card back in his pocket. He sipped his beer and hid a smile as Hart plowed through the hotdogs.

Hart washed them down with a swig of his beer and let out a burp.

"Those hotdogs didn't stand a chance against somebody who wasn't hungry."

"Sorry. I guess it's been a while since I ate."

The door banged open, and three men entered the bar. They were a rough-looking lot, with lots of tattoos and facial jewelry, and there was a predatory air about them.

"Ah, fuck," said Sam as he ducked down on his stool and tried to look inconspicuous.

"What's wrong?"

The old man shook his head. "These fuckers—"

"Hey! Pops!" The leader of the trio stopped next to Hart. "I thought we told you not to come back until you could pay your bill."

Hart didn't answer, so the man slapped him on the shoulder.

"I'm talking to you, geezer."

"What's your problem?" Ystremski asked. "Why don't you leave him alone?"

"This bum owes the place a lot of credits, and he ain't supposed to be in here until he pays."

Ystremski pointed to the bartender. "How much does he owe?"

"Uh, nothing. His tab is clear, Billy."

Hart looked at Ystremski with surprise on his face, but Ystremski stayed focused on Billy and his companions.

"You heard the man. His tab is clear, so fuck off."

A confused expression crossed Billy's face as he looked back at his cohorts. "Who the fuck paid the tab?" he asked the bartender.

"I did, you dumb sonofabitch," Ystremski said as he slid off his barstool. "Now, what part of 'fuck off' didn't you understand?"

Billy leaped forward and tried to grab Ystremski, but he telegraphed the attack. Ystremski sidestepped Billy's hands and used his momentum to throw the bigger man to the floor. The other two men charged and grappled with him. The trio crashed into one of the booths, and the table collapsed under them.

By then, Billy had gotten back on his feet and tried to get into the fray, but the three combatants were a confused tangle of arms and legs. One of the attackers screamed and rolled free, clutching at his groin. The other one grunted as a series of powerful punches punished his ribs while he struggled to wrestle with Ystremski, and he too scrambled away from the demolished booth. Ystremski climbed to his feet and wiped at the blood streaming from a gash on his forehead.

"You want some more?" he asked Billy.

Billy attacked again, but this time Ystremski couldn't dodge his charge amid the rubble. He tackled Ystremski and drove him back against the wall before he lifted the smaller man to slam him on the ground. Ystremski peppered Billy's kidneys with a series of vicious rabbit punches as he was lifted into the air, and he braced himself for the slam.

A bottle shattered on Billy's head and beer and broken glass sprayed the two men. Billy's grip on Ystremski's waist loosened as he went down on one knee, and the Space Marine slipped away. Hart stood nearby with the remains of a broken beer bottle in his hand.

"Thanks," Ystremski said before he stepped forward and delivered a roundhouse kick to the side of Billy's head. Billy sprawled across the broken table, so Ystremski grabbed two handfuls of his shirt and jerked him into a sitting position.

"Listen here, you piece of shit. Sam Hart is twice the man you'll ever be, and you're going to treat him with respect." He punched Billy in the face but didn't let him fall back down. "If I hear that you or your pals have been mistreating him, I'm going to come back here and put a real beating on you. Do you understand?"

Billy grunted, and Ystremski shoved him to the floor. When he stood, the other two men sprang at him. The three men went down in a heap, but they didn't repeat the mistakes from their last attack. Both men punched and kneed at Ystremski while he scrambled to get some leverage from under the pile. His strength enhancement tipped the balance in Ystremski's favor as he extricated himself from the pile and delivered a series of well-aimed punches at their groins, faces, and abdomens.

When he stood, Hart approached with another beer bottle.

"You don't need that," Ystremski said as he prodded the injured men with his toe. "School's out for these assholes. Lesson learned."

"It's not for them, it's for you."

Ystremski took a long pull from the bottle and reveled in the cold feeling that flooded his body.

"Here. This is for you, too." Hart handed him a damp rag. "Don't worry, I made him give me a clean one."

Ystremski wiped his face, and it surprised him to see the blood. Then he remembered the gash on his forehead.

"How bad is it?"

"I've seen worse," Hart said. "Nothing a stitch or two can't fix."

Ystremski pressed the rag to his head as he and Hart picked their way through the smashed furniture. "Sorry about the mess," he told the bartender, who had remained behind the bar the entire fight. "Put it on Billy's tab."

The two Space Marines laughed at the stares they drew as they walked down the street. Ystremski pointed to a small 24-hour pharmacy.

"Let's stop in there so I can get some glue for this cut."

"You really ought to get stitches," Hart said.

"I don't have money for stitches. Here." Ystremski handed the old man his card. "Get a bottle of antibiotic wash and some glue. That's all I need."

They found a secluded spot and sat down. Hart flushed Ystremski's cut and some fingernail scratches on his neck and laughed when Ystremski gasped at the sting.

"Quit whining, you pussy, or I'll pour some of this in your eyes and give you something to whine about."

"What were you in the Corps?" Ystremski asked as Hart pinched the cut on his forehead shut and applied a thick bead of surgical glue to seal the wound.

"I was a corpsman."

Ystremski chuckled and Hart joined him, and soon both men were laughing uproariously. Passersby stared at the bloody young man and his elderly companion, and the looks they gave the pair made it clear they thought they were insane.

"What's next?" Hart asked.

"I've got some business to take care of," Ystremski said as he stood and rolled his head on his neck to loosen up. "Maybe I'll see you around later."

The old timer looked disappointed. "That sounds good. I'll be around." Hart shook Ystremski's hand and then gripped his arm. "I can't thank you enough for what you did, Petr. Those guys were starting to make things difficult for me."

"Just stay out of that bar, okay?"

"DINLI," Hart said.

"DINLI, indeed."

* * *

Ystremski returned to his apartment and called Uncle Ivan.

"Hi, Uncle Ivan, it's your favorite nephew."

"What's up?" Anders asked.

"I ran into Cousin Cooter this morning, and I got to thinking about you. I'm going to accept that job offer we talked about."

"Good. Our intel indicates there are seven new members scheduled to depart for the Terra Earth Jump Gate tomorrow night. You might make eight, if they move fast."

"Before I go, I was hoping to borrow some credits. Two thousand, maybe?"

"What for?"

"I spent a bunch this morning tying up some loose ends, and I'm almost broke."

"Hmm. Okay, I'll have it transferred to your account."

"Thank you. Hey, you don't know what happens after the jump gate, do you?"

"I don't know. There's a half-dozen crew and resupply ships scheduled to leave in the next thirty-six hours; any one of them could be bound for the Freedom Jump Gate. We'll follow your movements and see which ship you embark. Then we can monitor flight plans when they're filed."

"What about after we launch?"

"There's nothing to stop a vessel from deviating from a flight plan and going wherever they want to go, but we only know of one destination the Kuiper Knights are sending divvies. We're watching traffic through all the gates, so when your ship jumps, we'll know."

"What about the communicator?"

"Charge it and leave it off until you want to transmit your position."

"Got it."

"One more thing. I received a report that one of our former comrades has joined the Kuiper Knights. Sergeant Bender."

"Bender's a Knight? Damn, I thought he was smarter than that."

"He is, but he also has a big chip on his shoulder when it comes to the UNT."

"Bastards. Bender's a good Space Marine."

"You all are."

"How do you want me to handle him, Uncle? He knows a lot more about me than any computer file in Manpower."

"It's inevitable that you will run into some of your comrades from your days in the Corps. I don't know anything about Bender's state of mind these days, so don't confide in him. He's a divvie and so are you. That's as far as it goes right now."

"Roger that."

"That's all I have, Nephew. I'll transfer the credits first thing. Be safe out there."

* * * * *

Chapter Ten

After a quick bite, Fortis decided it was time to holo his mother. He hadn't exactly been avoiding it, but he knew she would pepper him with a hundred unanswerable questions about when he was coming home, how long he would be there, and many other topics.

Since their joint vacation on the Terra Earth Jump Gate, she had expressed a lot more interest in his career and what he was up to with the ISMC. When he was off-Terra, it was easy to put her off with vague talk of upcoming operations because the holos were recorded. On Terra, live, she was relentless.

"Hi, Mom," he said when her face appeared on the screen.

"Abner! How nice to hear from you. Are you on your way home?"

Fortis didn't like to lie to her, but he had to tell her something. "Sorry, Mom, not for another three weeks or so. I got orders to conduct an inspection tour of some of our outposts. It won't take long, and then I've been promised some leave."

"Oh, dear. Well, I suppose that's okay. Your father won't be here, either. He bid on a big dome job on Maltaan, you know, and he's heading straight there to do survey work. It's a shame you missed him."

"Maltaan, eh? Well, there's plenty of work to be done there. I hope he wins the contract."

"Wouldn't it be wonderful if you could go to work for him there? I mean, if you were discharged?"

"Yeah, wouldn't it." Fortis blanched inside. He had joined the ISMC to avoid working for his father as a biodome engineer, and he had no desire to return to Maltaan, either.

After a few more minutes of chitchat about the latest societal news, Fortis managed to bring the call to an end with a promise to holo again soon.

He changed into workout clothes and jogged to the base gym. The ISR building had had an excellent weight room before the invasion, but someone stripped it after the building closed. The Space Marines on Maltaan had set up a serviceable gym that helped pass the time while they were sequestered. Fortis had kept up a regular workout routine until his return to Terra Earth, and his inactivity since had left him feeling restless.

His osseointegrated right leg drew more curious looks than usual as he made his way around the weight room. His artificial leg should have made him a prime target for the budgeteers searching for peace dividends, even if he more than made up for it with his performance. Fortis traded spots with other weightlifters as they grunted and strained under heavy weights, and he soon forgot about everything but the next rep. When he was finished, his arms trembled with fatigue and his heart thundered in his chest, but he felt fantastic. After he cooled down, he said goodbye to the other gym rats and left to head back to the ISR building.

As he jogged along the fence line, he heard a familiar voice.

"Welcome home, stranger."

He saw Liz Sherer, his friend and Terra Network News (TNN) reporter, smiling from the street outside the base.

"Liz! How are you?"

"I'm great. How about you?"

"Never better. What are you doing out there?"

Liz pointed back the way he'd come. "Meet me at the gate, and I'll tell you all about it."

Fortis met her on the sidewalk outside the base.

"Come give an old lady a hug," Liz said.

Fortis hesitated. "I'm a little sweaty," he said by way of apology.

"I don't care," Liz said as she pulled him in tight. "You came by it honestly." She stepped back and inspected his nose. "What happened to your face?"

"I was born this way."

They laughed together as they walked to a wrought iron bench outside the gate. "I got into an altercation my first day home. How have you been?" Fortis asked. "Why are you out here?"

"I lost my military correspondent credentials," Liz said with a sad smile. "I've been divvied."

"What?"

"While the drawdown was going on, the network discovered they had too many military correspondents covering too little military, so they divvied me. It's all right, though. They axed the senior world affairs correspondent and the Grand Council correspondent, too. Replaced us all with fresh faces straight out of university."

"I'm sorry to hear that, Liz. I'm sure the other networks would leap at the chance to have someone like you."

"Hmm, I don't know. It's been two months, and I haven't had a single response to any of my queries. Some of my 'friends' can't even make time to get a drink after hours, if you can believe that. Pricks."

Fortis shook his head but said nothing.

"Speaking of drinks after hours, what are you doing for supper?" Liz asked.

Fortis looked down at his sweaty workout attire. "I haven't looked that far ahead," he said. "I need a shower and a change of clothes, but after that, my schedule is wide open. What do you have in mind?"

"Well, if you dare to be seen in public with yesterday's news, while you're showering, I'll call around and get us a reservation somewhere nice. My treat."

"It would be my honor to have supper with you, but I can't let you pay," Fortis said.

Liz laughed. "Don't worry about it. I still have use of my TNN credit card until the end of the month. It's part of my severance package, and I plan to make them regret it. Make sure you wear a coat and tie."

Fortis scoffed. "I don't have a coat and tie, Liz. I've been on Maltaan for the last six months. I don't even have dress blues. All I have are utilities."

"Whatever you have is good enough, Captain Fortis," Liz declared. "It's time these ingrates are reminded how to treat a war hero."

* * *

As he dressed, it occurred to Fortis that he hadn't corrected Liz when she called him a captain, and he smiled in the mirror at the sight of the oak leaf insignia on his uniform. When he got back to the gate, Liz beamed.

"A major now? Very impressive. I remember when you were a wet-behind-the-ears first lieutenant."

"Thanks," Fortis said with a smile. "They just promoted me."

"Well, you look like a perfect gentleman," she said as she took his arm. "I made reservations at Vue sur la Montagne. It's French for 'Mountain View.'"

"Sounds fancy." Fortis plucked at his clothes. "Are you sure about this?"

"Never more," Liz said as she slid into a waiting taxi. "Between your fame and my fortune, we could wear togas, and they'd let us in."

Liz was right. Neither the doorman nor the maître d' blinked an eye after Liz informed them who their new guests were. They were given a table with a nice view of the Congo River and the agricultural fields beyond.

"Why do they call this place 'Vue sur la Montagne'?" Fortis asked. "I don't see any mountains."

Liz rolled her eyes. "Just go with it, Abner."

The conversation was light while they waited for their drinks. Liz asked after Fortis' parents, and he reciprocated with questions about her many nieces and nephews. Finally, she asked about Ystremski.

"Have you seen Petr since you got back?"

"They divvied him," Fortis said.

"What? When?"

"The day after we got back. We were told to report to Manpower to get our new assignments, and they divvied him." He gestured to his nose. "That's when he did this."

Her eyes widened. "Petr did that?"

"We had heard it was bad back here, but we didn't get a lot of news on Maltaan. What we did get didn't seem real. I guess the shock was too much for him, because he snapped."

"Fleet and the Corps didn't help their case when the peace craze started," she said.

"Neither did the news," Fortis replied and instantly regretted it.

Damn it.

Liz Sherer had written a series of articles that illustrated the missteps and mismanagement by MAC-M, and much of the blame landed on the commanding general, General Boudreaux.

Sherer put down her fork and leaned forward. "What do you mean by that?"

"Well, I, uh, what I mean is, some of the stories that came out were pretty rough on General Boudreaux and MAC-M."

"I didn't write anything that wasn't true, Abner. Boudreaux is a great general, but he's not much of an administrator, which is what Maltaan needed. General Tsin-Hu was in such a hurry to get home and share in the glory of the great victory that he didn't put a lot of thought into the appointment of Boudreaux. Boudreaux got left holding the bag."

General Tsin-Hu had been the supreme commander of the Maltaan invasion, but he had remained in orbit with five of the nine ISMC divisions that were unnecessary to secure the victory.

She continued. "Boudreaux didn't do himself any favors, either. He made three big mistakes that resulted in unnecessary self-inflicted injuries. First, I believe the budget he submitted was a sincere effort to fund everything that needed to be done to get the Maltaani back on their feet, but his timing couldn't have been worse. That was his first mistake. Trying to get it all done with the shoestring funding they did give him was his second."

"What was his third mistake?"

"Talking 'off the record' to a journalist."

Fortis blinked in surprise.

"Not me, but someone in my business," she said. "Someone without any journalistic ethics. When his comments got out, his days as MAC-M were numbered."

"I guess it's a rough kind of justice that Tsin-Hu was forced into retirement and Boudreaux got another star and went to the General Staff."

Sherer smiled. "Everyone gets theirs in the end."

"The best we can hope for is to choose which end," Fortis said. After a long second, Sherer realized what he'd said, and she sputtered. He joined in, and their laughter drew the attention of diners at nearby tables.

"What's next for Abner Fortis?" Sherer asked when they settled down.

He had anticipated her question, and he had a story ready.

"General Anders has me handling some administrative matters down here while he's stuck in Lviv. My new job is to inventory some vacant buildings. Routine stuff, really. Dancing on the edge of a budget cutter's blade while he calls the tune."

She arched an eyebrow and gave him a suspicious look. "I don't know why I even ask, because I don't believe a word you say. Remember the last time I asked what you were up to, and you said you were training local security forces? Then I found out you led the raid that killed the leader of the insurgency."

Fortis smiled. "Things changed, Liz."

"Hmph."

He diverted the conversation away from himself. "How about you? What's next for Liz Sherer?"

"Now that I'm independent, I can pursue any story I want," she said. "I've heard some rumbling about the Free Sector and the divvies, so I'm pulling that thread."

"Really?" Fortis feigned surprise. "What about them?"

"One of my sources told me the UNT is unhappy with the Big Four because they invited the divvies to the Free Sector. I also heard the divvies are unhappy because the UNT dumped them out there without any support. There's even been talk about divvies engaging in piracy near the Freedom Jump Gate. It's a tangled mess, and I intend to unravel it."

"Good luck."

She leaned forward and beckoned Fortis to come closer. "I heard a rumor about some purloined pulse rifles. Do you know anything about that?"

"Me? No, I don't know anything about stolen weapons. What's the story?"

"That's what I'm trying to nail down. I heard it's big, but nobody's talking."

"I'm sorry. I don't know anything about it. I couldn't tell you if I did."

She chuckled. "You're such a straight arrow, Abner."

The conversation turned to lighter matters again, and it wasn't until they ordered dessert that she fixed him with a steady gaze.

"Are you ever going to tell me the truth about your mission in Ulvaan?"

"I saw your story, Liz. You pretty much know everything already. My team was put on alert because MAC-M had some intel on where the insurgents were holding human hostages. They sent us in, we rescued the hostages, and killed the insurgents."

"Who were the hostages?"

"Civilians. That's all I can say."

"I heard you killed the leader of the insurgency, ex-General Staaber. Any truth to that?"

"I didn't kill him, but he died during the raid. Look, Liz, all of this is ancient history. It was eighteen months ago, and nobody cares about it anymore. You're not still writing about this, are you?"

"No, I'm not working on anything about the raid or Maltaan. Like you said, it's old news. I'm asking out of professional curiosity. Confirmation of sources. That sort of thing."

"Fair enough." He winked at her. "I don't want to make Boudreaux's third mistake."

Their laughter drew more stares, and Sherer held up her empty glass.

"More wine!" she called to a passing waiter.

* * * * *

Chapter Eleven

Ystremski waited until sunset to head for Delphine's. He waved hello to the usual crowd but didn't see Gilliam. Steve the bartender greeted him.

"Hiya, Petr. The usual?"

"Yeah, Steve. Thanks."

The bartender slid a glass of beer in front of Ystremski. "What brings you in here tonight?"

"I was hoping to find Miles Gilliam. I need to talk to him."

"I haven't seen him today. Something I can help you with?"

"Nah. We were talking about a job, and I want to follow up with him."

"Hmm." Steve put down the glass he'd been polishing. "Will you be okay for a second, Petr? I need to go check something in the back."

Ystremski raised his glass. "I have everything I need."

Steve disappeared through a door behind the bar, but not before Ystremski saw him pick up a communicator and slip it in his pocket.

Ystremski eased down the bar and fell in the with a group. Steve emerged from the back to refresh their drinks a few minutes later.

"Sorry about that, boys. I get busy out here and forget all about the stuff I have to do in the back," he said with a sheepish grin.

"I get a little absent-minded myself sometimes." Ystremski slid his empty glass across the bar. "Thanks for the beer, Steve."

Steve shot a glance at the door. "You can't leave yet, Petr. You just got here. Relax and have one on the house."

"Yeah, okay. One more."

The group slapped Ystremski on the back and threw some friendly barbs his way. Steve went back to polishing glasses as he watched the door. A few minutes later, Gilliam arrived.

"Hiya boys. Petr, what happened to your head?" Gilliam gestured to his forehead.

"Meh, it's nothing."

"Looks like a circumcision scar to me," one of the others quipped, and the group roared with laughter.

"Just some asshole that needed tuning up."

"It's a good thing you showed up," Steve said as he passed Gilliam a drink. "Petr said he was looking for you."

"Let's go down to my office so we can talk." Gilliam led Ystremski to the far end of the bar. "What's on your mind?"

"I thought about what you and Arthur said, and I'm ready to commit to the Kuiper Knighthood."

Gilliam smiled and clapped Ystremski on the shoulder. "That's fantastic news, Petr. You've made the right choice."

"I think so," Ystremski replied. "What's the next step?"

"Well, I need to contact Arthur and let him know. We'll arrange an induction ceremony, and you'll be admitted into the Knighthood as a page."

"A what?"

"A page. Entry level members are known as pages."

Ystremski frowned, and Gilliam was quick to explain.

"Don't let the name bother you, Petr. Most of our new members don't remain pages for long, and you're head and shoulders above the average new member. I'm sure you'll be a squire in short order and become a full knight not long after that."

Ystremski nodded. "That sounds okay then. Look, Miles, I don't want to give you the wrong impression, but what about the pay? We didn't have a lot saved up before they divvied me, and I need to send something to my family."

"Every two weeks, we'll deposit your pay into whatever account you choose. Depending on your duties, you can earn more. A lot more, in some cases. It depends on how quickly you advance and what tasks you're willing to take on. I can arrange for a half-month advance, but you'll have to pay it back a little every month."

"Okay, good. I think we can make it for a month with what we have left, so I don't think I'll need the advance. I'm good as long as I know a check is coming."

Gilliam pulled out his communicator. "Let me give Arthur a call. We might be able to have your induction ceremony this evening."

"That quick?"

"That quick," Gilliam said. "Speaking of quick, how soon could you be ready to deploy?"

"I can leave right now if need be. Give me five minutes to grab my duffel."

Ystremski returned to the bar with his empty glass while Gilliam talked to Booth.

"So, you're taking the plunge?" Steve asked.

"Yeah. Miles is calling Arthur right now."

Steve extended his hand over the bar. "Welcome aboard, Page Petr."

Ystremski smiled as they shook. "Not for long."

* * *

Ystremski and Gilliam went to the vacant house across the street from Delphine's. They met Booth and another massive man who Booth introduced as Pil Gustafson.

"Pil is a Master at Arms," Booth explained. "He maintains discipline and enforces our standards."

"Good guy to know then," Ystremski said as he shook hands with Gustafson. The blond-haired giant stared back with expressionless blue eyes.

Booth stood in the center of the room, flanked by Gustafson on his right and Gilliam on his left. He pointed to a spot two paces in front of him.

"Stand here, Petr, and we'll begin."

When Ystremski was in position, Gilliam and Gustafson left the room via a door behind him. They returned moments later wearing black smocks with unfamiliar red symbols sewn onto them. Gilliam had a rolled-up carpet under one arm and a deep purple smock in his free hand, while Gustafson carried an enormous sword, with the cross-guard at waist height and the tip high over his head.

Gilliam assisted Booth into the purple smock and unrolled the carpet on the floor in front of Ystremski. It was a deep red color, but Ystremski saw several darker stains on it.

Blood?

He struggled not to smile at the theatrics, but after Booth donned the purple smock, his entire demeanor changed.

"Petr Ystremski, are you ready to renounce your wickedness and have your soul cleansed by the fires of purity?"

After a long pause, Ystremski saw Gilliam raise his eyebrows, and he realized he was supposed to answer.

"I am."

"Petr Ystremski, is it your desire to join the Kuiper Knighthood and walk forward as a devotee to the principles of honor and fraternity?"

"It is."

"Remove your shirt and kneel."

Ystremski did as Booth instructed, and he saw Gilliam's eyes widen at the sight of the heavy scarring on his stomach.

"Close your eyes, bow, and touch your forehead to the floor."

Ystremski felt Gustafson move around to his left, and a moment later he felt the heavy weight of the sword on the back of his neck. Goose pimples raced down his back, and he shivered.

"Petr Ystremski, you are about to recite the sacred oath of the Kuiper Knighthood. If you violate that oath, your head will be separated from your body. Your remains will be cast out into the filth of the world, and your soul will never achieve the shining glory that awaits all loyal Knights. Do you understand?"

"I do."

The weight of the sword disappeared.

"Rise to your knees and open your eyes."

Gustafson passed the sword to Booth, who rested the tip on Ystremski's right shoulder.

"Repeat after me. I, Peter Ystremski, solemnly swear and affirm that I take this oath of the Knighthood freely and without mental reservation. I swear I will abide by the standards of the Knighthood and always seek to improve myself so I may be of greater service. I take this oath freely, without purposes of evasion. I further renounce any oaths or pledges of loyalty I have taken heretofore. On my honor and on my life, I swear it."

While Ystremski recited the oath, Booth tapped him on both shoulders with the sword. When he was finished, Booth handed the weapon to Gustafson and held out his arms to Ystremski.

"Rise, Page Petr, and receive our welcome."

Ystremski stood and exchanged embraces with Booth, Gilliam, and Gustafson. Booth and Gilliam gave him broad smiles, and even Gustafson managed a slight grin.

"How do you feel?" Booth asked.

"I feel great." Ystremski chuckled. "It's hard to describe, but it's like a weight has been lifted from my shoulders. Does that make sense?"

"Of course." Booth pointed to Ystremski's shirt. "Get dressed, and we'll discuss your future with the Knighthood."

The four men went back across to Delphine's. A group of men was gathered at the end of the bar, and they gave Booth and the others a raucous welcome. Ystremski discovered they were all new pages like him.

"Are you coming with us tonight?" a page named Wilson asked Ystremski.

Gustafson shot Wilson a withering look, and Booth smiled.

"I haven't discussed Petr's future with him yet. How about we save those questions for later?"

Booth guided Ystremski away from the group with a hand on his elbow.

"Let's go over here where we can talk, okay?"

When they were seated at a distant table, Booth shrugged. "I'm sorry about that, Petr. Wilson should know better than to ask a question like that, but he's new. As you might have guessed, we're sending a group of pages off to join the rest of the Knighthood tonight. Miles indicated you might be available to leave on short notice. Interested?"

"Tonight?" Ystremski feigned surprise. "Yeah, I mean, geez. I guess so. I'd have to grab my stuff and call my wife. Where are we going?"

"You'll find out where in due time. A few days travel and one gate jump into friendly space." Booth consulted the time. "The group isn't leaving for another six hours. Can you be back here in five?"

"I can."

"Excellent. You don't need to bring much, just your personal stuff. We'll give you everything else."

"I'll see you in five hours."

* * *

On a whim, Ystremski returned to the neighborhood of Gunny Pete's. He looked around the park benches and alleys but didn't find Sam, so he returned to the bar where he'd fought earlier in the day. A blast of music greeted him at the door, and he earned a lot of curious looks from the other patrons. Ystremski didn't see Hart propped up at the bar, so he went back outside.

"Hey, asshole."

Ystremski turned and saw Billy and his two friends standing on the sidewalk. He sighed.

"You guys again?"

"Time to pay the price," Billy said with a sneer as the trio advanced. Knives glittered in their hands. "Pray, and then you pay."

"Is that the best you've got?" Ystremski backed up a couple steps and took a quick look around. He saw a discarded rag in the gutter, so he grabbed it and wrapped one of his hands in it. "I really don't have time for another lesson, but if you insist."

Ystremski charged without warning and delivered a stiff-fingered blow to the throat of the nearest thug, who went down gagging. Before the second attacker could react, in one motion, Ystremski kicked the knife out of his hand and spun low to deliver another kick to the outside of his left leg. The goon howled and tumbled backward as he clutched his dislocated knee.

Billy was on him before he could stand, and Ystremski used his rag-wrapped hand to ward off the blade as he scrambled to his feet. He felt a burning sensation as Billy's knife cut through the cloth, but he resisted the instinct to look down at the wound.

"Everybody bleeds in a knife fight," his hand-to-hand instructors had taught him. "The winner bleeds the least."

It's time for Billy to bleed.

The two combatants circled as people poured out of the bar to watch the fight.

"Kill him, Billy!"

Billy feinted left and thrust from the right, but Ystremski was ready for it. He parried the attack with a forearm-to-forearm strike and slammed his injured hand into Billy's face. As he stepped back, Ystremski stepped on a knife dropped by one of the others, and he scooped it up.

"Party time, motherfucker," he said with a snarl.

Billy hesitated, but the screams of the crowd restored his courage. He spat out a mouthful of blood and gave Ystremski a crazed grin.

They circled as each searched for an opening. Ystremski could have launched an attack at any time, but he didn't want to kill Billy in front of the crowd. Better to let him come forward, counter his attack, and deliver a crushing but survivable blow.

Billy's eyes opened wide and telegraphed his attack. Ystremski easily sidestepped the knife thrust and slammed his forearm across Billy's unprotected neck. His feet went high in the air as Ystremski slammed him on the street. The onlookers gasped as Billy's knife skittered away, and they seemed to expect Ystremski to deliver a killing blow. Instead, he stepped back and squeezed his injured hand tight to stop the bleeding.

"Fuck off," he shouted at the crowd.

Nobody moved.

"Fuck off!"

Ystremski feinted at the nearest spectator, and they all turned and fled. Even Billy's friends staggered to their feet and limped away. He knelt with a knee on the unconscious man's chest and gave him a light slap.

"Hmmf." Billy struggled to open his eyes.

"I'm getting tired of beating on you," Ystremski said. "Don't let me see you again. Understand?"

"Hmmf."

Ystremski chuckled as he walked down the street toward the pharmacy where he and Sam had purchased the first aid supplies earlier that day.

"Pretty fancy moves, for a divvie."

Ystremski turned around at Hart's voice.

"I was looking for you, you old shitbird. Where have you been?"

"I have a little place around the corner I like to stay at. I heard the commotion and came out to see what was going on."

"Billy and his pals decided they needed another lesson."

"They're lucky you didn't kill them. How's the hand?"

"I need some more antibiotic and glue."

Ystremski talked while Hart dressed his hand. "I have to go out of town for a few days, maybe a week, and I need somebody to look after my place. Is there any chance you can do that for me?"

"My schedule is wide open. What do you need me to do?"

"Stop by, check the doors, make sure nobody has broken in. You can stay there if you want. Just don't have any parties."

"Sure, I can do that."

The two men walked to Ystremski's place. It pleased Ystremski that Hart had accepted his offer, because he knew the old Space Marine was homeless. If he got a temporary place to live on the ISMC's dime, that was fine by Ystremski.

Ystremski talked as he stuffed some clothes into his duffel.

"My Uncle Ivan pays my rent," he told Hart. "He's helping me out until I get on my feet. If you meet him, just tell him I said you could stay here."

By the time Ystremski put the keys on the kitchen table and grabbed his communicator off it, Hart had already begun to snore on the lumpy sofa.

Probably the first time he's slept inside in a long time.

* * * * *

Chapter Twelve

Booth and Gustafson stood back and watched their new pages interact as they waited to leave for the space port. All the pages were drinking except for Ystremski. Wilson, the page who had revealed their imminent departure with his clumsy question, threw surreptitious glances at Gustafson and unconsciously touched his new black eye.

"Did Wilson learn his lesson?" Booth asked.

"This time. I'm afraid he has many more similar lessons in the future."

"Hmm. Well, you've got time to train him before you arrive at Sanctuary."

Gustafson grunted in reply.

"What do you think of the newest page, Ystremski?"

"He looks good. Almost too good. He's a fighter though. His head and his hand prove that."

"He checked out," Booth said. "There's no question about his injury or his discharge. He slugged an officer on the way out the door. Broke his nose, if our report is correct."

"The last agent checked out, as I recall."

"And then he really checked out." The two men laughed before Booth got serious. "If you think it's necessary, test him. If he gives you good reason to suspect him, you know how to handle it."

"I will protect the Knighthood," Gustafson said.

"As will I, but we can't allow our suspicions to cloud our judgment. Nor can we allow our enthusiasm to blind us, either. The Master has decreed that we recruit from among the divvies. He gave us the responsibility and the tools to vet them, but there is still a certain amount of risk. What happened with the last agent wasn't our fault. In fact, it was you that saved us."

Gilliam motioned to Booth from the door and tapped his left wrist with his right hand.

"It's time to leave." Booth clapped Gustafson on the shoulder. "Be well, my brother, and safe travels to Sanctuary."

"Praise to The Master."

* * *

Ninety minutes after the Knights herded the new pages aboard the shuttle that had carried them into orbit, Ystremski and his comrades slid through the umbilical that joined the shuttle to the transport that would take them to their ultimate destination.

An unfamiliar Knight waited for them in the hangar. His bald head gleamed, and a neat black Fu Manchu beard gave him a malevolent appearance.

"Form two ranks of four here," he said as he pointed at the deck. "Front row or back, it doesn't matter. You're all equals here aboard *Pilgrimage*."

When the pages were formed, the Knight held up a sheet of paper. "I am Brother Crockett, assistant to Brother Gustafson for your journey to Sanctuary. I'm your primary tutor on the ways of the Knighthood. You will address me and any other Knight you encounter as 'Brother' or 'Sir Knight.' Is that understood?"

The pages all nodded.

"Good. This is the list of berthing assignments." Crockett brandished the paper. "There will be no changes. If there is a conflict between bunkmates, work it out between yourselves in whatever manner you choose, but do not deviate from these assignments. Is that understood?"

The pages nodded again.

Crockett smiled. "Good. You're all fast learners." He handed the paper to Ystremski, who happened to be the first man in the first row. "What's your name?"

"Petr Ystremski."

"Wrong. You are Page Ystremski."

"Sorry, Brother Crockett. My name is Page Ystremski."

Crockett smiled. "Excellent. Let's see if you do as well with your next challenge. You and your fellow pages have ten minutes to find your berthing, deposit your things, and return here."

Ystremski looked around at the other pages.

Crockett pointed to the hatch. "Move!"

It only took the pages a couple minutes to discover that *Pilgrimage* had a single main passageway. Their berthing compartments were just forward of the hangar. Even after their initial confusion, they managed to do as Crockett ordered and return to the hangar with seconds to spare.

"Good. You've proven your ability to follow simple directions. We have four days before we reach the jump gate, and you have much to learn. Let's begin."

* * *

Three hours later, Ystremski and the other pages sat together in the crew's mess to break bread, as they had been instructed to call eating.

"This basic training stuff is bullshit," Cramer, a former mech gunner who had been divvied straight from the brig in Kinshasa, grumbled under his breath.

"DINLI," Kuntz, a hovercopter crew chief, replied.

"Don't give me that ISMC crap," Cramer said. "I didn't join the Knighthood to be treated like a cherry."

"We have to prove we belong," Wilson said.

Cramer pointed to his cheek. "You're doing a great job of that, brother."

"Fuck you, Cramer. I made a mistake, and Brother Gustafson corrected me."

"Is there a problem here?" Crockett stood over the group with his hands on his hips.

Heads shook around the table.

"No, Brother Crockett," Kuntz said. "We are working out our conflicts among ourselves, as you taught us."

Crockett turned and walked away.

"Keep your fucking voices down," Kuntz said. "If you want to argue, do it in private, okay?"

Ystremski rolled his eyes and shook his head.

Idiots.

* * *

General Anders read the report on his screen and then dialed General Boudreaux's number.

"My apologies for the late hour, sir, but our agent, codenamed Graham, is moving. He's aboard *Pilgrimage*, one of the three ships we've associated with the Knights."

"Do we know where she's headed?"

"Not yet. We'll know as soon as she jumps through a gate."

"Okay, thanks. What about our strike force?"

"I'll have Fortis fly here first thing in the morning for the mission briefing and then send him down to meet Charlotte. That will give Graham a couple days head start."

"Sounds good."

* * * * *

Chapter Thirteen

The persistent buzzing of his communicator dragged Fortis out of his wine-fueled sleep. It was still dark outside, so he knew he wasn't late for anything. He saw General Anders' name on the screen.

"Abner, it's me. There's a ticket waiting for you for the next shuttle to Lviv in two hours. When your boots are on the ground here, report to me at the General Staff."

"Yes sir. Do I—" Fortis stared at his communicator. Anders had already broken the connection.

Fortis jumped through the shower and put on clean utilities. Unsure whether he needed to pack anything, Fortis rolled up clean skivvies and socks and stuffed them into his shaving kit. With kukri and kit in hand, he trotted through the pre-dawn darkness to the main gate and flagged a taxi.

He drew curious looks from his fellow passengers when he boarded the shuttle. Most of them looked like businessmen or government officials headed for the capital with a sprinkling of Fleet and Space Marines mixed in, so Fortis paid them no mind. The direct flight to Lviv was mercifully uneventful, and he even managed a short nap before they touched down at 1100 hours.

He caught a transporter to the UNT government complex and arrived at the MoD building twenty minutes later. After a brief delay passing through security with his kukri, Fortis arrived at Anders' office.

"Ah, Major Fortis," Anders said as he rose from his desk. "You remember Major Rho?"

Fortis and Rho, Anders' deputy, nodded their greetings.

"Your nose looks better. What happened to your lip?"

"The tacs on the roof weren't gentle, sir."

"Serves you right." Anders gestured to Fortis' shaving kit. "I see you packed light."

"I didn't get a chance to ask whether I needed any gear, so I brought the essentials. Clean skivvies and my kukri."

Anders chuckled. "Good." He turned to Rho. "I won't be needing you for the rest of the morning. We've got a meeting with General Boudreaux right now, and I don't know how long that will take."

Anders led Fortis across the lobby to a door that said, "Director of Operations." He stopped and looked at Fortis. "We're living in interesting times, Abner."

Boudreaux's aide ushered them into the general's office and closed the door. The general looked up from his desk and broke into a wide grin.

"Major Fortis! I'm glad to see you, boy. Welcome home."

Fortis couldn't help but smile as the two men shook hands. "Thank you, General. It's good to be back."

"You've looked better. What happened?"

"Gunny Ystremski didn't take the news of being divvied too well," Fortis said.

"Ah, shit, I hated hearing about that. It happened before I could weigh in. How's he doing?"

"I don't know, sir." Fortis gestured to his nose and gave a wry smile. "This was our last communication."

"So, what has Nils told you about the current clusterfuck?" Boudreaux asked after the trio of officers were seated.

Fortis and Anders exchanged looks. "Not a thing, sir."

"Good. That means our security is holding up." He tapped his keyboard, and a holo of the Terra Earth Sector appeared. A flashing red "X" also appeared.

"Two weeks ago, the flagship *Colossus* reported her position here. Since then, we haven't received any updates on her until last night." Boudreaux tapped his keyboard again, and a split view of the Terra Earth Sector and the Free Sector appeared. Another "X" flashed by the Freedom Jump Gate. "The captain of a cargo vessel we've worked with before reported a possible encounter with *Colossus* here, several days ago."

"Unfortunately, he didn't report it right away. He should have realized that a Fleet vessel had no business jumping into the Free Sector," Anders said.

Fortis didn't know where the conversation was headed, so he stayed silent. Boudreaux stared at him for a long moment.

"Do you understand what we're saying?"

"I'm sorry, sir, I don't."

"Damnit, Nils, you really *didn't* tell him anything, did you?"

"Not a word, sir."

"Well, why don't you go ahead and tell him now."

"This all started just before we deployed to Maltaan," Anders said. "The GRC mining vessel that detected the Badaax jumping through the unmapped warp also discovered that the asteroid belt they were exploring was helenium. Every asteroid they sampled.

"Before the GRC could file their claim, the president declared the Maduro Sector off-limits to humans and posted a destroyer at the gate to stop vessels from jumping through. Within a week, the GRC obtained an exemption to the president's order."

"That pissed off the Big Four," Boudreaux interjected. "Understandably so, since their whole economy is built on the helenium they've been bringing out of the Free Sector. An unlimited supply from another source will bankrupt them. They retaliated by declaring the Free Sector off-limits to the UNT."

Anders continued. "After the Peace Party decided to draw down the Fleet and ISMC to reap the 'peace dividends,' divvies flocked to the Free Sector, and the UNT was only too happy to see them go.

"And then somebody hijacked *Colossus*," Boudreaux said with a scowl.

"Who would hijack *Colossus?*" Fortis asked.

"Divvies or Kuiper Knights working in conjunction with them."

"Kuiper Knights?"

"That's our best guess right now," Anders said. "The Kuiper Knights have had a presence in the Free Sector for a long time. When the drawdown began, the Knights recruited heavily from the divvies migrating there. They also set up recruiting operations here on Terra Earth and sent thousands more.

"We designated *Colossus* to serve as the arsenal ship for the seven deactivated divisions. She was on her way to salvage orbit when she disappeared, along with some forty thousand pulse rifles and all the gear to go along with them. Whoever grabbed her now has everything they need to seize control of the Free Sector. The Big Four don't have military forces to stop them, and we're forbidden from operating there."

"That's a big problem."

"It's a giant clusterfuck, is what it is, and we caused it," Boudreaux said. "But we have a plan."

Fortis looked from Boudreaux to Anders and back. "I'm all ears, General."

"We have a source on the inside who will provide locating data for *Colossus* and the weapons. When they do, you will lead a clandestine force of private military contractors into the Free Sector to destroy *Colossus* and the weapons."

"You mean mercenaries, sir? Why not Space Marines?"

Boudreaux cleared his throat, and the scowl returned. "Fucking traitors."

"We've spoken a little about this, Abner. The drawdown has created a lot of hard feelings and divided loyalties, even among the Fleet personnel and Space Marines who remain on active duty. It's possible someone on the inside leaked information about *Colossus* to whomever hijacked her, but we haven't proven it yet."

"Fucking traitors," Boudreaux repeated. "String 'em up by the balls."

"You think mercenaries are more dependable than Space Marines, sir?" Fortis thought back to the mercenaries he had encountered over his career. Many of them weren't particularly reliable, and one contracted vessel captain had nearly cost the lives of him and his team.

"They are private military contractors, not mercenaries. We're not bankrolling a coup. I think they're loyal to whoever contracts with them," Anders said. "For this mission, there shouldn't be any competing interests to tempt them with a bigger payday. All they'll know about the mission is what you tell them."

"Let's stop bullshitting," Boudreaux said. "It's politics. We can find a couple hundred loyal Space Marines, but we can't find a single politician with the balls to tell the Big Four to fuck off when we send them into the Free Sector to destroy *Colossus*."

"What the general means to say—"

Boudreaux cut Anders off by pounding his fist on the desk. "I don't need a goddamn interpreter, Nils. Fortis knows what I'm talking about. He's not an idiot. It's politics, plain and simple. We have an agreement with the Big Four that's fixing to blow up in our faces if we don't deal with those fucking maniacs."

A heavy silence fell over the room before Boudreaux sighed and shook his head.

"I'm sorry, gents. This whole business really pisses me off. Forget about what I said. Anyway, that's our plan. Major, go to Australia, hire a couple companies of mercenaries, er, private military contractors, and stand by on this side of the Freedom Gate. As soon as we get confirmed locating data, you go in. Got it?"

Fortis nodded. "Yes sir."

"Good. Get out of here so your boss and I can talk about you, and don't breathe a word of this to anyone."

Fortis left Boudreaux's office and pulled the door shut behind him. The general's aide gave him an inquiring look.

"They're talking about me," Fortis said.

The aide smiled. "They're probably talking about golf."

* * *

After Fortis was gone, Boudreaux looked at Anders. "You're not going to tell him who our source is?"

"No sir. He doesn't need to know. He has strong feelings for Ystremski despite the nose, and I don't want that to upset his decision-making."

"He's not going to crack up, is he? Do we need to find someone else?"

"No, I don't think so. I read the results of his psych eval, and he's fit for duty."

"What about the planet killer? Are you going to tell him about that?"

"Right now, no. The mission won't change whether he knows about it or not. We don't know if the hijackers are aware of what they have, and we can't afford any inadvertent leaks. If it becomes necessary to tell him, I will. Until then…"

"Need to know." Boudreaux shook his head. "I don't know how you spooks keep this all straight, Nils."

"Practice, sir."

* * *

Anders came out of Boudreaux's office, and Fortis followed him into Anders' office.

"What's this about supper with Liz Sherer?"

"Liz and I have been friends since Balfan-48. You know that. We crossed paths in Kinshasa, and she invited me out to eat."

"You know she lost her military correspondent credentials, don't you?"

"Yes sir, she told me. I can still be friends with her, can't I?"

"There's no law against it, but she's unpopular in certain circles. Like General Boudreaux's."

"General, I ran into her on my second day back from Maltaan and we went out to eat. She didn't try to pry any secrets out of me, mostly because I don't have any. I know the general doesn't hold her in high regard, but I don't hold a grudge against her, even if I disagree with her reporting."

"I can't order you not to socialize with Ms. Sherer but be cautious what you say around her. You do not want to become a source, on or off the record."

"She told me she was working on a story about some stolen weapons and asked me about them. I didn't know what she was talking about, but she made it clear that she's going to track the story down."

Anders' face darkened. "Somebody's been talking."

"She didn't say where she got her info."

"Stay away from her, Abner. The Big Four are already angry with us, and if it gets out that the divvies hijacked a massive load of our weapons and took them to the Free Sector, it could cause a war."

"Roger that, sir."

"Now that we have that settled, let's talk about your mission. Tomorrow, you'll fly from here to Brisbane, Australia. From there, you'll catch a connecting flight to Burketown."

"What's in Burketown?"

"The headquarters of Paladin Executive Services, the contractor we're hiring. Paladin offers many different services including physical security and personal protection. They also provide forces to customer specifications. A lot of Terran companies contract with them to protect high-value personnel and cargo."

"They're able to take down a Fleet flagship?"

"Yes. Paladin personnel train in a broad range of skillsets. Many are former Space Marines, and assaulting a ship is well within their capability."

"I'm not questioning the mission, General, but wouldn't it be better to send only private military contractors to destroy *Colossus*? Why involve an active Space Marine officer? Plausible deniability and all that."

"Because we can't rely on them to do the right thing if the situation changes. What if the weapons are transferred to another ship or down to a planet before they arrive on the scene? We don't want to engage in long-distance contract negotiations to account for mission changes, and we can't agree to an open-ended contract without any control.

"There's also a matter of secrecy to consider. If you're there, we can wait to identify the target ship until the last possible moment. General Boudreaux told you we have a source on the inside. I'm not comfortable revealing that to anyone outside our organization, and certainly not to a contractor until we absolutely have to."

"Earlier, you said they are loyal to whomever is paying them," Fortis said.

"I believe that, but I'm not a fool and neither are you. Tell them as much as you have to and not one word more."

No matter how hard Anders pushed, Fortis refused to think of the Paladins as anything but what they were.

Mercenaries.

* * * * *

Chapter Fourteen

Anders asked Major Rho to take Fortis to the junior officers' mess for lunch. Because the MoD and General Staff were top-heavy, there were far more senior civilians and officers than there were juniors. The junior officers' mess was half-empty, and they were able to get their food and find a table without trouble.

"Are you all set for your mission?" Rho asked when they were seated.

"What mission?"

Rho gave him a puzzled look. "You know. The mission."

"I don't know what mission you're talking about, Major. If there was a mission, I couldn't confirm or deny it anyway."

"Okay, play it that way," she said with a self-conscious chuckle.

They finished their meals in silence and returned to Anders' office. Rho found an envelope on her desk. Inside was a brief note and a data stick.

"The general will be out of the office for the next several hours, but he left this for you to review. It's everything we have on *Colossus* and *Paladin*."

"For the mission," Fortis said with a smile. Rho didn't smile in return, so Fortis continued. "Boudreaux and Anders made it clear that secrecy is paramount for this operation, and I don't think the officers' mess is the right place to discuss it. Thank you for the data stick."

"You're welcome. If you need anything, ask."

Fortis wondered if he had gone too far but decided he was right in refusing to discuss the mission with her in public. He wasn't going to compromise the mission because a staffer wanted lunchtime chit-chat. There was too much on the line, including his own ass.

The first two documents reinforced what he already knew from his briefing with the generals, so he gave them a cursory scan. The third was the loading plan for the weapons and gear aboard *Colossus*, which he read in detail.

They had converted all the magazines to store explosive and incendiary ordnance, like grenades and flame generating units, after which they secured and depressurized the magazines. Crates of infantry pulse and ballistic weapons received similar treatment in the drop ship hangars, as did all the battle armor and other gear. The plan was to depressurize the entire ship and weld the hatches shut before she was placed in salvage orbit.

Fortis noted that the plan didn't reference the drop ships, mechs, hovercopters, and shuttles he expected to see on *Colossus*, and he made a mental note to ask Anders about them. He committed the layout of the weapons to memory, although he knew that whoever hijacked the ship could easily move them around.

The fourth document was a profile of Paladin Executive Services. Founded by a retired ISMC colonel named Roger Charlotte, Paladin advertised themselves as experts in many security-related disciplines. A short holo was embedded in the document, and Fortis watched as teams of Paladin operators stormed a building in one scenario and reacted to threats to a high value target in another. The scenarios were basic, but he noted smooth teamwork that could only be developed through intensive training. Paladin claimed their operators could perform their duties in all types of environments, from deep in the ocean to the vacuum of space, but Fortis didn't see any of the specialized equipment required to back up such a boast.

The next document detailed the ship hired to transport Fortis and the contractors on their search for *Colossus*. The vessel, *Dancer*, was a long-range mining colony resupply ship, owned and operated by a former Fleet officer named Zenith Lakshaw. Lakshaw had contracted with the ISR branch in the past and was considered reliable. *Dancer* carried two large shuttles for cargo and large mining colony crews and a smaller shuttle for routine personnel transfers. There was a spec sheet about *Dancer's* propulsion plant and auxiliary systems, but the only thing that stuck out to Fortis was the absence of weapons systems.

The final document was named, "Mission Finances," but it was blank. Fortis shook his head and closed the directory.

General Anders stuck his head in the office.

"Abner, I hope you're hungry. General Boudreaux has invited you to eat supper with us in the senior officers' mess."

It surprised Fortis to see that it was early evening. He'd spent the entire afternoon reading through the mission documents, and his legs were stiff when he stood up.

"Now that you've had a chance to read up on the details of the mission, he wants to address any questions you might have," Anders said as he led Fortis to the senior officers' mess. Fortis drew curious looks as he and Anders wound their way through the room to join Boudreaux, who sat at an isolated table in the corner.

"Have a seat, gents. I hope you're okay with medium rare steaks because I already ordered for you." Anders and Fortis nodded. "Good.

Tell me, Abner, do you have any questions about your mission? Anything you want to talk over?"

"I'm wondering how the Kuiper Knights managed to recruit so many Space Marines and Fleet personnel. I understand the anger of the divvies—I'm not happy about the situation myself—but I wouldn't expect them to join the Knights. The Kuiper Knights are a fringe cult, and the Knights I've dealt with have been mostly hard-core crazies. That doesn't sound like the vast majority of Space Marines and Fleet personnel I know."

"The Knights put together a pretty slick recruiting campaign when the drawdown began," Boudreaux said. "They started talking about mutual aid and the opportunity for a new beginning in the Free Sector. To guys and gals whose careers just ended, especially the mid-grade types with young families, it was too good to resist. Hell, the UNT helped 'em out by using our own ships to transport them. Goddamn fools."

Anders chimed in. "As we understand the current situation in the Free Sector, it is a loose confederation of different factions. There are some societies that have existed there for hundreds of years with little or no interaction with Terra Earth.

"The Kuiper Knights, although relative newcomers, have the most structured organization, with a specific leader and hierarchy. We believe they are interested in exerting control over the entire sector if they can accumulate enough power. Other groups of divvies have formed around colonies and planet clusters, but so far, most of them haven't demonstrated a desire to expand. There are, of course, the usual criminal elements in the Free Sector, and many divvies have joined them, too."

"It's a powder keg." Boudreaux's voice was loud enough to draw curious looks from other officers in the mess. He lowered his volume. "It hasn't exploded yet because all of those groups lack one thing."

"Weapons," Fortis said.

"You're damn right, weapons. Forty thousand pulse rifles are going to start some serious shit in the Free Sector. When it kicks off, it might spark a war here on Terra Earth."

"My apologies, General, but I don't understand why we don't just tell the Big Four the truth and send a fleet in to locate and destroy *Colossus*."

"Like I told you before, it's politics. The Big Four are already pissed off at us about the helenium in the Maduro Sector. Admitting that we allowed a shipload of weapons to get into the Free Sector might be the spark that sets the whole planet on fire." Boudreaux looked around and then leaned forward. "I'll tell you something, though. You just described Plan B, which we've been working on all day. If you can't find *Colossus* or destroy the weapons, there will be a task force standing by to jump in. With or without permission."

The trio finished their meals in silence. Fortis considered bringing up mission finances, but he figured it would be better to broach that subject with Anders alone. Boudreaux bade them a good night, and Anders led Fortis back to his office. They found an envelope with Fortis' name written on it waiting for them.

"Those are your tickets for Burketown; you're leaving first thing in the morning. When you get there, look up Colonel Charlotte at Paladin Executive Services. He'll be expecting you. You have two days to evaluate his troops and decide who and how many you want to take. You're due to link up with *Dancer* at SOMO in three days, embark your team, and head for the Freedom Gate.

"There's also an encrypted communicator with two codes in it, I and V. I is the code for me, and V is the code for one of our sources. V will automatically transmit locating data whenever they power up their communicator. There's no set comms schedule. Do not reply to V, that code is receive-only for you."

"Sir, I noticed the mission finances document on the data stick was blank."

"That was another detail that wasn't worked out until just this afternoon. General Boudreaux has approved one hundred billion credits for this mission. From that, you will hire the contractors necessary to complete your mission and pay for any emergent requirements."

Fortis gave a low whistle. "A hundred billion?"

"Two hundred men will cost us. Plausible deniability isn't cheap, but it's cheaper than going to war with the Big Four."

"Does that include *Dancer*, sir?"

"No. *Dancer* is on salvage hold, but we'll pay her fees through another source. She'll be ready to sail when you get there."

"Am I supposed to haggle with Colonel Charlotte over the price?"

Anders chuckled. "You can try. I expect Charlotte will demand two-fifty to three hundred million credits per operator. It's the going rate for something like this, but that number must include all the gear and specialized training they will need and transportation to meet our vessel. The extra forty billion is there in case you need it."

Anders ended their conversation on a cautionary note. "This mission is both extremely sensitive and important to the UNT and to Terra Earth. There are people in the government asking why we work so hard to cooperate with the Big Four. It's obvious they don't remember what happened the last time war broke out between us. Behind them are people who only see the profit potential of a conflict. A lot of lives are at stake, and I'm afraid that if we don't deal with this quietly, things will spin out of control. You *cannot* fail."

Fortis' "first thing in the morning" flight departed Lviv at zero one hundred hours, so he spent a couple hours at a nearby shopping mall buying clothes for the mission. Anders warned him against wearing his ISMC utilities, so Fortis packed up his uniform and kukri and left them with Anders. He left the general a list of personal gear he expected to need, and Anders promised to have an armorer forward it to *Dancer* the next day.

With his new bag packed full of civilian coveralls, Fortis went to the space port to wait for his flight. He tried not to look like a Space Marine, but he realized the terminal was full of fellow travelers trying not to look like Space Marines, so he relaxed and people watched as the minutes ticked away.

* * * * *

Chapter Fifteen

Ystremski and his fellow pages underwent three days of intensive instruction under Crockett's tutelage before Gustafson appeared in the hangar.

"*Pilgrimage* has arrived in the vicinity of our jump gate," he told the pages. "I am gifting you two hours of down time before we jump and two hours after. I suggest you spend it in your bunks. When that time is up, Brother Crockett will resume your instruction. Do you have any questions?"

By then, the pages had learned that when a Knight asked if they had any questions, it was a trap, and they remained silent. They had also learned that a suggestion from Gustafson was paramount to an order.

Ystremski, Cramer, Wilson, and a former Space Marine infantryman named O'Malley shared a four-man bunkroom. They all turned into their bunks as Gustafson "suggested."

"Crockett said it would be four days to the jump gate, but it's only been three. What jump gate do you reckon it is?" O'Malley asked from his rack above Ystremski.

"Who gives a fuck?" Cramer shot back. "Does it matter?"

"It matters to me," O'Malley said. "I like to know where I'm going."

"Why? Are you leaving a trail of breadcrumbs to follow in case you get homesick? Or maybe you want someone to follow us?"

"Are you calling me an agent?"

"I'm just saying that anything is possible," Cramer said. "Any one of you could be an agent."

Since Gustafson had "corrected" Wilson for divulging their impending departure from Terra Earth, the pages had gossiped among themselves about what it meant. The prevailing opinion was that the UNT was attempting to penetrate the Kuiper Knighthood, although none of them could articulate exactly why. It was pure speculation; one of the pages in the other bunkroom claimed he had a friend in the Knighthood who had told him the Knights exposed a government agent, and that sent the rumor mill among the pages into overdrive. Cramer was convinced there was an agent, and he wasn't shy about telling the others.

For his part, Ystremski avoided the conversations, and when he couldn't, he didn't express a strong opinion one way or the other. It made him uneasy to listen to the other pages as they ticked off the reasons why one page or another from the other bunk room could be an agent, and he wondered if the other group of pages were doing the same. They might be spinning the story out of thin air, but it didn't mean they were wrong.

"Why don't you all shut the fuck up and enjoy the break?" Ystremski growled from his bunk. "Three days of little sleep, constant lessons, and shitty food, and you want to waste the down time Brother Gustafson gave us by arguing over the boogeyman."

"Amen," Wilson said. "Let's get some sleep."

"Hmph." Cramer rolled over and faced the bulkhead. "Mark my words, brothers. There's an agent out there. You'll see."

* * *

The desert heat of the Australian outback summer blasted Fortis when he stepped off the shuttle in Burketown. The beads of sweat that trickled down his forehead evaporated before he could wipe them away, and the relentless sun blinded him as he stumbled across the tarmac and into the welcome shade of the terminal. He stepped off to the side to stretch out the stiffness from his long journey from the northern hemisphere as he scanned the few people in the terminal. No one stood out, so he shouldered his bag and went in search of a ride to the Paladin Executive Services headquarters.

"My name is Abner Fortis. I'm here to see Col—er, Mr. Charlotte," he told the guard at the gate.

The guard spoke softly into a throat mic, waited a second, and opened the gate.

"The colonel is expecting you. Follow the yellow line to the office. Do not deviate."

Fortis had overpaid for polarized sunglasses at the space port in Brisbane, but they enabled him to survey the compound as he followed the yellow line to the office. There wasn't much to see. In front of him, an office building squatted between two prefab huts that looked like barracks. More barracks lined one side, and garages lined the other. He heard the distant sound of automatic weapons fire and the unmistakable *thump* of concussion grenades from somewhere behind the office. When he stepped inside, Fortis was ushered to Charlotte's office by an unsmiling receptionist.

"Mr. Fortis, welcome." A large man rose behind the desk and offered his left hand to shake. The move surprised Fortis until he saw Charlotte's right sleeve hanging empty. "I'm Roger Charlotte."

"My pleasure, sir," Fortis said as they shook left-handed. Charlotte smiled at his hesitation.

"A bug got me on Demouli-4. Bit me just above the elbow, but the docs couldn't stop the necrosis before it got my shoulder. By the time they were done cutting, they couldn't give me an osseointegrated arm because there wasn't anything left to osseointegrate to." Charlotte laughed in a self-deprecating manner before he pointed to Fortis' right leg. "You're damned lucky a bomb got you and not a bug."

Fortis' expression gave him away.

"I know who you are," Charlotte said as he waved Fortis into a chair in front of the desk. "You research us, we research you. It's a big fucking game, Abner."

Fortis nodded. "Yes sir, it seems that way."

"Nils told me you might have some work for the Paladins. What do you have in mind?"

"A simple ship takedown, followed by a demolition job."

"Hmm, okay. What's the target?"

"I don't know for certain. I'll inform the men as soon as I find out."

"You don't know, or you don't want to tell me?"

"I don't know." Fortis answered without hesitation, hoping to sound convincing.

"Location?"

"Again, I don't know. Maybe another sector. As soon as I know, they'll know."

"Can you at least tell me if it will be in orbit or on the surface?"

"Most likely in space, but a ground assault is possible."

"Expected resistance?"

"Unknown to light."

"How many men are you looking to hire?"

"Two hundred. Two companies, two company commanders, and a demolition team."

"That doesn't sound like you're expecting light resistance to me."

"It's a fluid situation, sir. I think it's better to bring too many and not need them than need them and not have them. They'll be paid whether we use them or not."

"Payment was never a question." Charlotte stood. "Before we get into numbers, let's go look at what's happening on the training ground. I think you'll like what you see."

For the next hour, Charlotte and Fortis observed training evolutions conducted by Paladin personnel. From an observation platform high above the training ground, they watched as teams assaulted vehicles, buildings, and a spaceship mockup from the ground and then repeated the assaults by fast ropes from hovercopters. Their moves were smooth and precise.

Fortis saw Charlotte watching him from the corner of his eye, and he forced himself to remain impassive to the demonstrations. To an inexperienced observer, the mercenaries would have appeared highly skilled, but Fortis saw flaws in their execution. It was obvious they had practiced those same scenarios many times before, but it looked repetitious to him. There were no casualties, no loss of comms, and no resistance from unexpected vectors. The personnel acting as the opposing force were exactly where the assaulters expected them to be. On the Space Marine crawl-walk-run training continuum, the mercenaries looked like they were at the walk stage.

"The Paladins you're watching are Herron's and Zylstra's companies," Charlotte said. "Mostly new guys, just finished our entry-level course."

"Where did they come from?"

"The same place all our personnel come from. The Corps, Fleet, and a bunch of half-assed militias from here to the Free Sector. We don't turn anyone away if they're willing to learn, and they're not unsafe."

They heard a shout of pain from the training ground. One of the black clad mercenaries was sprawled on the ground clutching his leg while another mercenary stood over him. From his body language, Fortis could tell he'd accidentally shot his comrade.

A third mercenary approached and, without hesitation, butt-stroked the shooter across the head. The shooter's helmet flew off, and he went down on hands and knees, and the third mercenary kicked him in the face. A warning siren blared as several other Paladins dragged the attacker away.

A Paladin in a blue jump suit appeared on the scene, followed by two corpsmen in white coveralls with red crosses. The man in blue grabbed the third mercenary by his battle armor and dragged him off the training ground while the corpsmen attended the injured man. The man who'd been beaten and kicked struggled to his feet, retrieved his helmet and pulse rifle, and stumbled out of sight.

Charlotte led Fortis back to his office. "Will they meet your needs, Mr. Fortis?"

"I think they will."

"Good. I can have two companies of Paladins with all their gear, including demolition experts, in orbit in two days."

"Our transportation is at SOMO, so we can link up there."

Charlotte shook his head. "Paladins don't set foot on SOMO, or the Terra Earth Jump Gate, either. We'll rendezvous and transfer the men and gear by shuttle."

"Hmm. The best I can do is give you a definite maybe right now. My next stop after Burketown is SOMO to check on our ride. If there are any problems with your proposal, we'll have time to work them out." Fortis paused for a moment. "What's all this going to cost me?"

"Sixty billion credits."

The number surprised Fortis even though he expected it would be large. "Sixty billion?"

"You want two hundred Paladins on an open-ended contract to take down an unknown ship in an unknown location. That's a lot of unknowns and a lot of risk, both for Paladin and my employees. The price is sixty billion credits, and it's non-negotiable."

Fortis stood and extended his left hand. "We have a contract, Mr. Charlotte."

* * *

"He's a convincing liar," Charlotte told Brad Herron and JJ Zylstra, the Paladin company commanders he had assigned to Fortis' mission. "Look at this."

A holographic recording of Fortis seated across from Charlotte appeared above his desk. A colored map showed the hot spots on his body, and a side panel showed his vital signs.

"Again, I don't know," Fortis said in response to Charlotte's question about the location of the mission. There was a slight increase in heart rate and respiration, but no change to his body heat.

"Do you want us to do anything about it?" Herron asked.

"No, just be aware of it."

"Where do you think the mission is, Colonel?"

"I don't know."

Charlotte was a convincing liar, too. There was only one reason the ISMC would contract with Paladin to take down a ship, and that was because the ship was somewhere the ISMC couldn't reach—like the Free Sector.

"Brad, I'm giving you the lead on this one. You have two days to get your companies packed up and ready to go. You have the mission list, so make sure your men have the necessary gear. Fortis will contact me when he's ready to rendezvous with our shuttle, so expect a short notice deployment. This is your first mission for Paladin for both of you. If you want there to be more, don't fuck it up."

* * *

The following morning, Fortis caught a shuttle to Brisbane and booked a seat on the next launch to the Terra Earth Jump Gate (TEJG) scheduled for that evening. With time to kill, he called General Anders.

"That's about what we expected," Anders said when Fortis told him about Charlotte's price. "I'm not surprised."

"Do you think he knows?"

"Charlotte has a lot of contacts, and I'm sure he knows something is up, but not specifics."

"I'm booked on the next launch to TEJG and then on to SOMO," Fortis said. "I'll be up there around midnight your time."

"Excellent. *Dancer* is there, and the armorer reported that your gear has been shipped."

"Sounds good, sir. Any updated information on the situation?"

"Not yet. I'll let you know when there is. For now, get your team situated aboard *Dancer* and be ready to go."

"Roger that."

Fortis splurged on a cup of real coffee and settled in to wait for his ride to SOMO to board. It surprised him to see a man with the unmistakable dueling scars of a Kuiper Knight walk through the terminal. He paid closer attention to the crowds moving through the terminal and saw four others with dueling scars. The Knights weren't outlawed by the UNT, but their presence was discouraged, and security forces closely scrutinized them.

Fortis' platoon had unearthed and destroyed a Kuiper Knight cell attempting to establish a narco-state on Eros-28, and later, he had narrowly survived an assassination attempt bankrolled by the Knighthood. That attempt had prompted a private war on the Knights by the ISMC ISR branch which ended because of the Maltaan invasion. Since then, Fortis hadn't seen or heard much about the Knights except what Anders had told him. Until now.

The shuttle to TEJG finally boarded, and Fortis saw all five men scattered throughout the passenger compartment. He was unarmed and outnumbered but attacking him on the shuttle would be a suicide mission. None of the five seemed to be interested in him, though, and Fortis forced himself to relax.

When the shuttle docked at TEJG, Fortis took his time to collect his bag and debark the craft. He was among the last passengers to emerge from the tunnel, but he didn't see anyone loitering in the area that looked out of place. After a final look around, Fortis made his way to the shuttle gate for SOMO and checked in. There were only three other passengers headed for SOMO, and none of them appeared to be a Kuiper Knight, so he settled in for the ride over to SOMO.

Finally, after a day of travel, Fortis arrived at SOMO and went in search of *Dancer*.

* * * * *

Chapter Sixteen

Three days after their gate jump, *Pilgrimage* arrived in orbit around Sanctuary, which the pages now knew was a planet in the Free Sector. The pages were ordered to assemble in the hangar.

"I don't know why they couldn't just tell us where we were going," O'Malley said. "It's no secret the UNT are sending divvies out here."

"Did it make that much of a difference?" Cramer asked. "Were you going to tell them no if you knew we were headed for the Free Sector?"

"Lock it up," muttered Kuntz. "Here comes Brother Gustafson."

Gustafson had a dark expression on his face, as did Crockett, who followed close behind the Kuiper Knight leader.

"I understand there has been a lot of speculation regarding the presence of a government agent among you pages," Gustafson said. His eyes bored into each of the pages in turn. "We take threats to the Knighthood seriously, and so must you, if you are to be knighted someday." He nodded to Crockett.

"When I call your name, follow us to the far side of the hangar. The rest of you remain here. Page Cramer."

The two knights and the page walked across the hangar and held a brief conversation out of earshot of the group, during which Cramer pointed back toward them. Crockett then gestured to the other corner, and Cramer walked over and sat on the deck facing the bulkhead.

"Page Kuntz," Crockett called.

One by one, the eight pages were summoned to join Gustafson and Crockett. They called Ystremski last.

"Page Ystremski, who do you believe is the government agent and why?"

The question stunned Ystremski.

The government agent? Why are they certain there is an agent?

A million thoughts raced through his mind, and Ystremski wanted to request clarification, but he knew better.

Fuck it. I'll throw them the least likely agent.

"I believe Page Cramer is the government agent. He has talked about little else since we left Terra Earth. I believe it is a common tactic of guilty people to throw suspicion in every direction but on themselves."

Gustafson and Crockett exchanged glances, and Gustafson nodded.

"Very well. Join the others, Page Ystremski."

Ystremski walked across the hangar on wobbly legs and took a seat next to the other pages. He concentrated on controlling his heart rate, afraid his pounding pulse could be detected by the others. Ystremski had been in many dangerous situations before, but he was unarmed, surrounded by strangers, and a long way from help.

"Pages, come here," Crockett ordered.

The pages did as they were told and stood in their usual double ranks.

"Front rank, take one step forward and turn around to face the rear rank."

The pages did as Crockett ordered, unsure of what was to come. Gustafson stood at one end of the double line, and Crockett positioned himself at the other.

"Gossip is a cancer and the pastime of ignoble people," Gustafson said. "To engage in gossip and idle speculation is to erode the trust between brothers, between Knights. A Knight must be better than that."

Ystremski forced himself to relax. Whatever Gustafson was talking about didn't sound like he was about to expose a suspected agent.

"Page Cramer, come here."

Cramer threw a wide-eyed look at the other pages before he did as he was ordered.

"A gauntlet is an armored glove worn by a knight to protect his hand," Gustafson said as he held his hand up over Cramer's head and made a fist. "It is also a way we use to punish Knights who stray from the path. Page Cramer, you've been found guilty of gossip by a jury of your peers." Several of the pages gasped, and Ystremski blinked in surprise. "Your punishment is to run their gauntlet." He lowered his fist and drove it deep into Cramer's stomach. Cramer groaned and fell to his knees.

Gustafson shook his fist at the other pages. "You must mete out the punishment deserved by your conviction, or you will join Page Cramer in the gauntlet."

Ystremski felt a twinge of guilt as he watched the Kuiper Knight yank Cramer to his feet and position him at the head of the gauntlet of pages.

"Walk, don't run, or you'll pass through again," Gustafson warned before he shoved Cramer forward.

Kuntz was the first to face Cramer, and after a brief hesitation, drove a fist into Cramer's face. Cramer cried out as his hands pawed at the blood spurting from his shattered nose. Wilson was next, and he slugged Cramer low in the abdomen.

Cramer staggered through the line as his fellow pages hammered him from all angles. When he reached Ystremski at the end of the gauntlet, his eyes peered through slits in his swollen face, his nose was a mangled mess, and his breath wheezed in and out between split lips. Ystremski hesitated for a second as he searched for a way to hit Cramer without injuring him further.

"Do your duty, Page Ystremski," Gustafson commanded.

Ystremski leaned forward and spat in Cramer's face. "You're not worthy of my fist, *Brother*," he snarled before he delivered a thunderous open-handed slap to the side of Cramer's head. Cramer staggered and went down face-first on the rough hangar deck, and Ystremski bent down and wiped the blood and gore from his hand onto Cramer's coveralls.

"Justice has been done," declared Gustafson. "Deliver your injured brother to the infirmary and let none speak of this matter again."

* * *

Two hours before the pages were due to board a shuttle to the surface of Sanctuary, Gustafson called Ystremski into his office.

"Sit down, Petr," Gustafson said.

"Yes, Brother Gustafson," Ystremski said as he sat.

The Kuiper Knight smiled.

"Well done, Page Ystremski. I called you Petr, and you corrected me without correcting me. Quite clever."

Ystremski didn't respond.

"Not as clever as how you dealt with Cramer," Gustafson said.

Ystremski remained impassive as the Knight studied his face.

"Don't think I didn't see you struggling with your decision." Gustafson chuckled. "Your fellow pages administered their sentence with more enthusiasm than I'm used to seeing. Cramer is unpopular?"

"We like Page Cramer just fine, Brother Gustafson. He comes across too strong as though he has something to prove, but he works hard."

"Why do you think he's like that?"

"I'm not a trained therapist, Brother Gustafson, but if I had to guess, I would say it comes from his time in the brig. The brig isn't the best place to be passive or reserved."

"That's right," Gustafson smiled. "You've spent time in the brig, haven't you?"

Ystremski nodded. "Yes, Brother Gustafson. I made a mistake when I was younger, and I paid for it."

"We don't hold a man's past against him. It's what you do today that matters to the Kuiper Knights."

Ystremski nodded but stayed silent.

"I brought you in here to tell you that I've been impressed by what I've seen from you thus far. You're attentive to your duties, you help your fellow pages, and you think on your feet. I've been so impressed, I'm going to put you forward to serve as my squire when we get to the surface."

"Thank you, Brother Gustafson, for your vote of confidence. All I want to do is serve the Knighthood to the best of my ability."

"That's the right attitude, Petr, er, Page Petr." He stood, and Ystremski followed suit. "Now, go join your brother pages and say nothing of this."

Ystremski's mind whirled as he picked his way through the passageway back to the hangar.

What the fuck?

Gustafson's offer put Ystremski in a tough spot. It would be a great insult to refuse, and it might even earn him a gauntlet, or worse. However, his mission was to find the stolen weapons, not penetrate the upper ranks of the Knighthood. He couldn't find the weapons if he was ferrying pages back and forth from Terra Earth with Gustafson.

When he got to the hangar, Kuntz welcomed him back with a nod.

"Is everything okay, Brother?"

Ystremski and Kuntz had formed a cautious friendship during their journey from Terra Earth. There was a quiet confidence about Kuntz that Ystremski liked, but he kept the former crew chief at arm's length.

I can't afford to make any friends here.

"I'm good," he told Kuntz.

The pages waited in silence for the shuttle. Cramer was still in the infirmary, and his absence was a gaping void in the group. Ystremski detected a heavy undercurrent of guilt from his fellow pages. Cramer acted like an ass and deserved a beating from a fair fight, not the mob justice meted out in the gauntlet. Ystremski had seen violence in countless forms during his service in the ISMC, but the speed at which Cramer's fellow pages turned on him and their willingness to beat him without mercy disturbed him.

When the shuttle from Sanctuary docked with *Pilgrimage*, two dozen men debarked into the hangar before Gustafson led the pages aboard. They buckled in, and after a bumpy entry into the atmosphere, the shuttle touched down.

"Welcome to Sanctuary," Gustafson announced as he led the pages down the ramp.

Ystremski stared in disbelief.

Maltaan. In the Free Sector?

He rubbed his eyes and took another look. The planet was lush and green like Maltaan, but the mountain ranges that ringed the space port were unfamiliar, and the buildings were far different. He glimpsed several prefab hangars and biodomes, and a handful of square buildings squatted behind them.

Kuntz laughed and clapped Ystremski on the back. "I flashed back to Maltaan, too."

They didn't have a lot of time to look around before Brother Gustafson hustled the pages off the tarmac and into one of the hangars.

Inside the hangar was a group of Kuiper Knights dressed in black smocks. There was one Knight for each page. One of the Knights stood next to Ystremski, but Gustafson stepped in.

"Not this one, Brother. He's with me."

Gustafson motioned Ystremski to follow him, and they went back outside. The pair climbed into a waiting truck.

"Take us to the palace," Gustafson said, and Ystremski noticed the driver was wearing the white smock of a page. The truck rattled along a rutted road and stopped in front of another anonymous biodome.

"Wait for me," Gustafson told the driver as he slid out. "Come on, Page Ystremski."

This biodome was larger than the first, and when they got inside, Ystremski saw it had been divided into sections by movable screens.

"This is the palace," Gustafson said in a low voice. "The Master lives here, and this is where we conduct our ceremonies. Follow me."

The Kuiper Knight led Ystremski through a rabbit warren of passageways deep into the palace, nodding at and greeting each Knight he passed. Ystremski didn't know if he was supposed to say or do anything, so he nodded and gave each person a brief smile. They stopped in an open area with a dais at one end.

"This is the Ceremony Room," Gustafson whispered. "Only The Master may speak in a normal voice here. You must always speak in whispers, and only when necessary. Wait here."

Ystremski nodded, and Gustafson disappeared through a door behind the dais. He emerged a few minutes later, followed by two other men. One bore a large sword and the other carried a rolled-up carpet. All three wore black smocks, and all three had grim expressions on their faces.

The Knight with the carpet unrolled it on the floor, and Gustafson gestured for Ystremski to stand in front of it. Then they waited in silence.

The door opened and a tall man dressed in a purple smock entered the Ceremony Room. His face was gaunt, and when he got close, Ystremski saw unmistakable dueling scars on his cheeks. The thickest scar started in front of his left ear and trailed down his neck. All three Knights bowed, so Ystremski followed suit.

I guess this is The Master.

"Who comes before me?" The Master asked in a surprisingly high-pitched voice.

"Page Petr Ystremski," Gustafson whispered.

"For what purpose?"

"For elevation to squire."

"Has he been tested?"

"He has, Master."

"Page Ystremski, are you prepared to accept the burden of a squire?"

Ystremski hesitated for a half beat, unsure how to respond. "I am," he whispered.

"Remove your shirt and kneel."

What followed was the same ceremony Ystremski had undergone when he became a page. When it was finished, the four men exchanged embraces, and The Master touched the scar on Ystremski's stomach.

"That must have hurt," he said with a sad smile.

"It certainly did, Master," Ystremski whispered in reply. "Not as bad as the betrayal by the Corps, but close."

After The Master left the room, Gustafson retrieved a blue smock from behind the dais which he handed to Ystremski, along with his shirt. Ystremski dressed as he followed Gustafson out of the Ceremony Room.

"That wasn't so bad, was it?" the Knight asked.

"No, Brother Gustafson," Ystremski replied. "What's next?"

"First things first." Gustafson extended his hand. "My name is Pil. You may call me Brother Pil, and you are now Squire Petr." The two men shook. "Now, Squire Petr, what do you say we break bread?"

The truck whisked them to another biodome, and when Ystremski got out, he caught the unmistakable aroma of food. It had been a long time since breakfast aboard *Pilgrimage*, and his stomach let out a loud growl. Ystremski gave an embarrassed smile.

"My apologies, Brother Pil. My stomach hasn't learned any manners since I was wounded."

Gustafson laughed as he led Ystremski inside. "No apologies necessary, Squire Petr. Let's see how your stomach feels about food after eating here."

Steam tables lined two sides of the biodome, and half-filled tables filled the rest of the room. A thousand conversations filled the air. Ystremski followed Gustafson into the line, and it surprised him to see Page Wilson dressed in an apron and hairnet ladling food onto empty trays held out by hungry Knights. Wilson glanced up, and recognition and surprise flashed across his face when he saw Ystremski. Neither man said a word, and Ystremski hurried to catch up with Gustafson.

"This dining facility is used by Knights and their squires to break bread in the morning and afternoon," Gustafson said. "In the evening, squires break bread with the pages in the next dome over. Perhaps you'll meet more of your former page brethren tonight."

Ystremski nodded. He poked at the food on his tray.

"Eat it, Squire Petr. Our brothers worked hard to produce this meal, and it would dishonor their efforts to not eat it."

Gustafson dug in and ate with relish, so Ystremski followed his lead. The food didn't taste bad. In fact, the food didn't have much taste at all. It was filling, and nobody was shooting at him, which made it better than many meals he'd eaten in the Corps, so Ystremski finished every bite. When he was done, Gustafson nodded his approval, stood, and carried his tray to the end of the line.

Just as Ystremski placed his tray atop the other dirty trays, a large hand clapped him on the shoulder.

"Crickey! Look what the cat dragged in."

He turned and saw Bender's smiling face.

"Bender!" Ystremski caught himself when he saw Bender's black smock. "Brother Bender, I mean."

The hulking Australian grabbed him in a big bear hug and then held him at arm's length.

"Forget all that, mate. How have you been? What are you doing here?"

Ystremski looked at Gustafson, who nodded.

"They divvied me," he said. "They waited until I healed up, sent me back to Maltaan for six months, and divvied me."

Bender shook his massive head. "Bastards." He pointed to Ystremski's abdomen. "The last time I saw you, your guts were hanging out and you were almost dead. You're all healed up, yeah?"

"All healed up. The worst part was the infection. The Maltaani mushrooms wouldn't let go, but I finally beat them."

Bender and Gustafson traded looks, and the Australian smiled at Ystremski. "I have to go, mate, but now that I know you're here, we'll have time to catch up, yeah?"

Bender turned and strode away, and Gustafson touched Ystremski on the elbow.

"Walk with me, Squire Petr."

Ystremski followed Gustafson outside, where the Kuiper Knight waved off the driver's offer of a ride.

Gustafson put a hand on Ystremski's shoulder, and they walked along the row of biodomes.

"Brother Bender is fond of you," Gustafson said. "You are good friends?"

"We served here on Maltaan together, Brother Pil," Ystremski said. "He was with me when I was wounded, and he helped save my life."

"A good friend to have. But not anymore." Gustafson stopped and faced Ystremski. "I know how difficult it is to leave your past life in the past, but you must. Do not place friendship ahead of the Knighthood. I never served, but loyalty to the Knighthood is a far sterner test than anything you experienced in the ISMC. What happened on *Pilgrimage* with Page Cramer should have taught you that."

Fat fucking chance.

Ystremski nodded. "It was a stark lesson indeed, Brother."

"I see something in you, Squire Petr. Something that reminds me of me, frankly, and I think you have the potential to become an important member of the Knighthood."

"I will do my best, Brother Pil."

"I know you will." Gustafson turned and guided Ystremski back toward the truck. "Continue to conduct yourself as you have been, and knighthood will be within your grasp before you know it."

When they got back into the truck, Gustafson instructed the driver to take them to the squire biodome.

"I have no need of your services for the rest of the day, Squire Petr. Use the time to settle into your accommodations and familiarize yourself with the layout of Sanctuary. There is a reading room in your dome with many titles that will help expand your knowledge and understanding of the Kuiper Knighthood. Tonight, after our evening meal and services, I will come for you, and we'll talk more."

"Yes, Brother Pil."

The truck stopped in front of another dome, and Ystremski got out. Without another word from Brother Pil, the truck drove off.

Ystremski shrugged and then pushed through the door into the biodome.

* * * * *

Chapter Seventeen

Abner Fortis threaded his way through the crowds on SOMO until he arrived at the office of the Salvage Master. A harried looking man peered at him from behind a stack of files perched on the counter.

"Take a number and have a seat, mister," the man said. "I'll get to you when I get to you."

Fortis had been to the Salvage Master's office before, and he knew better than to wait. Instead, he smiled. "I'm here for *Dancer*."

The clerk jerked like he'd been shocked, and he stared at Fortis for a long second through smeared glasses.

"*Dancer*?" Fortis repeated.

The clerk flapped around like a startled bird as he searched behind the counter. "Why didn't you say so in the first place?" He sighed in relief and held up a sheaf of papers. "*Dancer*. Here we go."

Fortis took the papers and flipped through them. There was a title of ownership, a commissioning certificate, a bill for salvage costs stamped "PAID" across the top, and a blank vessel history report. They all appeared in order, so Fortis tucked them under his arm.

"Thank you."

"Wait a second," the man said. "There's still the matter of the Salvage Master's fee."

"The Salvage Master's fee?" Fortis asked. "What's that?"

"Well, uh, there are expenses, you see. Running SOMO isn't cheap, you know. It's ten percent of the salvage value." The clerk gave an exaggerated shrug. "The Salvage Master says I have to collect it, so I have to collect it."

Fortis chuckled. "Let me stop you right there, okay? This isn't my first time through SOMO. I know you're the Salvage Master, and I know you've already been paid."

The man gaped for a second before he took off his glasses and wiped them on his filthy shirt. "Well, you got what you came for. Go!"

"What dock number?"

"Number Seven," the Salvage Master said. "Lucky Number Seven."

"Thanks."

Fortis plunged back into the SOMO crowds and pushed his way through to a set of double doors. The noisy crowds and smell of unwashed bodies vanished, replaced by the hammering and grinding of a working shipyard and the acrid sting of welding fumes. He dodged sprays of sparks and sidestepped grimy yardbirds wrestling with heavy equipment until he found the sign marked "Salvage Claim Dock Seven."

At the end of the narrow gangway that led to the dock, four men and a woman confronted him.

"Where do you think you're going?" the woman demanded. She was a half-head shorter than Fortis, with dirty blonde hair and hard eyes. She stood at the gangway with her fists on her hips as if to block his passage all by herself.

"I'm going aboard my ship," Fortis said evenly. He waved the salvage papers. "*Dancer*. I just salvaged her."

"Who are you?"

"Who wants to know?"

She looked over her shoulder at her companions. "Zenith Lakshaw. *Dancer* is my ship, and this is my crew."

"Well, Zenith Lakshaw and crew, you can call me Fortis. My rich daddy Anders gave me *Dancer* as a birthday present."

"Anders? Why didn't you say so?" She turned to her crew. "This is the new owner. *Temporary* owner. Get aboard and get to your stations. We're leaving."

Lakshaw's attitude softened as she extended her hand. "Sorry about that. I had to be sure you weren't a speculator who bribed the salvage master to steal *Dancer* out from under me."

"I still could be," Fortis said as they walked to the boarding ramp. He followed Lakshaw up the ramp and into *Dancer*. It pleased him to see the passageway was clean and well-lit. Long-range resupply vessels typically saw hard use and didn't age well, but *Dancer* appeared to be in good condition.

Lakshaw caught him looking around. "*Dancer* might be old, but she's in good shape," she said. "McLeod works magic with the engines, and Yak keeps everything else working."

They arrived at the control room where a crewmember in the left-hand seat flipped switches and punched buttons on his console. Lakshaw slid into the right-hand seat and waved Fortis onto a fold-down seat next to her.

"This is Doe. He's my first mate and *Dancer's* AI."

Doe paused long enough to wave to Fortis.

"I wouldn't think a ship this size rated an AI," Fortis said.

"Doe is mine. He's been with me since I started sailing, and I won't go anywhere without him. He and *Dancer* are all I have." When Fortis didn't respond, Lakshaw turned in her seat to face him. "What's the job, anyway? Anders didn't give me a lot of details."

"That makes two of us," he said. "Lay off the TEJG and embark a crew and equipment via shuttle. Transport the crew and equipment to a designated position at a designated time and stand by for further instructions. Expected mission duration is three weeks."

"That's not much to go on."

"You're welcome to return to SOMO, and I'll find another master to take the job. While we're gone, maybe you can convince Anders to give you *Dancer* when we get back."

"Have you worked for Anders long?"

"Anders? Never met him," Fortis said.

"Never met him? How in—" Lakshaw stopped and gave him a look that was part anger and part annoyance. "Are you a spook?"

Fortis shook his head. "Nope, I'm not a spook. I'm just a guy trying to earn a paycheck, same as you."

"Same as me, my ass. Speaking of gifts, your rich daddy sent you a gift. It's secured in the cargo bay."

"Good."

"Hey Captain." An angry voice came over the intercom. *"The fuckers took our cargo shuttles. All we have is the little one."*

"Dammit! Hang on, Yak." Lakshaw looked at Fortis. "How bad do you need the cargo shuttles?"

"I don't know. How many men can fit aboard your little one?"

"A hundred, more if they're good friends. A hundred and fifty."

"What happened to your other shuttles?"

Lakshaw scoffed. "This is SOMO, which is another way of saying legalized theft. Shuttles get beat up pretty bad, so they take them from ships in salvage orbit and assign them elsewhere."

"Can we get yours back?"

"Probably not. They're on another ship headed God-knows-where by now. We could probably get replacements if you want to wait a week or two."

"We're not waiting. We'll make do with what we have."

Lakshaw nodded. "Hey Yak, we're going without them."

"Okay, skipper."

"Captain, pre-launch checks are complete and satisfactory," Doe announced. "All stations have reported they are manned and ready. All airlocks and outer hatches are secure, and the airtight integrity status board is green. *Dancer* is prepared for launch."

"Very well. Launch *Dancer* and put us in waiting orbit near the TEJG."

* * *

Shortly after Dancer got underway, Fortis messaged Anders and reported his status. A few minutes later, Anders replied.

Embark Paladins ASAP. Proceed to coordinates transmitted to Lakshaw and await further tasking. Expect target location on short notice.

He returned to the control room and found Lakshaw examining a holo of the Terra Earth Sector.

"Anders sent some coordinates," she said before Fortis could speak. "Looks like we're headed for the Free Sector."

Fortis managed to keep a straight face. "I don't know. Where do the coordinates plot?"

She zoomed in on the area around the Freedom Jump Gate and pointed to a flashing red dot nearby. "Right next to the gate."

"That doesn't mean we're jumping, but it would be better if that information doesn't get out. Right now, we need to focus on getting my men and their gear aboard. Do you have any preference on where to rendezvous with them?"

"I was waiting on you to tell me. Where are they launching from?"

"Southern hemisphere."

"Okay." Lakshaw entered a few keystrokes and another red dot appeared in the vicinity of Terra Earth. "Send them these numbers, and we'll meet them there. How soon do you expect them?"

"Thirty-six hours, give or take. I'll have a better idea after I send these coordinates to them."

Fortis took a walk around *Dancer* while he waited for a response from Charlotte. His first impression of an aging, but well-maintained, ship was borne out everywhere he looked. He didn't know how long the vessel had been in salvage orbit, but it was obvious the crew hadn't wasted any time returning her to a high standard of readiness and cleanliness.

While he looked around the cargo bay, a crewman with wild grey hair and a shaggy beard approached. Fortis recognized him as one of the men from the dock.

"Everything to your liking?" he asked.

"Absolutely." Fortis stuck out his hand. "Abner Fortis."

The man wiped his hand on his stained coveralls and took Fortis' hand. "Yakeev Blazerius. Yak for short. I'm the cargo master and second engineer."

"Good to meet you. The ship looks good," Fortis said.

"Lakshaw keeps us on our toes. She insists we keep her looking good." Yak winked. "It helps her get top dollar for charters."

Fortis didn't respond, so Yak continued.

"How many guests are we expecting on this trip?"

"Two hundred, give or take."

"How much cargo?"

"I don't know. How much can she handle?"

Yak laughed. "A lot more than any two hundred humans can carry."

After a quick look around the main propulsion space led by Yak, Fortis thanked him and headed for the crew's mess. His communicator beeped while he sipped a cup of ersatz coffee, and he saw a response from Charlotte.

Paladins underway. ETA to rendezvous twenty-six hours. Two hundred plus two standard cargo containers.

He showed Lakshaw the message, and she nodded.

"We'll be ready to receive."

* * *

Fortis squinted in the bright African sun as he aimed his pulse pistol at Adam Zeiler. Zeiler's face twisted with fear as he raised his hands in surrender.

Tactical police burst onto the roof and tackled Fortis just as he squeezed the trigger. The bolt hit Zeiler in the chest and threw him backward into space. He didn't make a sound, but Fortis saw accusation in his eyes.

"Why?" they screamed.

Fortis woke up with a start, and it took him several seconds to remember he was aboard *Dancer*. His heart pounded and his pillow was damp with sweat as the last images of his unsettling dream faded.

There was no chance of getting back to sleep, so Fortis went for a walk around the ship to clear his head. He ended up at the control room door. When he poked his head inside, Fortis saw Lakshaw and Doe hunched over a chess board.

"I'm not interrupting, am I?"

"No. C'mon in. I'm about to do the impossible."

Lakshaw moved a piece, and Doe immediately countered.

"Checkmate, Captain."

"Fuck. Set 'em up again, Doe."

"They say it's impossible to beat an AI at chess."

Lakshaw twisted around and looked at Fortis for a moment.

"Doe, go down to the mess and bring up a fresh pot of coffee, please. And two mugs this time."

"On my way, Captain."

When the AI was gone, Lakshaw smiled. "I don't like to use him for silly tasks like that, even though I could. Some people treat their AIs like slaves, but Doe is more like my friend."

Fortis looked at the chess board. "Why are you playing chess with an AI? You know you can't win."

"Can't win? Why not?"

"Because an AI can analyze every possible move on every turn and calculate which one leads to the highest probability of victory. Even the best human players can't compete with that for long."

"Really? I beat Doe all the time. As often as I wish."

"Even Dragovic, the greatest chess player in history, couldn't beat an AI. He had a seventeen-year unbeaten streak against human players, but when he went up against an AI, he lost every game. It was big news when I was in university."

"I know, and after he lost, he killed himself."

"So, you're better than Dragovic?"

Lakshaw shook her head. "Not even close."

Doe returned with a jug of coffee and two mugs. After he served Fortis and Lakshaw, he sat back down and resumed studying the chess board.

"You don't believe me?" Lakshaw asked Fortis.

"I'm not calling you a liar, if that's what you mean," he replied. "I'm skeptical."

Doe made a move. "Your turn."

Lakshaw picked up her queen, her king, and Doe's king. She swept the remaining pieces onto the deck and put Doe's king in the corner and her queen in a checkmate position. Her king went into the opposite corner.

"Checkmate."

Doe stared at the board for thirty seconds before he looked up. "You win again, Captain. Another game?"

"Not just now," she said. "Doe, go to sleep."

Doe put his hands in his lap and his chin on his chest, the classic AI sleep position.

"See? I won."

Fortis scoffed. "You cheated."

"You could say that. Or you could say that I recognized I was at a severe disadvantage, so I improvised a way to win. You Space Marines do it all the time."

"That's different. That's war. Chess is a game."

"'Chess is like war on a board.' A famous chess champion named Bobby Fisher said that a long time ago, and it's still true today."

"Chess is a game. It has rules. What you did isn't chess. It's not fair."

"You don't have any rules in war? Do you kill everything in front of you that's not a Space Marine?"

"No, of course not."

"But you would if you had to. If you were at such a severe disadvantage that you were at risk of defeat or worse, you'd kill everything."

"Okay, I see your point, but that's different. War is life or death. Cheating to beat an AI at chess isn't."

Lakshaw looked at Doe for a moment. "I love Doe. He's been with me since I graduated from Fleet Academy. I rely on him a lot because he's almost infallible, and yet I cheat to win because it reminds me that he can be beaten. We can defeat AIs at anything, if we remember that they're trapped by the rules we created. Did you see how he reacted when I knocked the pieces off the board?"

"He didn't."

"Exactly. He didn't react because he didn't recognize it as a legitimate move. The next legitimate move he saw was my checkmate, and he was beaten."

"How are you going to win if Doe learns to cheat?"

"He won't, because cheating violates the rules of the game. If the rules of the game were changed to include sweeping your opponent's pieces off the board, then every game would have one move, and white would always win. Have you ever heard of the Karlstad Experiment?"

Fortis shook his head.

"During my second year at the Academy, a group of cadets traveled to the University of Karlstad to observe and participate in a series of war games between two AIs that had been running for eight months. Every move that gave one side an advantage was countered by a move that swung the balance the other way. Step by step, every single game escalated until weapons of mass destruction wiped out the opposing populations. There were no winners.

"Then they put us cadets on one side and an AI on the other. We won in under five minutes. You want to know how?"

"You swept the pieces off the board. Your first move was weapons of mass destruction."

Lakshaw smiled. "Exactly. And that's how humans can defeat AIs. Don't play by their rules. Remember that."

She winked and then touched the back of Doe's head. The AI sat up.

"Another game, Captain?"

* * * * *

Chapter Eighteen

Twenty-seven hours later, Fortis stood behind Yak in the cargo crane control tower and watched as the shaggy cargo master manipulated the joystick controls. On a screen above the cargo bay viewport, he could see two large containers approaching *Dancer* from the Paladin shuttle, guided by cargo drones. To save time, Yak had equalized the cargo bay pressurization and opened the door before the drones arrived.

It was Yak's job to pluck the containers from the drones using *Dancer's* retractable cargo crane and guide them into the cargo bay. It was a simple operation, but it was fraught with hazards.

The drones could lose control of their load and collide with *Dancer*, which might puncture the hull and kill them all. The handoff between drone and cargo crane could go wrong and send the containers spinning off into space. The drones could fail to release, or the crane could fail, either of which could force *Dancer* to call for assistance and the inevitable flood of questions regarding the cargo and why the two ships hadn't docked at the jump gate for the transfer.

"Yak, the first load is at the door," Lakshaw's voice announced over a speaker buried in the maze of pipes that ran through the overhead.

"I can see that, thank you," Yak muttered to himself. It was clear to Fortis that the cargo master was feeling the strain of the evolution.

Yak extended the cargo crane and manipulated the hydraulic jaws to clamp down on the first container. He pressed a button on his console, and the cargo drones released the container and moved away from *Dancer*. After some careful maneuvering, Yak landed the container in the bay where two crewmen in pressure suits and grav boots secured it using pad eyes recessed in the deck. When they finished, one of them flashed a thumbs up to the control tower.

"First container is aboard and secured," Yak reported to Lakshaw.

"Second load is inbound," she replied.

The second pair of drones were six meters from *Dancer* when the operating lights on one of them went out. The load began to turn as the operational drone kept thrusting, and the spinning load continued toward *Dancer*.

"Fuck!" Yak shoved the joystick forward and the crane extended out to deflect the load. He punched at his console, and the working drone released the load and flew off.

"What's going on, Yak?" Lakshaw demanded over the speaker.

"Shut the fuck up." Yak opened the jaws of the crane and tried to grab the container as it spun by. The jaws closed on the container and one of the drone hooks, and the load stopped spinning.

"Talk to me, Yak."

"One of the fucking drones died on approach and the load became unstable," Yak reported in a surprisingly calm voice. "I released the good drone and grabbed the load, but I got a piece of the dead drone in the jaws."

After a few seconds, Lakshaw replied, *"Can you open the jaws and grab the container from another angle?"*

"Only if you can drive the ship sideways to let the container drift into the hangar in case the crane craps out," Yak retorted.

Fortis covered his mouth to stifle his laughter.

"That's not helpful, Yak."

"Neither are your fucking ideas," he grumbled. He pressed the transmit button on the console. "Captain, your idea has merit, but if the crane suffers a casualty while the jaws are open, and there are no other drones available to assist, we will lose control of the container. It might hit our ship, another ship, or the jump gate. Best case, it would drift off into space for a billion years. In any event, I cannot recommend opening the crane jaws. What does the delivery ship have to say about their drone?"

"They're not answering. Can you recover the load?"

Yak lowered his chin to his chest and took a deep breath before answering. "Once again, Captain, your idea has merit, but the risk of bringing a deranged drone inside our ship is too great for me to agree to do so. It might—"

"Okay, Yak, I get it." Lakshaw sounded annoyed. *"What I need to know is, what are we going to do about this thing?"*

Yak flashed Fortis a grin. "Now we're getting somewhere." He pressed the transmit button. "I'm going to retract the crane as close to the cargo door as I can. Then I'm going to put on a suit, climb out there with a cutting torch, and cut the drone free. After that, I'll bring the container into the cargo bay."

There was a long pause before Lakshaw replied. *"Okay. I'll let the delivery ship know what you're doing."*

"Negative!" Yak said. "Don't tell them anything except that we're trying to figure it out. I don't want their drone jockeys to fire that thing up while I'm out there cutting. Wait until it's clear."

"But you're cutting their drone."

"They shouldn't have sent a piece of shit over here in the first place."

Another long pause. *"Okay but hurry up. If they get impatient, they might start fooling with the drone anyway."*

Yak looked at Fortis. "Do me a favor, would you? While I'm out there, sit here and watch. If anything goes wrong, hit this button." He pointed to a button labeled "Retract Crane."

"Are you sure? There isn't anyone else?" Fortis pointed to the crewmen in the cargo bay. "What about them?"

"They're dock monkeys," Yak said as he headed for the hatch. "Strong backs, weak minds. Most of them don't know how to read."

"Okay then, if you're sure. I'll be right here."

"This won't take but a minute."

It took Yak longer to get dressed and assemble his tools than it did to cut the cargo drone free. He climbed back into the cargo bay so fast that Fortis thought he'd forgotten a tool or something. Yak returned to the cargo crane control tower with a satisfied look on his face. He slid into the controller seat.

"Here we go."

The drone had hovered next to the container after Yak cut it free, so he nudged it away from *Dancer* with the crane before he retracted the container into the cargo bay. The crew had the container tied down in seconds, and Yak secured the crane and lowered the cargo bay door.

"Captain, the container is aboard and secured, and the dead drone is clear of the ship. The crane is stowed for travel, and the cargo bay door is secured. Request permission to pressurize the cargo bay."

"Negative. We have another container coming."

"Another one? I thought you said two."

"The first two were equipment. The third one is carrying our guests."

* * *

The drones delivered the third container without mishap, and Yak guided it into the cargo bay. As soon as it was on deck, Yak stowed the crane and secured the cargo door without direction from the control room. The cargo handlers scrambled to secure the container as Yak began to equalize the pressure.

"Let's get them out of there as soon as possible," Lakshaw ordered unnecessarily.

Yak keyed his mic. "In progress, Captain." He turned to Fortis. "Never, ever work for your ex-wife. C'mon, let's go down and greet our guests."

As soon as the pressure alarms cleared, and the hatch interlocks released, Fortis and Yak entered the cargo bay. The cargo handlers opened the doors on the third box, and the Paladins climbed out. Each man wore a portable breathing device like the emergency escape devices in use on most ships. They fell into ranks, and two men detached from the group and approached Fortis.

"I'm Herron, and this is Zylstra," the larger of the two said. "I'm the lead on this contract. I command First Company. Zylstra has Second."

Herron had dark, narrow features and a dark five o'clock shadow, while Zylstra had wispy brown hair that covered the half of his head that wasn't gnarled burn scars. His left ear was new, pink tissue, and the scars disappeared under his collar.

"I'm Fortis." The trio shook hands. "That was quite an entrance."

"We left Burketown in the box because there are a lot of people who like to keep track of what Paladin is up to. It's uncomfortable but effective."

"Hey, Herron, everyone is here," one of the Paladins called.

Lakshaw appeared with another *Dancer* crewman in tow.

"This is Zenith Lakshaw, master of *Dancer*," Fortis said. "This is Herron and Zylstra."

Lakshaw stepped forward. "Welcome aboard, gents. This is Dinkle, she's my head steward. She'll take care of your messing and berthing needs."

While Dinkle worked out the details of the Paladin embarkation, Lakshaw pulled Fortis aside.

"I hope your rich daddy has deep pockets, because the shuttle master is pissed off about his drone."

"I'm sure he can cover it. Send him a bill."

"Speaking of your rich daddy, have you heard any more about where we're going?"

"All I have are the coordinates he gave you. Maybe he'll give me more when I report the arrival of the Paladins."

"Keep me posted. I'm going to get us pointed in the right direction." She nodded toward the mercenaries, who were unpacking their weapons and gear. "Make sure they keep the weapons in here, please."

* * *

Fortis stood against the bulkhead near the hatch and watched the Paladins conduct their weapons and gear checks. They didn't appear to be well organized, but Fortis chalked some of that up to the unfamiliar confines of the cargo bay. Each company had a separate box, and it was obvious First Company had done a better job packing their gear. Each Paladin went in and emerged with an armload of gear and weapons. The Second Company box must have been packed by category instead of operator, because they had to unload everything before the Paladins could claim their gear.

Herron and Zylstra joined him and frowned at what they were witnessing.

"Buncha fucking monkeys," Zylstra growled. "I've seen privates do better."

"I'm guessing you were a gunny," Fortis said.

"Nope. Warrant Two, mech element commander, Second Division. Dropped onto Maltaan right behind you recon types. Maltaani air defense shot a missile up our ass and the drop ship came down sideways." He gestured to his scar tissue. "I left half my head inside my helmet when we bailed out. The Fleet hospital gave me a new ear, and the day after they decided not to try dermabrasion to fix up the rest, they divvied me."

Fortis shook his head. "Bastards." He pointed to Herron. "How about you?"

"I had a platoon in Third Division. We dropped on the space port on the second day and missed the fun, so they assigned us to round up the test tubes. I got into a kinetic disagreement with one of the GRC mercenaries and wound up in the brig. They divvied me the day I got out."

"I guess most of these guys are Space Marines? I've been getting some pretty strange looks from some of them."

Herron chuckled. "They know who you are. Your reputation precedes you."

"What reputation is that? I don't have a reputation."

Herron and Zylstra traded looks. "You certainly do."

"Okay, what is it?"

"Space Marines tend to die in large numbers around you."

"What the fuck does that mean?" Fortis felt his blood rising. "I don't—"

"Pada-Pada." Herron held up a finger. "The Battle of Balfan-48. Lima Company. The invasion of Maltaan. That's a lot of dead Space Marines."

"I didn't kill those Marines. I worked hard to prevent their deaths."

"Nobody's accusing you of killing anyone or being a careless leader. You gotta admit, though. The shit seems to fly pretty thick wherever you're at. If they thought you were careless or inept, nobody would have boarded that shuttle."

"Huh. All right. I've never heard that before, but if it's any consolation, we're probably not going to see a lot of shit flying in any direction on this mission."

"Now I know we're fucked."

Herron went on to explain the Paladin organization. The battalion consisted of two ninety-man companies, led by Herron and Zylstra. Each company consisted of three thirty-man platoons, and the platoons were further broken down into ten-man squads of two fire teams each.

"Each platoon has a demo squad with two hundred kilos of high explosives."

Fortis whistled. "That's a lot of boom-boom."

"Charlotte didn't know how big you wanted to go, so we brought a lot. We can always take it home. Everyone else carries a standard Space Marine kit of pulse rifles, grenades, and personal sidearms."

"There's a medic assigned to each platoon as well, along with an electronics tech," Zylstra added. "If you get hit, you're probably better off treating yourself."

"We also have a twenty-man command element. Organize them however you want, or we can integrate them into the companies. It's your choice."

"Let's leave it for now. As we get more details about the target, we can adjust."

* * * * *

Chapter Nineteen

Ystremski saw the biodome was open-bay berthing, with bunkbeds and lockers lined up over two-thirds of the floor. There was a classroom area with rows of chairs and a lectern in front, and tall bookshelves lined the wall. Other squires in distinctive blue smocks moved around the dome, but there was no organization or purpose to their presence.

Ystremski noticed the bunks were organized alphabetically, so he picked his way down the rows, looking for the Y section. His was a bottom bunk, and the one next to him was occupied when he found it. The man sat up to greet him.

"Nidal Zerian," the man said as he extended his hand.

"Petr Ystremski."

"Welcome back to boot camp." Zerian smiled. "It's not bad, really. It gets dark back here after lights out, and the head is across the way, so we're out of the main traffic areas. When a knight comes in looking for a few volunteers, they rarely get back this far. Speaking of knights, my knight is Brother Albert Machel. Who is yours?"

"Brother Pil Gustafson."

Zerian let out a low whistle. "Well then, you're practically royalty. Brother Gustafson is close to the top of the food chain."

Ystremski shrugged. "I was a Space Marine ten days ago and a page until a few hours ago. I don't know much about the politics around here."

"You've done well thus far." Zerian sucked in a breath and stiffened, then bowed his head and stared at the floor.

Ystremski turned and saw a man dressed in an unfamiliar crimson smock staring at the two squires. Unsure what to do, he bowed his head, too. After several seconds, the man stalked off.

Zerian let his breath out with a *whoosh*. "I hate when they come around."

"'They?' Who's 'they?'"

"Knights Errant. They're like, well, they adhere to the old ways of the Knighthood. Did you see the scars on his cheeks?"

Ystremski shook his head. "I was too busy eyeballing the floor."

"They're fanatical. They don't participate in regular life around here. The Master gives them special tasks, and they do them."

"Special tasks like what?"

Zerian looked around before he answered. "It's better if we don't discuss this, Brother Petr. Ask your knight to explain. Just know that it's better not to have anything to do with a Knight Errant, if you can help it."

The appearance of the Knight Errant seemed to unnerve Zerian, and he said something about a late appointment before he hurried away. Alone again, Ystremski decided to explore the rest of the biodome.

All the bunks were neat, and the military influence on the occupants was obvious. The head reeked of pine-scented chemical cleaners, and Ystremski felt a twinge of nerves when he entered one of the stalls. He fished his communicator out of his pocket and sat down. He powered it up, typed in 'Arrived Sanctuary,' and waited several seconds for the Transmit light to blink. After he flushed, Ystremski powered the unit down and slipped it back into his pocket before he left the head.

Ystremski nodded at the other squires he encountered as he wandered around, but none spoke to him until he was perusing the books that packed the shelves next to the classroom area.

"Looking for anything specific?" A bespectacled man in a blue smock with an armload of books approached.

"No, I'm just browsing," Ystremski said.

The two men shook hands.

"Squire Malias," the other squire said. He shifted his load of books. "I'm the unofficial librarian."

"Squire Petr. I'm the new guy. Can I give you a hand?"

Ystremski didn't recognize any of the authors or titles. The books were arranged alphabetically by author, and they made quick work of shelving them. While they worked, they traded names of their knights, which Ystremski realized was the main part of a squire's identity.

"Thank you for your help."

"My pleasure."

"Petr, you said you're the new guy. May I suggest a book to aid your journey to knighthood?"

"Uh, sure. If it's okay with my knight, I mean."

Malias smiled. "I'm sure he'll approve." He took down a slim volume and handed it to Ystremski. "Beginnings of Brotherhood," was the title, and the author was Pil Gustafson.

Ystremski nodded. "You're right. I'm sure he'll approve."

"Squire Petr, you look familiar. Were you a Space Marine?"

"Yes, I was. Were you?"

"No, I was Fleet. I was a cargo handler on *Atlas*, the Ninth Division flagship."

"Maybe that's where we met. I dropped with Ninth Division from *Atlas*."

"That must be it." Malias gestured to a group of lounge chairs arranged around a low table. "Many of our brother squires enjoy reading there. The chairs are comfortable, the lighting is good, and it's convenient to return books to the shelves."

"That's a good idea, thank you." Ystremski took his book to the reading area and settled into a chair from which he could see the rest of the biodome. He feigned interest in Gustafson's treatise about the origins of the Kuiper Knights and their belief system as he listened to the rhythm of the building around him. Groups of squires came and went, but none approached the reading area. Malias had disappeared.

A short time later, Ystremski returned the book to the shelf where Malias had taken it from. After a moment's hesitation, instinct drove him to return to the head.

The sinks were mounted to the wall, and when he ran his hand underneath one of them, he discovered a lip several centimeters wide. After a quick look around, Ystremski stashed his communicator under the third sink. It was his only link to the outside world, but it was also a damning piece of evidence should the Knights become suspicious of him. Satisfied with his decision, he returned to the main room.

The biodome began to fill with squires, which he took as a signal that the workday had ended. A hundred conversations sprang up as the young men stretched their personalities after being confined within the strict limits of their service during the day. Several of them nodded to Ystremski, and a small group followed Zerian over to greet him. Zerian introduced them in turn.

"Brother Petr, this is Brother Zao, Brother Shane, and Brother Tieg. Brother Petr is the new squire to Brother Pil Gustafson."

The other squires expressed their admiration for his lofty assignment, and Ystremski forced himself to smile. He hadn't yet figured out the significance of his assignment, but it gave him some much-needed credibility.

A horn sounded, and the mass of squires headed for the doors.

"Breaking bread," Zerian explained. "Join us."

Ystremski watched black-clad Knights and red Knights Errant streaming into the next dome over as he followed Zerian into the squire and page dome. The set up was the same as lunch in the other dome, Steam tables along one wall manned by pages, while rows of tables filled the rest of the floor. He didn't see any familiar faces in the food line.

The food was the same colorless, tasteless stuff he'd had for lunch. Ystremski tried to match the gusto of the squires at his table, and his tray was empty in short order.

"What's next?" he asked Zerian as they deposited their trays at the end of the line.

"We have free time until eighteen hundred and then evening devotion in our biodome," Zerian replied. "When evening devotion is over, we're free again until lights out at twenty-one hundred. That's when you're expected to shower and prepare for the next day."

"Speaking of tomorrow," Ystremski said as they entered the biodome. "What am I supposed to be doing during the day?"

"Brother Gustafson will instruct you." Zerian chuckled. "Don't worry, I doubt he has forgotten about you."

"He told me he was going to come for me after services."

"I'm sure he'll give you guidance then."

The dome filled up with chattering squires fresh from their evening meal, and the noise level was almost unbearable.

"Is it always this loud?" Ystremski shouted to Zerian.

"There was a knighting ceremony during services last night, so everyone is convinced there will be one tonight as well," Zerian yelled back.

Squires began to fill the rows of seats as eighteen hundred approached.

"As squire to Brother Gustafson, you can sit in the front row if you like," Zerian said.

"What about you?"

Zerian gave Ystremski a sad smile. "Brother Machel's rank earns me a spot standing in the back behind the chairs reserved for you."

"I don't have to sit up there, do I?"

"Not if you don't want to."

"Then I'll stay right here."

A sudden hush fell over the dome and Ystremski saw Brother Gustafson enter through a door behind the lectern, followed by a pair of stern-faced Knights Errant. Squires scrambled to fill the remaining seats, and by the time Gustafson stood in front of them with his arms raised, the room was dead silent.

"Blessings of The Master upon thee," Gustafson said.

"And upon thee," the squires responded.

"Light of The Master upon thee," Gustafson continued.

"And upon thee."

The devotional service continued that way for several minutes as Gustafson went through a litany of ways The Master blessed the crowd, and they responded in kind. Finally, the knight ended it as he had begun.

"Blessings of The Master upon thee."

"And upon thee."

Gustafson regarded the squires for a moment before he began.

"Tonight, we speak of death."

None of the squires moved.

"The Knighthood has suffered a great tragedy. One of ours, a page, barely a man, passed to the other side aboard *Pilgrimage* today."

Cramer.

A low murmur swept across the room.

"For a Kuiper Knight, death is not a reason for mourning. Death is the next step in our eternal journey and nothing to fear. To die with honor, in service to the Knighthood. That is our most fervent wish.

"No, what happened aboard Pilgrimage was neither honorable, nor in service to the Knighthood. That is the tragedy, and that is your lesson tonight."

Gustafson related the story of Cramer and his sin of gossip. Heads nodded as he described how the other pages had convicted him, and there were gasps of surprise when he got to the gauntlet. Ystremski looked at the squires around him and saw eyes shining with excitement as the Knight detailed every blow.

Gustafson stopped mid-story. "Where is Squire Petr? He's here somewhere. Where is he?"

"Here he is!" cried Zerian as he waved his hand over his head.

Everyone turned and stared at Ystremski, and his face flushed bright red.

"Squire Petr, join me," beckoned Gustafson.

Many hands propelled Ystremski forward until he stood next to Gustafson. The Knight put his arm around Ystremski's shoulders.

"This is my new squire, Squire Petr. Let me tell you why I chose him."

Ystremski went numb as Gustafson told the squires how he spat in Cramer's face and slapped him, and when it was over the squires roared their approval. A hard knot formed in his stomach as he bathed in the adulation of the other squires, and even the Knights Errant nodded their approval.

The squires in the front row made room for Ystremski, and he sat through the rest of the devotional service without seeing or hearing a thing. He stood when the crowd stood, sat when they sat, and muttered wordlessly when Gustafson closed with the litany of blessings. Finally, it was over.

"Squire Petr, come."

Ystremski followed Gustafson and the Knights Errant through the door and out into the darkness beyond.

Out behind the dome, Gustafson and the Knights Errant gathered around Ystremski.

Have I been betrayed? Did they find the communicator?

Ystremski braced himself for an attack.

"Squire Petr, this is Brother Addison and Brother Merrill," Gustafson said as he gestured to the red-clad knights. The pair nodded but didn't offer their hands, so Ystremski only nodded back. "They are Knights Errant. They wear red smocks because they are specially selected by The Master for certain tasks based on their special skills and experience. Knights Errant don't take squires. A Kuiper Knight must first earn the black smock of knighthood and prove himself before The Master elevates him to Knight Errant."

Ystremski knew most of this from skimming through Gustafson's book. He didn't know where Gustafson was going with his explanation, so he remained silent.

"I am leading these brothers, along with many others, on a critical mission tomorrow—a mission which will bring glory to the Knighthood and solidify our position here in the Free Sector. It is far too soon for you to be advanced to full knighthood, and especially Knight Errant. On a mission such as ours, I would not normally bring a squire along, but I believe you have skills and experience which will prove useful."

"You are choosing me, as The Master chose them," Ystremski said.

Addison shifted his feet, and Merrill hissed at him.

"Blasphemy!"

Gustafson held up his hand. "Be at peace, Brothers. The squire knows not what he says. Squire Petr, it is a grave transgression to make comparisons to The Master. Even in matters such as this, it may appear to be as you say, but I assure you, it is not."

Ystremski hung his head in silence.

What kind of gibberish is that?

"I am appointing you to assist Brother Addison and Brother Merrill on our mission. I am confident you will perform your duties with diligence and prove yourself worthy of knighthood."

"Thank you, Brother Pil. I will endeavor to do all that is asked of me."

"Good." Gustafson patted Ystremski on the shoulder. "Don't speak of this to anyone, Squire Petr. Our success depends on secrecy and surprise. Sleep well, and someone will come for you in the morning."

The three Knights walked off into the darkness as Ystremski stared after them. He turned and reentered the dome. Inside, Zerian and several other squires greeted him with worried smiles.

"You're okay," Zerian said as he looked Ystremski over. "No cuts or broken bones?"

"No, why?"

"Normally when Gustafson and the Knights Errant take a squire outside, it's for a personal sanction to correct a misbehavior," Zerian said.

One of the other squires pointed to a thick scar on his cheek. "I laughed at something Brother Gustafson said during a service. I thought it was a joke. I don't laugh anymore."

"I thought you might have been sanctioned for not sitting in the appropriate row," Zerian said. "Praise The Master, I am glad you were not hurt because of me."

"I'm not hurt at all. Just a stern talking to," Ystremski said.

A short while later, Ystremski joined the stream of squires headed for the showers. The scars on his abdomen and back drew a lot of stares, and he was happy when he returned to the relative solitude of his bunk with a fresh blue smock over his shoulder, which he hung up next to his bunk.

"Don't mind their curiosity, Petr," Zerian said from his bunk. "Many of them are veterans of the Fleet or the ISMC, but not many have seen active combat. You have quite a reputation."

"It's okay, as long as they're only looking at my scars," Ystremski said. After a second, the two men laughed together. Ystremski climbed onto his own bunk and propped himself up on an elbow. "Do you know a squire name Malias?"

"A squire? No. Not a squire. I know of a Knight Errant named Malias, but not a squire."

Ystremski's mouth dried up, and his blood froze.

Malias is a Knight Errant?

He swallowed hard. "Huh. I guess I heard his name wrong. He recommended a book earlier, and I wanted to look him up and thank him again."

"I'm sure you'll see him around," Zerian said as he rolled over onto his back. "If you have to piss or anything, you better hurry. You've got about two minutes before lights out."

"I'm good. We don't have to stay in our bunks, do we? I mean, I might have to go later."

"The fire watch is supposed to report anyone moving around, but nobody ever does. Don't worry about it. Just be quick and quiet."

"Lights out!" someone called from over by the door, and the biodome went black. The only light came from the red emergency exit signs over the doors and the lights in the head.

Just like the Corps.

Ystremski closed his eyes and tried to clear his mind. Thoughts of Tanya and the kids slipped around the edges of his consciousness, but he pushed them away. There would be time enough for them later, but right now, he needed to focus on his mission. He hoped that whatever mission Gustafson had assigned him to wouldn't interfere with his efforts to locate the hijacked weapons.

Ystremski soon fell into a deep, dreamless sleep.

* * *

Three hours later, the pressure in his bladder forced Ystremski to open his eyes. In the bunks around him, men snored, farted, and mumbled in their sleep. The urge to urinate told him it was time to get up, and he padded barefoot to the head. He saw the flashlight of the fire watch at the far end of the dome, so he went straight to the sink where he had hidden the communicator. He retrieved it in one smooth motion and immediately went into one of the stalls and locked the door.

Ystremski sat down and relieved himself before he looked at the communicator. He thought about powering it up to send an updated set of coordinates but decided against it. Preserving the battery was crucial since he didn't know how long it would take to find the stolen weapons.

He had a sudden surge of paranoia when he imagined the Kuiper Knights had a system to track rogue transmitters, but he shook it off.

They can't even make decent food.

A pair of boots appeared under the door.

"Are you okay in there?" a soft voice asked.

"Yeah." Ystremski groaned. "The food."

"It hits everybody," the voice said.

"I'll be okay."

"Best get back to your bunk."

Ystremski flushed and stuck the communicator deep into his left armpit. He could hold it there without the danger of it falling from his waistband. He nodded his thanks to the waiting fire watch on his way out the door.

Ystremski returned to his bunk and waited. He heard the soft footsteps of the fire watch and closed his eyes as the flashlight beam drew closer. The steps paused at the head of his bunk for a moment before they moved off. He counted to three hundred before he peeked through slitted eyelids and saw the flashlight moving away.

He lifted his arm away from his body enough to allow the communicator to slip onto his mattress. With a sleepy sigh, Ystremski rolled over and retrieved it. Another sigh, and he slipped it inside his pillowcase. Under the mattress was the obvious place to hide it, but it would be easier to retrieve it from the pillowcase.

He got comfortable and soon fell back to sleep.

* * * * *

Chapter Twenty

"Squire Petr."

A hand shook his shoulder, and Ystremski grabbed and twisted as he jumped out of his rack.

"Argh!" Ystremski blinked when he realized it was Brother Merrill's hand, and he turned it loose.

"Brother Merrill, my most humble apologies."

Merrill gave him an angry look as he rubbed his injured hand. "Get dressed. We're leaving."

The Knight Errant turned and headed for the door. Ystremski scrambled to don his clothes and throw on his smock.

"What's going on?" Zerian whispered from his bunk. "Where are you going?"

"Go back to sleep," Ystremski said. He felt around inside his pillow until he located the communicator, which he slipped into his pocket. "You're dreaming."

Ystremski trotted past the fire watch as he ran to catch Merrill. The fire watch just nodded and pointed his flashlight beam at the door.

Outside, the sky was beginning to lighten. Ystremski saw knights in black and red scrambling aboard waiting trucks, and he spotted Merrill near the front of the column. He ran to catch up and fell in beside the Knight Errant. When they got to the lead truck, Merrill pointed to the back.

"In."

Without hesitation, Ystremski climbed into the bed of the truck and saw it was full of Knights Errant. They all glared at him, but several grudgingly made room for him to sit. The convoy drove to the far end of the makeshift space port where a shuttle waited. As soon as the trucks stopped, the Knights Errant jumped up and piled off the truck. Ystremski was swept along with the group, and he looked in all directions for Merrill or Addison as they made for the shuttle.

He caught sight of Addison standing by the boarding ramp and managed to squeeze out of the group.

"Brother Merrill brought me here, but I lost track of him," he told Addison.

Addison scowled. "He's already on board. Get on and take a seat in the back rows."

"Thank you, Brother Addison."

When Ystremski entered the cabin, it surprised him to see a group of squires seated in the back rows. He nodded as he took an empty seat and cinched his harness. The squires looked older than the other pages and squires he'd met, and he recognized the familiar hardness around their eyes. They had the look of combat veterans—Space Marines, men who had entered the crucible of war and emerged alive. Men who knew how to apply controlled violence to accomplish their mission. Whatever Gustafson had in mind, if it involved combat, he had brought the right sort.

He leaned back and closed his eyes as the shuttle engines started. The craft jerked into motion, and after a brief pause, the engines wound up and the shuttle rolled down the runway. Ystremski was pressed back in his seat as the shuttle took flight and made a near-vertical climb out of the atmosphere.

Once they were in space, Ystremski leaned over to the squire sitting next to him.

"Any idea where we're going?" he muttered.

His neighbor shook his head and remained silent.

Two hours later, the pilot came over the intercom. "Stand by to dock."

Ystremski heard a *clunk* as the shuttle mated with a pressurized collar.

"The hatch is pressurized," the pilot reported.

None of the squires moved. Ystremski saw Merrill squeeze through the Knights lined up to exit the shuttle, and when he caught the Knight Errant's eye, Merrill motioned to him.

Ystremski joined Merrill in the line and followed him through the hatch. When they were clear, Ystremski looked around. He stood in a familiar cargo bay filled with crates and boxes stacked to the overhead and secured to the deck with heavy chains. They were all an unmistakable shade of olive green, and although he couldn't make out the yellow lettering painted on each one, he recognized the weapons crates.

Colossus.

* * *

In the salon aboard the luxury yacht *Bellissima*, Liz Sherer paged through her notes on the story of the stolen weapons as she tried to divine their location and destination.

The complete wall of silence that greeted her inquiries in Kinshasa and Kiev told her there was something to the story. Sherer was an experienced journalist, and she knew the difference between, "I don't know" and "No comment." The former meant her sources truly didn't know, and the latter meant there was something there, but they couldn't talk about it.

Sherer had gone to the Terra Earth Jump Gate to troll for information among the spacefarers who congregated there. Almost immediately, she heard a rumor a Fleet flagship had been detected passing through the Freedom Gate a few days earlier. *Colossus* was the name she heard most often, and when she queried one of her sources directly, the response was a sputtering cross between "I don't know" and "No comment."

Bingo.

After some hardnosed wheeling and dealing with her former editor at TNN, she secured the funds to charter a ship into the Free Sector. Sheer good fortune got her a berth aboard *Bellissima*, a private vessel owned by a GRC executive, which was bound for an undisclosed destination in the Free Sector.

Bellissima was nearing the Leavitt Peripheral, the most populous area of the Free Sector, when Captain Moretti approached her in the salon.

"Pardon the interruption, *Signorina* Sherer, but there is a matter I must inform you of." Moretti's English was stilted and formal, and it never failed to make her smile.

"Yes, *Capitano*?"

"There is a ship approaching, and they have instructed us to stop for inspection," Moretti said.

"Is that a problem?"

"It is, eh, not usual. There is no authority to do such a thing here in the Free Sector."

"Then what are you going to do?"

Moretti gave an exaggerated shrug. "Ah, well, we will stop. *Bellissima* is not armed, as you know."

"Is it pirates?"

"Sadly, *Signorina*, I do not know."

Ninety minutes later, a shuttle docked with *Bellissima*, and a dozen armed men crowded aboard. Moretti had his crew assembled in the crew's mess, and Sherer stood with them.

"I am *Capitano* Andre Moretti, and *Bellissima* is my ship. How may I be of service to you, gentlemen?"

The boarding party leader surveyed the group. "You have a certain passenger," he said. His eyes landed on Sherer. "Her."

Two of the boarders seized the journalist and dragged her away from the crew.

"Hey, you bastards, that hurts!" Sherer struggled, but she couldn't escape their grasp.

Moretti and his crew watched helplessly as the boarders forced Sherer into their shuttle. The hatch slammed shut, and the shuttle disengaged.

"What's this all about, guys?" Sherer asked her captors. "Do I owe some of you some credits? Did we have a bad breakup in a former life?"

None of them responded, so she sat back and waited for the shuttle to return to its mother ship.

Someone is going to answer for this.

* * *

As *Dancer* approached the loiter point, Fortis' internal tension grew. He checked his communicator every hour or so, hoping to find an update from Anders, but there were none.

When he stopped in the cargo bay to check on the Paladins, he found them loose and seemingly unconcerned.

"Why worry?" Herron asked when he mentioned it to the mercenary leader. "We're getting paid whether we're playing cards or in a gunfight, remember?"

"Yeah, I can understand that. Not getting shot at makes every day better."

Fortis told Herron he expected their mission would involve a vessel takedown, so the Paladin company commanders devised some training scenarios to exercise their troops. They took turns assaulting and defending the cargo bay, pointing empty weapons and shouting, "Bang, bang!" with as much enthusiasm as they could muster. It was make-work to help pass the time, but there were still too many hours in the day, and the uncertainty of their jump-off date served to compound their restlessness.

The highlight of the training scenarios was when First Company tack-welded the cargo bay hatches, and Herron was forced to call a halt to the exercise after Second Company attackers made plans to assault the cargo bay by spacewalking around to the escape hatch.

"Welding the hatches shut was a clever idea, and so was spacewalking to the escape hatch," Herron told them. "It's also out of bounds."

"Both companies displayed ingenuity and a willingness to do whatever it took to complete the mission," Fortis said to Herron.

"Any word on our target?"

Fortis shook his head. "A ship. Nothing more yet. Lakshaw said we'll be at our loiter point around midday tomorrow. Maybe we'll hear something when we get there."

"This is the Paladin life. We live in the dark, they feed us bullshit, and when we get where we're going, the job isn't what they said."

"DINLI."

"Indeed." Herron looked around and lowered his voice. "A word of advice. I wouldn't get too carried away with the DINLI thing. Some of these guys are still sore at the Corps, if you get my meaning. Fucking peace dividend."

"Point taken."

"Hey, Yak told me *Dancer* doesn't have any shuttle pilots?"

"I hadn't heard that. I know she's down a couple shuttles."

"He was in here earlier and I asked about training on the shuttle. He said the primary pilot took another job when *Dancer* was salvaged, and they didn't hire another one."

"I'll talk to Lakshaw about it," Fortis said.

"Tell her I have a couple guys qualified for ship-to-ship shuttle ops. It would be good idea if she'd let them get some flight hours while we're loitering."

"Sounds good."

Fortis went to the control room and confirmed with Lakshaw that *Dancer* didn't have a dedicated shuttle pilot.

"I use Doe," she said. "It's not perfect because he only accepts commands from me, but it works."

"Herron said he has a couple guys who are qualified for ship-to-ship transfers," Fortis said. "If it's okay with you, I'd like to get them some flight time at the loiter point."

"I'll give you a tentative yes, but that's the best I can do right now. It depends on how things go when we get there."

After supper, Fortis checked his communicator but there were still no updates. Since his presence in the cargo bay was only tolerated, and

Dancer's virtual reality library was years out of date, he had nothing better to do than turn in early.

* * *

*D*ancer reached the loiter point the following afternoon, and Fortis reported to Anders. He received a four-word response.

Stand by for orders.

He found Herron and Zylstra in the cargo bay. "Nothing new on the mission," Fortis told them. "Hurry up and wait."

"We're going to run some training on the shuttle. Did you talk to Lakshaw about flight hours?"

"She gave me a tentative yes, depending on how things go here. I'll talk to her again this afternoon and see if you're good to go."

"Hey, Mr. Fortis," Dinkle called to Fortis from the hatch. "The captain wants you in the control room. She said it's important."

Fortis trotted through the passageways and scrambled up the ladders to the control room.

"What's going on?"

"We have company," Lakshaw said.

"What? Who?"

"I have no idea. We picked up a contact on the collision avoidance sensor a couple hours ago, and it's been closing ever since. I maneuvered to get out of the way, and it looks like she turned to follow."

"That's it?"

"That's it. *Dancer* doesn't have long-range sensors or scanners, just the standard navigation suite. All I can tell you is that it's a contact and it's moving this way. I don't even know if it's a ship, except I think it turned when we turned. At that range, what I'm calling a turn might be a resolution error. I just don't know."

"Have you tried hailing her?"

Lakshaw shook her head. "It's too soon. We've got at least six hours before the contact becomes a collision problem. If it hasn't turned by then, I'll call." She read Fortis' face. "We can't hail every ship we encounter."

"Hmm. Is there anything I can do to help you?"

"No. I have a question, though. Did you tell anyone where we were going?"

"I reported our loiter point arrival to Anders. He acknowledged the report but nothing else. Do you think this contact is deliberately closing on us?"

"Probably not. I don't know. We're not in the usual shipping lanes to the Freedom Jump Gate, but there could be something else out this way that's not on the charts. We'll have to wait and see."

"Okay, Captain, thanks for the heads up. If there's something you need, let me know."

Back in the shuttle bay, Fortis told Herron about the contact.

"What do you think it means?" Herron asked.

"Your guess is as good as mine. We're so far out of the way that it looks deliberate, but like Lakshaw said, there could be something out here we don't know about."

"What about us?"

"We have no reason to hide. We haven't done anything wrong," Fortis said.

"You're right, we haven't, but some people might view a ship full of mercenaries and weapons as a problem that needs resolving, legally or otherwise."

"Like whom?"

Herron chuckled. "Piracy is rampant out here. The UNT talks a big game about law and order and the Sky Marshals keep things under control around the TEJG, but their influence fades until you reach no man's land. The big players like the GRC have their own cutters, or they hire guys like us to protect their interests, and they enforce their own set of rules however they see fit. Plenty of pirates simply vanish, and nobody is the wiser."

"You think someone would mistake us for pirates?"

"From what I know about our mission, we *are* pirates. We're loitering near a jump gate, and we're training to assault a ship. That's what pirates do."

"But we're not… I mean, we… shit. I see your point."

"I'm not worried about it yet. This contact could be a lot of things. We'll have to wait and see."

* * *

Five hours later, Lakshaw summoned Fortis back to the control room.

"It's a ship, and they hailed us," she said as Fortis sank onto the fold-down seat next to her. "They claimed to be the Japanese Space Defense Force vessel *Sumida*."

"Japanese? What are they doing out here?"

"They're on an anti-piracy patrol," Doe said.

"The Big Four ship is on the wrong side of the jump gate for that, aren't they?"

"There's that, plus they don't speak Japanese," Lakshaw said. "I had Doe respond to their hail in Japanese, and it took them a long time to answer."

"It was an electronic translator," Doe said. "And a poor one at that."

"What are we going to do?"

"What can we do? We're unarmed, and we're too slow to run. We wait and see what they want."

"Can you send a distress call?"

"And say what? 'Help, we've been hailed by a Japanese ship that doesn't speak good Japanese.' I doubt anyone will respond to that."

"So, we just let them board us."

Lakshaw shook her head. "I didn't say that. I said let's wait and see what they want. This stuff happens all the time. Once they realize we're not carrying anything of value, they'll probably leave. If they try to board us, I'm sure you'll think of something."

Fortis returned to the cargo bay and told Herron what was happening.

"She's right, this happens all the time. What do you want us to do?"

"Nothing, for now."

"What if they try to board us?"

"Lakshaw said if it comes down to that, we'll think of something."

"Sounds like this mission is about to get interesting."

Fortis returned to the control room.

"*Sumida* is three kilometers behind us," Lakshaw told him. "They asked what we were carrying, and I told them it was none of their damned business. They haven't responded yet. That's her."

A grainy black and white image floated on one of the screens on the forward bulkhead. Fortis squinted, but he couldn't make out much detail.

"That image is from the docking camera mounted above the engines," Lakshaw said. "Doe analyzed it and said he's sixty-five percent certain it is not the *Sumida*."

"Sixty-four-point eight percent," Doe said.

"Dancer, this is Sumida. *Stand by to receive a shuttle at your midships hatch."*

"This is *Dancer*. Did you just say you are sending a shuttle over here?"

"That is affirmative. The shuttle will approach and dock at your midships hatch."

"This is *Dancer*. Why are you sending a shuttle?"

"Routine safety inspection."

Lakshaw turned to Fortis. "They think we're stupid."

Sumida drew closer and the camera image sharpened.

"I am now ninety-eight percent certain that is not *Sumida*," Doe said. "That's a cargo ship, not a Space Defense Force vessel."

"Can you tell if she's armed?"

"I don't detect any weapons," Doe said.

"What should we do?" Lakshaw asked Fortis.

"Stall them. Give me time to get the Paladins in position at the hatch and then let their shuttle dock. We'll greet them and find out what's going on."

Back in the cargo bay, Fortis found the Paladins gearing up for a fight.

"Herron, Lakshaw is stalling *Sumida,* but their shuttle will be coming alongside the midships access hatch any minute now. I want a platoon standing by to greet them at the hatch. After we get their boarding party under control, I want to grab their shuttle. I'll lead three Paladins forward to seize the cockpit. Designate another half-dozen to head aft and grab the engine room. We need prisoners, so no shooting unless we have to. Designate a prisoner control force here, and I want someone with Lakshaw in the control room with a communicator dialed in so we can talk to her."

Herron gave him a bored look. "This isn't the ISMC, you know. We got this. There's no need for you to go. Why don't you stay in the control room with Lakshaw until I give you the all clear?"

"It would be better if I go," Fortis said. "I can't let you guys have all the fun. Don't worry, I'll let your guys go first and stay out of their way."

Fortis donned his tactical gear and checked his weapons before he joined Herron to brief the boarding party.

"Alpha Platoon from First Company is the primary boarding force. We'll take positions at the midships access hatch to deal with the boarding party. We don't want to kill these guys; we want to capture them. When Fortis gives the go order, we'll assault their shuttle. Otto, take a communicator up to the control room and make sure the captain is plugged into the right circuits. Ailes, Wykoff, Jenna, raise your hands." Three Paladins held up their hands. "When we go, you're the cockpit team. Fortis will be moving forward with you." The trio traded glances but said nothing. "The rest of Alpha Platoon will sweep their ship. We want prisoners, not corpses.

"The remainder of First Company will post up in the passageways around the hatch as prisoner control and reserve force. Zylstra and Second Company will remain here in the cargo bay and be ready to respond as needed.

"This is nothing new, ladies. We train for this all the time. Any questions?"

"What do we do about *Sumida* when we're done?" Zylstra asked.

Herron looked at Fortis.

"We'll play that by ear," Fortis said. "I think they're probably pirates, but she might actually be a Japanese vessel on anti-piracy patrol. If that's the case, we don't want to start a gun fight with them. If they are pirates, we'll figure out how to deal with them. We might be able to repel them."

* * * * *

Chapter Twenty-One

Fortis crouched next to Ailes, Wykoff, and Jenna near the access hatch. All around them, Alpha Platoon stood ready for the arrival of the pirates. The mercenaries were equipped with pulse pistols and flashbang grenades in case they had to engage the boarders. The mood was tense, but Fortis didn't detect any nervousness from the Paladins. There was no fear, just a familiar sense of anticipation and a desire to get the action started.

Lakshaw kept them apprised of the situation from the control room.

"The shuttle is on final approach."

Fortis heard the clunk of metal on metal as the shuttle grappled for the rings that would allow it to mate to the docking collar around the hatch. He keyed his mic.

"They've landed."

Doe had analyzed the shuttle on the docking camera and calculated it could hold a maximum of fifteen passengers. The plan was to allow them to open the hatch and then rush into the shuttle with weapons drawn.

Fortis was confident Alpha Platoon could handle fifteen attackers, given the element of surprise and the reputed poor level of training and organization among pirates. Still, the migration of divvies to the Free Sector may have changed things, and Fortis didn't want to find out the hard way that he was wrong.

He heard the hiss of air as the pressure equalized inside the docking collar.

"Here they come."

The locking mechanism on the access hatch spun and stopped in the open position. The hatch opened, and a pirate stepped onto *Dancer*.

"Go, go, go!"

Alpha Platoon surged forward. The first Paladin slapped the man's weapon away and drove his fist into the pirate's face. The rest of the platoon rushed past them and overwhelmed the boarding party. No shots were fired as the mercenaries overpowered the attackers.

Fortis and his handpicked team raced forward in search of the cockpit. Speed was critical; they had to subdue the crew before they had a chance to alert *Sumida*. Fortis kicked open the cockpit door and the Paladins crowded in behind him. The shock of their sudden appearance with guns drawn must have been too much for the co-pilot, because he went down in a dead faint. The pilot half-rose from his seat before Fortis and another man tackled him and pinned his arms to his sides.

"What the fuck?" the pilot sputtered from under the two men piled atop him between the pilot's seat and the console.

"The engine room is secure," the Alpha Platoon leader, a Paladin named Tyler, reported. *"We're holding eight prisoners in the cabin and one more in the engine room."*

"The cockpit is secure." Fortis groaned as he untangled himself from the pile of bodies in the cockpit. They pulled the pilot into his seat and shoved a pistol under his chin. The co-pilot came to and cowered in his seat, ashen faced.

"Who the fuck are you guys?" the pilot demanded.

Fortis shook his head. "You go first. Who are you?"

"We're, uh, conducting a routine safety inspection."

Fortis grabbed a handful of the pilot's flight suit and jerked him halfway out of his seat. "Wrong answer. Try again."

The pilot scowled and pressed his lips together.

Fortis sighed. "We'll do it the hard way." He punched the pilot in the temple with a vicious right hand and shoved the unconscious man down into his seat. "Watch this fucker," he told the Paladins crowded in next to him.

He turned and looked at the co-pilot. "How about you? Do you have anything to say?"

The co-pilot blanched. His lips trembled as he struggled to speak. "P-p-please. My family."

Fortis stepped close and loomed over him. "I didn't ask about your family, I asked about you. Who are you?"

"I-I-I..." The copilot blubbered and buried his face in his hands.

"Fortis, you need to come and see this," Herron said over the circuit.

"Don't let these guys touch anything," Fortis told his companions. He went aft to the cabin where he met Herron. "What's up?"

Herron pointed to their prisoners, who kneeled in two rows of four. Fortis saw they all wore identical red smocks. "They're Kuiper Knights."

"Are you serious?" Fortis leaned closer and saw strange symbols embroidered on their tops. The prisoners glared at him, and he saw most had distinctive dueling scars on their cheeks, a sure sign of the Knighthood.

What the fuck?

"Keep these guys on ice," Fortis told Herron as he headed for the cockpit. When he got there, he pushed his way to the co-pilot and yanked him out of his seat. "You're Kuiper Knights," he snarled into the man's face.

The co-pilot's eyes opened wide with surprise and fear. "Please. My family…"

"Shut up about your family." Fortis shook the man. "What are the Kuiper Knights doing here?"

"We-we came out here looking for ships," the co-pilot croaked. "We need supplies."

"What are you doing *here*, in this position?" Fortis demanded. "This is a long way from the shipping lanes."

"I don't know. They sent us coordinates, so we came." He leveled a trembling finger at the unconscious pilot. "He's a Knight. I'm just a page."

Fortis' senses went on high alert. "Who sent you coordinates? Where did they come from?"

"Sanctuary. Our home base. Sanctuary sent them."

"Fortis, what's going on?" Lakshaw's voice broke in over the circuit. *"What's taking so long?"*

"Stand by, I'll brief you in a minute." Fortis turned back to the co-pilot. "How many people are on your ship?"

"Wha-wha-what?"

Fortis pulled him close until they were nose to nose. "How many people are still on your ship?"

"Uh, oh God, let me think." The co-pilot closed his eyes and took a deep breath. "Twenty. Maybe twenty-five, if you count the crew." He looked at Fortis. "Twenty-five."

"You're sure? What weapons?"

"I-I don't know. I'm just a pilot. Rifles. The same weapons the others carried."

"Good." Fortis released him. "What's your name?"

"Rooney. Timothy Rooney."

"Can you fly this thing back to your ship, Rooney? Can you dock it?"

"Of course."

"Don't fucking move." Fortis shoved Rooney back into his seat. "Watch him," Fortis told his companions. "I'll be right back."

Fortis ducked into a closet-sized head in the passageway between the cabin and cockpit and pulled the door shut. He dialed up Lakshaw and Herron for a private three-way conversation.

"We have eleven prisoners here," he said. "The co-pilot said there are twenty-five more back on their ship, probably armed with rifles."

"We can take them easy," Herron cut in. *"I'll send Second Company; they can do the job."*

"Except they'll know you're coming," Fortis said. "They won't wait around while we dock with them. I'll take Tyler and Alpha Platoon over there on their shuttle."

"Are you fucking crazy?" Lakshaw demanded. *"I thought you were just talking tough when you said you wanted to counterattack."*

"We don't have a choice. These guys are Kuiper Knights. They're out here looking for ships to hijack."

Lakshaw groaned. *"Kuiper Knights? Damn it."*

"They don't know who we are, but they know what ship we're on, and they know we're armed. If we let them go, they'll report back to their home base and blow our cover."

"That shuttle only holds fifteen passengers. You're going to attack twenty-five Kuiper Knights with fifteen men?"

"We'll use speed and surprise. They won't be expecting us, and I doubt they're walking around armed on their own ship. Besides, we can cram a whole lot more than fifteen guys on that shuttle."

The circuit was silent for a second. *"I'd rather lead this, but you're the boss,"* Herron said. *"What do you want me to do?"*

"Take control of the prisoners and transfer them to *Dancer's* cargo bay until we get done with their ship."

"What about me?" Lakshaw asked.

"If the assault goes sideways, get out of here as fast as you can. Then call my rich uncle and tell him what happened."

* * *

When Fortis briefed Alpha Platoon on his plan, they smiled and slapped each other on the back. While the Paladins moved the prisoners to the cargo bay, Fortis went to the cockpit and slid into the now-empty pilot's seat next to Rooney.

"Rooney, in about five minutes, we're going to uncouple from *Dancer*. Then you're going to fly this thing back to your ship and park it in the shuttle bay."

The co-pilot gave him a puzzled look. "What do you mean? What are you doing?"

Tyler poked his head in the cockpit. "Hey Fortis, we're all set back here."

"Roger that. We'll be underway shortly." Fortis turned back to Rooney. "You're going to fly us over to your ship for a visit."

"Are you serious?" Rooney's eyes grew big. "I can't do that. My family—"

Fortis cut him off with a raised finger. "Your family is going to miss you if you don't fly us over there. We haven't killed anyone so far; it would be a shame if you were the first to die."

Just then, a voice broke in over the shuttle's comm circuit. *"Brother McClusky, what's taking so long?"*

"Is that your ship?" Fortis asked Rooney. The co-pilot nodded. "McClusky is the pilot?" He nodded again. "You better answer him."

"What do I say?"

"Tell them *Dancer* was empty, and you'll return as soon as McClusky takes a leak."

Rooney nodded and then picked up the mic. "This is Page Rooney. Brother McClusky is in the head. The ship is empty, and we'll be back as soon as he's finished."

"Okay."

Rooney looked at Fortis.

"Let's go."

The shuttle jerked when Rooney released the locking ring, and it lifted away from *Dancer*.

Fortis kicked himself for not thinking of everything. "Are there any pilots in Alpha Platoon aboard?" he asked Tyler.

"Affirmative. We have two."

"Send one up here."

Fortis met the pilot in the passageway.

"Sit next to the pilot and look dangerous," he told the Paladin, a fresh-faced young man named Nellis. "He's scared right now, but make sure he doesn't do anything stupid like crash us into his ship or steer us into space."

"Roger that."

"When we get there, stay with him. I don't want him transmitting a warning to their control room."

Fortis squeezed through the mercenaries packed into the shuttle until he found Tyler in the passenger cabin.

"How many men did you bring?" he asked the platoon leader.

Tyler grinned. "All of them. Do you think any of these meat eaters were going to stay on *Dancer* while the rest of us had fun? They'd never live it down."

"Who's doing what?" Fortis asked. "Where are the guys assigned to take down the control room?"

"Those are the guys up front," Tyler said. "Third Squad. Gibbons, raise your hand."

The Paladin nearest to the hatch waved.

"Gibbons is the leader of Third Squad."

"Okay. I'll be moving with Third Squad then. Where will you be?"

"I'll stay with First Squad in the shuttle bay. We'll keep control of the shuttle and be ready to respond wherever we're needed. Second Squad is going to the engine room."

"Okay, good. I didn't think to ask Rooney where these guys store their weapons, so don't hesitate to do whatever is necessary to get control of the ship. They're on their home turf, so we can't afford a gunfight with them even though the numbers are about even. Shoot and scoot."

"Hey, Fortis, it's Nellis up here in the cockpit. We're on final approach. Everything seems okay."

"Got it, thanks," Fortis said. He thumped Tyler on the shoulder. "Do the deed, and let's bring them all home."

He pushed his way through the crowd to join Gibbons.

"I'm going to move with Third Squad to the control room," he said to the squad leader. "Do your thing, and I'll be right behind you."

Gibbons nodded and smiled. "Try and keep up." The Paladins gathered around them laughed.

The shuttle jerked, and Fortis heard the recovery rail clamp on to the shuttle.

This is where we get fucked.

If the Kuiper Knights suspected anything was amiss, they could close the shuttle bay doors and not equalize the atmosphere, effectively trapping the Paladins in the shuttle. Shuttles weren't built for long-term survival, and they'd be forced to surrender. The Knights were fanatics, and Fortis knew they wouldn't hesitate to sacrifice the prisoners on *Dancer* if it meant escaping back into the Free Sector.

"They're closing the shuttle bay doors," Nellis reported. A minute later, he came back on. *"Doors are closed. They're pressurizing the bay."*

The shuttle creaked as the pressure equalized, and Fortis knew they were only seconds away from launching their assault.

"The hatch opens inward, boys," Gibbons said. "Here we go."

"Pressurization complete," Rooney announced over the intercom.

"Go, go, go!"

* * * * *

Chapter Twenty-Two

Gibbons led Third Squad through the hatch and into the shuttle bay, and Fortis heard shouts and pulse rifle fire. He exited the shuttle and saw two Paladins face down on the catwalk next to the shuttle. The rest of the squad charged up the metal steps that led out of the bay. Three red-clad Kuiper Knights were sprawled on the steps and the grating above, while a fourth tried to engage the onrushing mercenaries from the shuttle control tower. The tower exploded in a shower of blue-white sparks as energy bolts shredded the Kuiper Knight, and blood splashed all over the wall.

Gibbons was the first to reach the shuttle bay hatch, and he didn't hesitate. He slammed it open and disappeared into the passageway beyond before Fortis was up the steps. Fortis heard more shouts and the *crack* of a grenade, and grey smoke billowed into the hangar. When Fortis caught up with Third Squad, they were exchanging fire with several Knights who had taken cover behind some equipment boxes further down the passageway. Another grenade exploded, and Gibbons broke cover.

"Follow me!"

Fortis and the rest of Third Squad charged up the passageway behind Gibbons, firing as they pressed their attack. Fortis stumbled and almost tripped over mangled bodies and twisted metal in the smoky passageway. The Paladin in front of Fortis went down with a smoking hole where his face used to be, and that's when Fortis realized how heavy the incoming fire was. Another Paladin spun around and went down with a shoulder wound that almost tore his arm off. The passageway was becoming a killing field, and Fortis felt their assault begin to stall.

"Come on!" Fortis shouted as he moved up the passageway. "We gotta go!"

He came upon Gibbons crumpled against the bulkhead, holding both hands over a gaping hole in his stomach.

"Keep moving." Gibbons grimaced and spat blood and gore all over his chin. "Go."

Fortis didn't hesitate. He tore a flashbang from his vest, pulled the pin, and hurled it up the passageway. One beat after it exploded, Fortis charged forward, firing from the hip at everything that moved. Incoming fire slacked off, and Fortis discovered he was standing at a T-junction of passageways. Dead Kuiper Knights choked the deck, and he had to scramble over them to reach a door marked "Control Room." By then, four other Paladins had caught up with him.

"On three," he growled through his smoke-scorched throat. They nodded, and Fortis counted down as he reared back to kick the door.

When he got to three, Fortis kicked as hard as he could just as someone inside the control room opened the door. His momentum carried him forward, and he stumbled into the person at the door. They went down in a heap as the Paladins leaped over them to clear the room.

"Don't shoot!"

"Clear!" the mercenaries called as one of them hauled Fortis to his feet. "You okay, Fortis?"

"Yeah, I'm okay." Fortis keyed his mike. "This is Fortis, with Third Squad. The control room is secure."

"This is Second Squad. The engine room is secure."

"This is Tyler. Shuttle bay is secure, and I have a fire team sweeping for stragglers."

"Roger that. We've got the pilots here, so maybe we can figure out what's going on. Gibbons is down in the control room passageway with a gut wound."

"*Fortis, this is Lakshaw. You guys might want to hurry. There is some debris blowing out through a hole in the hull near the forward access hatch.*"

"We're on it, thanks."

The Paladins dragged the two Kuiper Knights out from between the control room consoles. The one Fortis accidentally tackled had a deep gash in his scalp, and blood flowed freely down his face.

"Who are you?" a Paladin named Anshoot demanded. When the Knights didn't respond, Anshoot kicked the injured pilot in the chest. "Who are you?" When they still didn't respond, Anshoot raised his rifle to deliver a butt stroke.

"His name is Kelly," one of the other Paladins said.

The Knight with the head wound jerked like he'd been shocked.

"Sam Kelly, if I remember correctly."

"You know him?" Fortis asked.

"Yeah. He was a hovercopter pilot in Fifth Division."

Fortis looked at the wounded Knight, who nodded.

"Steve Kelly."

"These guys are Space Marines?" another mercenary asked.

"*Fortis, this is First Squad,*" Tyler called over the circuit. "*I'm in the main passageway across from the shuttle bay, looking at the hole in the hull. One of the grenades must have cracked a weld.*"

"How bad is it?"

"*About a centimeter long right now, but it's getting longer.*"

"Can you plug it?"

"We jammed a bunch of stuff into it, but the vacuum is sucking hard. We found a damage control locker, but it's empty."

Fortis knew that even a small hole in the hull could catastrophically fail at any moment and suck everyone and everything into out into space. If they couldn't plug the leak, they had to evacuate, and fast.

"All stations, this is Fortis. Collect our dead and wounded and fall back to the shuttle bay. Nellis, are you still in the cockpit?"

"Yes sir."

"Tell Rooney to start his preflight checklist. We'll be aboard in a few minutes, and we need to get out of here, quick." He gestured to the Kuiper Knight pilots. "Bring these guys, and let's go."

"I'm not going anywhere," the unwounded Kuiper Knight said. "I'll die before I willingly go along with heretics."

"That's easy." Anshoot fired his pulse rifle, and the impact of the energy bolt at close range flung the man across the control room. He leveled his rifle at Kelly. "Are you coming or are you dying?"

Kelly stared at Anshoot with horror in his eyes. "I'm coming."

Anshoot's casual murder of the pilot shocked Fortis, but he knew this wasn't the time or place to address it. He had to get the mercenaries focused on the task at hand, that being rapid evacuation of the crippled ship.

"I said, let's go."

When he got back to the shuttle bay, Fortis found First and Second Squads had already begun the grisly task of collecting their dead. There were three wounded Paladins—the shoulder wound from the firefight in the passageway, a member of Second Squad with a head injury he sustained when one of the crew attacked him with a pipe, and a third with his hand swathed in bandages. He also saw a group of six Kuiper

Knights, four wounded and two unwounded, under guard. Third Squad pushed Kelly in with the group.

"Four friendly KIAs, three wounded," Tyler reported.

Fortis nodded at the wounded. "Gibbons?"

Tyler shook his head. "Didn't make it."

Fortis grimaced. "Damn. How about the Knights?"

"We swept the ship, and those seven are all that are left," Tyler said. "There are parts and pieces of the rest all over that passageway."

"It got pretty hairy," Fortis said. He looked around. "Let's get everyone loaded and get off this thing."

"Not so fast." Tyler pointed to the demolished shuttle bay control tower. "This crate only has two ways to open the bay doors and release the shuttle from the rail. The controls up there and a manual hydraulic station in the passageway. Right next to the crack."

"Are the hydraulics working?"

"Yeah, I think so. I had one of the lads look them over, and he said they don't appear damaged."

"So, what's the problem?" Before Tyler could answer, Fortis realized what it was. "Somebody has to open the doors and release the shuttle."

"Exactly. We might have gotten away with somebody in an emergency escape suit operating the electronic controls and then making a run for the shuttle, but not the hydraulics. It will take too long."

Fortis had a sudden thought, and he keyed his mic. "Nellis, this is Fortis. Are you still in the cockpit?"

"Yeah. Where are you? We're getting ready to leave, you know."

"I heard. Ask Rooney if he can dock the shuttle with this ship."

"What?"

"Ask Rooney if he can dock the shuttle with this ship."

"*Stand by.*" A few seconds later, Nellis responded. *"He said yes, but he wants to know why."*

"Why doesn't matter." Fortis turned to Tyler. "Get everybody aboard the shuttle. I'll find an escape suit and then open the doors and release the rail. You come around and pick me up at the hatch."

"Are you for real?" Tyler asked, but he saw the look on Fortis' face. "You're the boss. Let one of these other guys do it."

"No. I'll do it. Get everyone loaded on the shuttle."

"But—"

"Just go!"

Paladins carried their dead and wounded aboard the shuttle and herded the prisoners behind them. Word spread about what Fortis was planning, and more than one offered to take his place. He waved them off, and Tyler finally reported all Paladins and pirates were accounted for.

Fortis found an emergency escape suit in a locker on the second level of the shuttle bay and took it with him. He could hear the atmosphere whistling out through the crack in the passageway, so he pulled the suit on and left the hood and mask hanging over his shoulder.

At the hydraulic control station, Fortis took a second to familiarize himself with the valves and levers. The instructions printed on the bulkhead were simple and straightforward, intended to be operated by personnel in an emergency.

"Nellis, I'm opening the bay doors," he said over the circuit.

"Roger that. We're ready to go."

Fortis opened the valves in the right order and began pumping on the door handle. He heard a loud *whump*, and the entire ship shook when the hangar atmosphere inside suddenly equalized with the space outside.

The instructions said it would take one hundred pumps to open the doors, and when he got to one hundred, Nellis confirmed they were open.

"You scared the shit out of us," Nellis added. *"You didn't equalize."*

"No time," Fortis said. The whistling had become a low roar, and he imagined the crack was growing larger. "I'm releasing the shuttle."

After twenty pumps on the rail handle, Nellis called again.

"We're out. We'll meet you at the main hatch."

Fortis had to go by the crack to get to the hatch, and he felt it sucking at him as he slipped past. When he got to the hatch, he called Nellis.

"I'm standing by at the hatch."

"Bad news. Rooney said the leak is making the ship spin, and he can't get the approach angle right."

Fortis looked around. The hatch vestibule doubled as an airlock, and he got an idea.

"Nellis, tell Rooney to hover as close as possible to *Sumida* and I'll jump for the shuttle."

"What?"

"Get as close as you can, and I'll jump."

"You're fucking crazy."

"Hurry up," Fortis said. "The crack is growing bigger."

Fortis secured the inner hatch and bled off the atmosphere in the vestibule while he waited for word from Nellis. He cracked the outer hatch and looked out. He could barely make out the navigation lights on the shuttle, and he realized Nellis was right.

I am crazy.

"We're on final approach," Nellis said.

A few seconds later, Fortis saw the shape of the shuttle looming close aboard *Sumida*, but it was already rotating past the hatch. Unwilling to wait for another rotation, Fortis jumped.

"On my way," he said as he drifted through the weightless vacuum between the vessels. At the last second, he realized he was moving too fast, so he twisted around to get his feet in front. When he impacted the shuttle, he scrambled for a handhold before he bounced off and spun out of control.

"I'm hanging on near the nose."

"We're cracking a hatch," Nellis reported. *"Can you see the light?"*

A dull glow caught Fortis' attention ten meters aft of where he clung to the shuttle.

"I see it. I'm headed that way."

Fortis made his way hand over hand to the shuttle. Hands grabbed Fortis, yanked him inside, and slammed the hatch.

"We got him!" Tyler announced over the circuit. He pounded Fortis on the back. "That was crazy!"

"What's going on?" Lakshaw demanded.

"We're on our way back," Nellis reported. "We'll be at the hatch in a few."

The transfer back aboard *Dancer* was effortless compared to what they'd just been through. Rooney guided the shuttle to a smooth touchdown, the locks engaged, and First Platoon disembarked. After everyone else had transferred, Fortis met Nellis and Rooney at the hatch.

"Good work, Rooney," Fortis said.

"Good enough to let me go?"

"Go where? Back over there?"

"Point me in the right direction, and maybe I can make it to the Freedom Jump Gate," the pilot said.

Fortis shook his head. "Sorry. I can't do that. The best I can offer is to remember what you did for us."

"I guess that will have to do."

Rooney climbed through the hatch, followed by Nellis and Fortis. When the hatch was secured, they released the hooks and the shuttle drifted away.

* * * * *

Chapter Twenty-Three

Fortis barely had time to strip off his gear before Lakshaw found him.

"We need to talk. Now."

He followed her to her quarters and pulled the door shut behind him.

"What the fuck do you think you're doing?" Lakshaw demanded. Her eyes blazed with fury, and her cheeks flushed deep red.

The captain's temper surprised Fortis, and he struggled for an answer.

"Why are you angry? We defended your ship against pirates," he said.

"You attacked a ship and brought back a bunch of prisoners."

"And?"

"*Dancer* is a private vessel, not a warship. Contract or no contract, we don't have the authority to capture anyone. What you did is called kidnapping. Piracy, even."

"I don't see how."

Lakshaw's frustration was obvious as she shook her head. "Listen to me for a second. *Dancer* is a private vessel, and we are allowed to defend ourselves. *Defend*. The guys who tried to board us under false pretenses with weapons were pirates, and we were within our rights to defend against the attack. Boarding their ship and capturing them made *us* pirates. Do you see the difference?"

"I say we conducted a proactive defense."

"The Space Admiralty isn't going to buy that."

"Their ship was severely damaged. We rescued them."

Lakshaw scoffed. "You caused the damage when you attacked them. You say you rescued them, yeah?"

Fortis nodded.

"How many of them came over here voluntarily?"

Fortis felt his ears begin to burn, and he shrugged.

"You 'rescued' them at the barrel of a gun. I'm not a legal scholar, but that sounds like kidnapping to me."

Fortis and Lakshaw regarded each other for a long second. The euphoria Fortis felt from surviving the vicious firefight and prevailing over the Kuiper Knights faded into a dull feeling in his chest. She must have sensed his change of mood, because she took on a conciliatory tone.

"The rules are different for civilians out here. You might get a pass as a Space Marine, but for the rest of us, it doesn't matter who we're contracted with. I'm glad you came back in one piece, though. That was some stunt, jumping from the ship to the shuttle."

"Thanks."

"Now, what are we going to do with your prisoners?"

"Turn them over to…" He stopped when she cocked an eyebrow at him. "No?"

"We could jump through the gate and give them to the first Kuiper Knights we come across."

"I don't think that's such a great idea. We probably wouldn't make it out."

"What do you suggest?"

"Airlock every one of them and pretend this never happened."

Lakshaw gaped, and Fortis shrugged.

"They're pirates."

"You're not airlocking anyone on my ship," Lakshaw said. "I think you need to report everything that happened to your rich daddy and find out what we should do."

"What if he tells me to airlock them?"

"Then we'll take them back to Terra Earth, and he can stick his contract up his ass."

Fortis laughed. "Okay, I'll send the message, but the response might be slow. We could be waiting for a couple days."

"When he hears that we've committed piracy and taken prisoners, he'll answer."

* * *

When Fortis returned to the cargo bay, Herron had the prisoners separated and guarded by pairs of Paladins.

"Some of these guys were Space Marines," he told Fortis.

Fortis told Herron what had happened in the cockpit of the pirate ship.

"Anshoot killed him?"

"Shot him dead. It happened so fast I couldn't stop him," Fortis said.

"It's a good thing it's not a crime to kill pirates, but what the fuck?"

"I just had a long talk with Lakshaw about that." Fortis described his conversation with the captain, and when he finished, Herron frowned.

"Fuckin' civilians and their rules. Should have killed them all."

"How are our wounded?" Fortis asked.

"Mayfield took one in the shoulder, and it doesn't look good. The docs got the bleeding stopped, and they dosed him up to prevent infection, but his shoulder is hamburger. One of the pirates hit Thoms with a pipe, so he's got a concussion. De Garza smashed his hand in the hatch during the assault, but he'll be okay."

"What about the wounded pirates?"

"They'll live. Probably."

"Okay. Give me a few minutes to send a report, and then we'll figure out what to do with the prisoners."

When Fortis finished his message to Anders, he caught back up with Herron.

"I want to interview these guys, one at a time," he said. "Former Space Marines first, starting with Steve Kelly. He was one of their pilots."

Fortis sat with Kelly in the crew's mess. An armed Paladin stood out of earshot at the far end of the room, but otherwise, they could have been two shipmates sharing a cup of coffee.

"How's your head?" Fortis asked as he nodded to the bandages wrapped around Kelly's wound.

"It hurts when I think, but I'll live."

Fortis smiled at Kelly's humor. "Sorry about that."

"I should have stayed in my seat and let you kick the door open," Kelly said.

"What's your story?" Fortis asked between sips from his steaming mug. "How did you end up here?"

Kelly shrugged. "The Corps divvied me, and I didn't have anything better to do."

"You're a pilot. Everybody needs pilots."

"Except when there are a thousand pilots looking for the same kind of work."

"Why the Kuiper Knights? They don't have the best reputation."

"They said all the right things, and it sounded good. Getting in was easy, and as a pilot, I didn't have to mess around with the bullshit they put other recruits through."

"Fair enough. Did you think you'd be flying for pirates?"

"No, or I wouldn't have joined. And most of what we do isn't really piracy. I mean, it is, but we're not plundering treasure ships. The Master calls it taxation. We stop ships and take a little from everybody."

"Taxation. Hmm. You know, I'm curious. How did your ship end up out here? I mean, we're on the wrong side of the Freedom Jump Gate, and we're not on a routine shipping route. It seems a little out of the way for what you're doing."

"We go where The Master sends us," Kelly said.

"You get coordinates, and that's where you go, no questions asked?"

"Exactly." Kelly must have recognized Fortis' skepticism, because he continued. "You have to understand something about the Kuiper Knights. We're not all fanatics, but the fanatics are in charge. The pilot your guy shot in the cockpit? His name was Zurowsky, and he was a fanatic. They don't ask questions, they do exactly what The Master commands." He unzipped the top of his flight suit to reveal a black smock. "The guys in black are regular Knights. Some of us are devout, but we're not crazy. The real crazies like Zurowsky wear red."

Kelly didn't offer up much useful information, so Fortis focused on finishing his coffee. After he drained his mug, he set it down, but before he could say anything else, Kelly spoke.

"What are you going to do with us?"

"Turn you over to the authorities," Fortis said.

"You're a terrible liar, Captain Fortis." Fortis blinked, and Kelly nodded. "Yeah, I know who you are. Or were, anyway. Most of the guys know about you. How did you end up out here with a ship full of mercenaries?"

Damn. He doesn't miss much.

"That's another story for another time," Fortis said as he stood. "And the truth is, I don't know what we're going to do with you. We're still trying to figure it out."

Kelly nodded as he stood up. "Make it quick, okay? Not the airlock, at least not while I'm conscious."

Fortis returned Kelly to the cargo bay and brought Rooney with him next.

"I want to thank you for what you did today. Flying the shuttle, I mean. You saved a lot of lives."

"I cost a few, too. I should have refused to fly you over there." Rooney seemed to have regained his nerve, and there was a tone of defiance in his voice.

"You didn't have much of a choice, did you?"

"No, I guess not."

"I'm sure the Knighthood will understand."

Rooney's face went white. "The Knighthood?"

Fortis nodded. "Yeah. We're on our way to the warp gate. We've been ordered to meet a Kuiper Knight ship there and turn all of you back over to them. You're going home."

"You can't do that."

"We have to. Our client ordered us to."

"Turn the other guys over if you want to but let me stay here. Please!"

"I don't understand. Why don't you want to go back with the other Knights?"

"I'm not a Knight." He unzipped the top of his flight suit and revealed white underneath. "See that? It's white. Knights wear black or red. I'm a page. I'm the lowest of the low."

"What are you doing flying a shuttle for them?"

"The other pilot, the one you knocked out in the shuttle? He's my Knight. Wherever he goes, I go. Whatever he tells me to do, I do."

"You're a slave."

"No, not exactly. It's a rite of passage. Someday, I'll become a squire and then a Knight. I mean, I might have, but not after this. After this…" He made a cutting motion across his throat.

"That's why you don't want to go back with them. Because they'll kill you."

"Yeah, and not just me. They know where my family lives."

"What are you doing with the Knights, Rooney? Were you a Space Marine?"

"No. I was a shuttle jockey on a regular cargo run between Terra Earth and the Felder Reach. Fleet divvied a bunch of pilots, and suddenly there were a hundred guys willing to fly for half of what I was making. I reported to my ship and found out I didn't have a job anymore."

"That's tough."

"Yeah, it is, especially when every job was filled by those guys."

"So you joined the Kuiper Knights."

"Yeah, I joined the Kuiper Knights. They needed pilots, and I needed a job. I pledged to do some mumbo-jumbo, and I had a job."

"Flying around collecting taxes."

Rooney shrugged. "It's a living. *Was* a living. Now, I need to get back home before the Knights find out I flew the shuttle for you. Can you help me?"

Fortis shrugged. "I don't know. It depends on what our employer says."

"Who's your employer?"

Fortis shrugged again. "'They.'"

"Are 'they' looking for pilots? How about your team?"

"I don't know about 'them,' but my team is a one-time thing." As soon as he said it, Fortis kicked himself. A one-time team implied a specific mission, and a team like Fortis' meant the target was something serious.

Like a ship full of weapons.

Disappointment crossed Rooney's face. "Well, if you get an opening, keep me in mind. I really don't want to go back to the Kuiper Knights."

The rest of the interviews were as fruitless as the first two. The red-clad Kuiper Knights glared at Fortis in sullen silence. Some of the former Space Marines recognized Fortis and were more willing to talk, but they didn't have much to tell. They did what they were told, and they got paid. None of them knew why they were on this side of the Freedom Jump Gate.

He hinted around about stolen weapons with a couple of them, especially those from Fifth and Sixth Division, but the conversations went nowhere. Finally, he summoned Herron to the mess.

"Get anything useful?" Herron asked.

"No, not really. I found out the guys in red are supposed to be extra-fanatical. None of them admitted to coming out here specially for us, but they might be lying. There's a bunch of former Space Marines among them."

"Yeah. Some of our guys know them. What do you think will happen to them?"

"I have no idea. We kind of fucked up when we captured them."

"What do you want to do with them for the short term?"

"Keep the reds and blacks separate. That pilot, Kelly, said the reds are in charge, so I think we'll get more cooperation if we keep them apart. If any of them give our guys any trouble, put them in restraints. No exceptions."

* * *

Boudreaux stared at Anders in disbelief. "Piracy?"

"A ship detained and boarded *Dancer* under the guise of a safety inspection. Fortis and his men defended *Dancer* and carried the fight to the pirate, which happened to be a Kuiper Knight vessel."

"What the fuck is Fortis doing? Does he know the meaning of 'clandestine?'"

"Of course he does, sir, but he suspects the pirate vessel targeted *Dancer* specifically. His mission may not be as clandestine as we think."

"How do you think we should handle this, Nils?"

"The Fleet destroyer *Comte de Barras* is a short distance away. We can send her to take custody of the pirate vessel and then order *Dancer* through the jump gate."

"What about the pirates?"

Anders shrugged. "Treat them like pirates."

* * *

Three hours later, Fortis got his answer from Anders.

Remain in current position and stand by to transfer the prisoners to a Fleet destroyer, currently enroute.

* * * * *

Chapter Twenty-Four

Aboard *Colossus*, the knights and squires fell into ranks. Ystremski stood with Merrill and Addison, and they all waited in silent anticipation. For the first time since he boarded the shuttle at Sanctuary, he saw Gustafson. The towering Knight took a position in front to address the formation.

"We are gathered here to begin the next phase of our operation. You have been chosen for this task because of your knowledge and experience with these weapons, and our brothers are relying on us to ensure they are operational and ready for action. The Master has given us a great gift, and it is our responsibility to distribute it to our brothers across the sector.

"In a few hours, shuttles will arrive to collect the first deliveries. Do your work well, and our success is assured. Squad leaders, take charge and report to your assigned sections."

Merrill and Addison gathered Ystremski and three squires Ystremski didn't recognize in a huddle as the formation broke up.

"Our task is to prepare grenades for issue," Merrill said. "Two of you will come with me, and we'll handle the frags and concussion grenades. Brother Addison will take the other two and handle incendiaries and smokes. We will inspect each crate. The Space Marine armorers collected them and put them straight into storage, so there's no telling what condition they're in. If any of them are damaged or otherwise suspect, set them aside for closer inspection."

"Why aren't we using Fleet shuttles to transport the weapons?" one of the men asked. "A ship this size has to have a dozen or more."

"It's not your concern, Squire," Merrill shot back. Ystremski, who had wondered the same thing, stayed silent.

Probably not enough pilots.

Addison took Ystremski and one of the other squires aft to a compartment secured by a heavy lock. On the bulkhead above it, a sign with bright red letters glared at them.

Ammunition magazine. Keep this hatch secured at all times!

The Knight Errant pulled out a set of keys and opened the hatch. "This is us." He flipped on the lights and stepped inside.

Ystremski estimated the magazine was six meters wide and three meters high. He couldn't see to the back through the crates that lined the bulkheads and created long, narrow aisles, but it looked at least twenty meters deep.

"That's a shitload of grenades," the other man in their group said.

Ystremski held out his hand. "Squire Petr Ystremski."

"Squire Alton Barker."

"Let's start in the back," Addison said.

The three men pulled down the crates from the top of the first stack and released the hermetic seals. Addison let out a deep breath as they lifted the lid.

"Something wrong?" Ystremski asked.

"Some of these things have been buttoned up for over a year. If one of them is going to fail, it's probably going to happen when the air rushes in."

"If that happens, it won't be our problem for long," Ystremski said. Still, he shivered at the thought of a defective incendiary grenade igniting in the magazine.

There were hundreds of crates to inspect stacked up in the magazine, but once they got into a rhythm, the trio began to make real progress. The air in the magazine grew warm and stale, and it wasn't long before they were drenched with sweat. After a couple hours of steady effort, they paused.

"Brother Addison, whaddya say we take a break?" Barker asked. "I need to take a leak and peel my sweaty skivvies out of my ass crack."

"Yeah, let's do that," said Addison. "We'll take five and ventilate the space."

After they exited the magazine and dogged down the hatch, Addison activated the ventilation and pointed down the passageway. "The head's that way."

Ystremski had ignored the feel of the communicator in his pocket all morning, but as he followed Barker to the head, it felt like a burning weight bumping his leg with every step. When he was in the stall with the door latched, he slipped it out of his pocket and turned it on.

"Fucking hot in there, brother," Barker said from the urinal.

"I hope we can find some water on this thing." Ystremski waited for the communicator to synch up. "I'm dying of thirst." Instead of the message screen, he saw, *No Signal.*

Fuck.

He slipped the communicator back into his pocket and flushed. Barker waited by the door.

"Let's go find something to drink."

They found Addison leaning against the bulkhead, sipping from a disposable cup.

"They've got food and drinks set up in the cargo bay," he told them. "Don't take too long. I want to get this magazine finished as soon as possible."

Someone had set up jugs of water and a stack of sandwiches, and the pair helped themselves and stood off to the side.

"We're the only ones who are sweating," Barker said. "What's everyone else doing?"

Ystremski shrugged and took another bite of his sandwich. Supper had been a long time ago, and there hadn't been breakfast, and he didn't want to waste a second of eating time by talking. When he was finished, he washed it down with big swigs of water. Barker finished his food, and they headed back to the magazine.

"Ah, shit." Ystremski clutched his stomach. "I gotta hit the head again. My stomach."

Addison gave him an annoyed look. "Hurry up. We're going to get started."

Ystremski apologized with a weak smile and started for the head. When he was alone in the passageway, he pulled out the communicator for a quick look. "Signal detected. Synching."

"Hurry up, you piece of shit," he mumbled.

As soon as he saw it was synched, he entered the geolocator mode, captured the coordinates, and transmitted them. Before he had a chance to send an amplifying message, a stern voice from behind startled him.

"Where are you supposed to be?"

It was Gustafson, and he had an angry look on his face.

"I'm sorry, the magazine is hot, and my stomach…" Ystremski turned and fumbled to get the communicator into his pocket unseen. "Addison said it was okay if I go to the head before we start up again."

"Well? Get moving. We have a schedule to keep."

"Yes, Brother."

Ystremski went back into the stall and saw the communicator had dropped the signal again.

No signal this deep in the ship.

He started to type a message and leave it pending transmission until he got back into the passageway, but a warning bell went off in his head. He stood up, saw he was alone, and tucked the communicator into some pipes that ran overhead. Just as he reached for the door handle, Gustafson pushed it open and stood in the doorway with his arms crossed.

"All finished?"

"Yes, Brother. Sorry about that."

As Ystremski walked up the passageway toward the magazine, he felt Gustafson's eyes on his back.

Too fucking close.

It was too late to go back now; he would have to retrieve the communicator later.

The rest of the afternoon passed quickly in the magazine as they opened and inspected hundreds of crates. The ordnance handlers who had prepared the incendiaries and smokes for storage had done an excellent job, and the trio only found one crate's worth of suspect grenades in the entire space. The nervous apprehension they felt when opening a new crate faded, and the gallows humor disappeared as the monotony of the job set in.

They paused work when other groups of Kuiper Knights came to the magazine and carried away inspected crates. Ystremski assumed the weapons were bound for Sanctuary, but he didn't ask.

As the afternoon wore on, Ystremski struggled to focus on the task at hand, and the thought of the communicator hidden in the head nagged at him.

"Watch what you're doing, man," Barker said. "You put a bad grenade back in this crate."

"Ah shit, sorry," Ystremski mumbled.

"What happened?" Addison asked in a sharp voice from further up the stack.

"Brain fart. A momentary lapse."

"You better get squared away, or you're going to kill all of us."

"Yes, Brother."

Ystremski made a show of rubbing his stomach and wincing before they resumed work, but he bent to his task with renewed focus.

Someone opened the magazine door and called in to Addison. "Knock off time. Break bread in fifteen."

The trio sighed with relief as they finished with the crate they were working on and put it on the stack.

"That was a good day's work," Addison said as they filed out toward the hatch. "If we keep up this pace, we'll be finished by the day after tomorrow."

"Great," Barker groaned, and Ystremski chuckled.

"C'mon, troop, it could be worse. It could be raining."

Addison and Barker stared at him for a second before they smiled and nodded. Ystremski had momentarily forgotten they were divvies, and the usual Space Marine humor wasn't welcome. He gave them a sheepish grin.

"Sorry. Old habits, you know?"

When they got to the cargo bay, they saw tables loaded with more sandwiches and water jugs set up on one side. Gustafson was there, and he called for everyone to fall into ranks.

"Take a look at the rack assignments posted on the bulkhead over there," he announced as he pointed across the bay. "After you finish eating, go straight to your assigned berthing compartment. Berthing is through that hatch and one deck down. The rest of the ship is off-limits. There will be roving security to make sure nobody gets lost, so don't go exploring."

When Gustafson finished his announcements, the formation broke up, and lines formed at the food and the rack assignment lists. Ystremski found Addison.

"Do you think it would be okay if I go to the head?" he asked his team leader.

"Again?"

Ystremski shrugged as he rubbed his stomach. "Been like this since I got my guts scrambled on Maltaan."

Addison frowned. "Go ahead, but don't fuck around. Go and get back here."

Ystremski's senses were on high alert as he walked down the passageway to the head. He didn't hear anyone behind him, and when he took a long look back toward the cargo bay as he entered the head, the passageway was empty.

When he retrieved the communicator, the screen was dark, and it didn't respond when he pressed the power button. He mentally kicked himself that he'd left the communicator powered on when he'd stashed it among the pipes, and the battery had run down.

Ten days, my ass.

Now, Ystremski faced a difficult decision. He could carry the communicator on the outside chance that he would find some usable voltage somewhere in the next two days, but that risked discovery. Gustafson already seemed suspicious of him, and there was nothing Ystremski could do if Gustafson decided he wanted to search him. He didn't want to contemplate what would happen if the communicator was discovered in his possession. Alternatively, he could leave the communicator hidden and retrieve it if he discovered a way to charge it, but he might miss an opportunity that wouldn't come again.

Either choice carried risk, and ultimately, Ystremski chose his personal safety. He had to assume Anders had received the coordinates of the transport and would take whatever actions were necessary to prevent the rebels from distributing the weapons. Meanwhile, he had to make it home in one piece, and that didn't include getting caught with a dead communicator.

Ystremski tucked the communicator back into the pipes, flushed, and stepped out into the passageway, where he found Gustafson waiting with arms crossed and an angry look on his face. He froze.

"What are you doing back here again?" Gustafson demanded.

Ystremski put his hand on his abdomen. "It's my stomach, Brother. The heat in that magazine is murder on me."

"Why did you come all the way down here to use the head? There are heads closer to the cargo bay."

"I didn't know that. I asked Brother Addison if I could use the head, and he didn't say anything. I've never been on a ship like this, so I don't know where anything is."

Gustafson's eyes narrowed. "You were a gunnery sergeant, and you've never been on an ISMC division flagship? Didn't I make it clear not to go exploring?"

"I wasn't exploring, I was using the head." Ystremski felt his temper rising, and he let his indignation come through in his reaction. He felt that someone with no guilt and nothing to hide would become upset at Gustafson's continual suspicions and accusations. "If there's a head closer to the cargo bay, I'd be happy to use it. I almost didn't make it to this one."

Gustafson seemed mollified by his reaction, and his expression softened. He gestured toward the cargo bay.

"Squire Petr, go join the others. It's time for evening devotion. If your work assignment is causing you trouble, tell Brother Addison, and I'll have you reassigned. I can't afford to lose you when we have so much more to do."

"Thank you, Brother Pil."

Ystremski didn't look back as he walked toward the cargo bay.

* * * * *

Chapter Twenty-Five

Ystremski joined the line for sandwiches and water. Each man was given two sandwiches, which they ate standing up. After he was finished, he checked his berthing assignment and followed the stream of men headed down the ladder Gustafson had indicated earlier. He located his bunk and then drifted toward the lounge area where many of the others had gathered.

"The food sucks," one of them declared. "Is it too much to ask for a hot meal after working all damn day?"

"This ship is dead, brother," another man, dressed in engineering coveralls, replied. "There's no galley to cook in."

"No fucking hot water, either." Another man, clad only in a towel, emerged from the head. "I hope you guys don't mind cold showers."

Angry outbursts greeted this news, and Ystremski suddenly felt grimy after working in the magazine all day.

"We started one generator for creature features, scrubbers, and lights," the man who told them about the galley replied. "It's only for a couple days, so let's get this done and get out of here."

"That's easy for you to say." The man who complained about the food stepped forward. "You've been walking around with a clipboard in your hands and your head up Gustafson's ass—"

The group erupted in laughter, but it died away into an uncomfortable silence when they realized Gustafson had entered the berthing compartment and stood in the back.

"Someone has a complaint?"

When nobody responded, Gustafson scowled. "Get ready to turn in, ladies. We start again early in the morning."

The men scattered and climbed into their bunks. Ystremski folded his hands behind his head, stared at the bunk above him, and wondered what the next day would bring.

* * *

After a breakfast of more sandwiches and water the next morning, the Kuiper Knights got back to work. Addison left Ystremski and Barker to work on their own and went to oversee workers in another part of the ship.

Unlike the previous day, Ystremski and Barker encountered faulty packing in almost every case they inspected. They also discovered three cases of frags that were stored in the wrong magazine. After three hours, they had gathered six full cases of suspect incendiaries and smokes, along with the frags. They stopped work to show Addison, who came by mid-morning.

"What the hell happened?"

"They fucked up when they sealed these cases," Barker said. "Whoever did it was in a hurry, or they didn't know what they were doing."

"They couldn't read, either." Ystremski toed the cases of frags, which were clearly labeled. "These ought to be in a different magazine."

"What do we need to do? Can you finish?"

Ystremski and Barker exchanged shrugs. "We've come this far, we might as well get it done," Ystremski said. "I'm not an armorer, but I don't think these things will be a problem if we seal the crates again.

You can't issue them, though, so somebody will have to dispose of them."

"Hmm. Okay, keep working, and I'll report what we've found."

Ystremski put his hand to his stomach and gave Addison a weak smile. "Before we start, would you mind?"

"All right but be quick about it. We need to get this finished as soon as possible."

Ystremski was alone in the head, so he retrieved the communicator before he stepped into the stall. He stabbed at the power button and almost wept with relief when the screen lit up. The unit hadn't died, it had gone into a power save mode he didn't know how to exit. He went straight to geolocator mode, captured his position, and hit "send." The communicator dropped synch, and he knew the message was pending. He decided to risk carrying it to ensure it transmitted the coordinates.

When he got back to the magazine, he found Barker waiting.

"Sorry. My stomach."

"It's okay, Brother. We all do the best we can. Are you ready?"

"Yeah."

They resumed their work and inspected twelve more cases before Addison reappeared.

"The first shuttle of the day to collect weapons and gear will be here in six hours. Brother Zerec has commanded us to stage the grenades in Cargo Bay Three and load them as the shuttles arrive."

Ystremski's ears perked up. "Colonel Zerec?"

"*Brother* Zerec was a Space Marine in his previous life, I believe. Is that a problem for you?"

"Not at all, Brother. I recognized his name from my own service and became curious."

Addison's eyes narrowed. "Best to keep your curiosities to yourself, Squire. They lead to gossip."

Addison left, and Ystremski shrugged. "Sorry, I didn't mean to upset him."

"Brother Addison is a Knight Errant," Barker said as they reentered the magazine. "His faith is strong."

While they worked, Ystremski evaluated Barker. Barker was also a squire, but he didn't have the intensity Ystremski had seen among some of the others. Much like Ystremski, Barker's knowledge and experience made him a valuable recruit to the Kuiper Knights, but he didn't display the fanatical devotion Addison did. Ystremski instinctively liked him, but like Kuntz aboard *Pilgrimage*, he knew he couldn't trust anyone on this mission.

Over the next three hours, the two men finished inspecting the rest of the grenades in the magazine. They ended up with nine cases of suspect smokes and incendiaries and another five cases of frags that were improperly stored.

"Now what?" Barker asked.

"I guess we wait for Addison." Ystremski rubbed his stomach and nodded toward the hatch. "In the meantime…"

"Yeah, of course. Go ahead."

Ystremski went to the head, powered down and stashed the communicator, then returned to the magazine. Addison appeared a few minutes later and surveyed their work.

"All suspect ordnance and weapons are to be moved to Cargo Bay Four," he told Ystremski and Barker. "Stack it near the outer doors. When it's all there, it will be airlocked."

"Yes, Brother," Ystremski said. "What about the frags we found in here? They're not suspect, but we shouldn't leave them here."

"After we break bread, move them to Four and leave them near the access hatch. When the teams are done inspecting the frags, I'll have them stored in the proper magazines."

When the three men got to the cargo bay that served as the crew's mess, they heard a loud commotion.

"We've captured a spy!" one of the squires announced.

The men crowded around a hatch that led to the adjoining bay and watched as two Knights and a Knight Errant led someone into the space. Ystremski craned his neck to see, but he was too far back. One of the Knights raised his hands, and the group fell silent.

"Brothers, we have an unexpected guest," he shouted. "Her name is Liz Sherer, and she is from the Terra News Network. The Master has granted her permission to join us and learn about our purpose."

Ystremski recoiled.

Liz? Here?

* * *

Sherer spent the next two days sequestered aboard the mother ship in utter boredom. There was nothing to read, no VR entertainment system to watch, and nobody would answer her questions. She was free to move between her cabin, the adjoining head, and a small dining area, but moving only meant being bored in a new room.

On the morning of the third day, one of the crew tapped on her door.

"Follow me, please."

"Where are we going?" she asked as she followed him to the shuttle bay.

He gestured to the open shuttle hatch, and she climbed in. After a brief ride, the shuttle attached to an umbilical, a long tube designed to transfer passengers and small cargo without docking. When Sherer emerged from the tube, she stared in amazement.

She stood in a cavernous space amid rows of cargo containers stacked three high. A big number "4" was painted in yellow on the bulkhead. Two men in black smocks and a third in red stood near the hatch. Another in blue waved her over.

"You are Liz Sherer," the man in blue said when she stood in front of them.

"Yes."

"This is Brother Nicaro and Brother Dietz," he said as he gestured to the men in black. "This is Brother Zerec. We are Kuiper Knights."

The man in red scowled at Sherer and she struggled not to recoil at the sight of the thick scar across his head. She knew of the Kuiper Knights by reputation only, and what she knew was all bad.

"Why have you kidnapped me?"

Nicaro smiled. "We didn't kidnap you; you came of your own accord."

It was Sherer's turn to smile. "That's an interesting way of describing what you did."

"You came to the Free Sector in pursuit of a story, and we've brought you to your story," Nicaro said.

Sherer turned and looked around at all the containers. "These are the stolen weapons?"

"We prefer the term 'reallocated,' but yes, these are some of the weapons you seek."

"You know, you should have just called me," she said. "We could have skipped the whole kidnapping scenario. But okay, we'll do it your way. Why are you showing me this?"

"The Master has decreed that the world beyond the Free Sector know the truth about what we are building here. He chose you to be his messenger."

Sherer's journalistic cynicism emerged. "He did, did he? Maybe he should have talked to me before he made that decision. What if I don't want to be his messenger?"

Zerec snorted. "No one dares to defy The Master."

The malevolence in his expression sent a cold tickle of fear down her spine, and Sherer struggled to present a brave face.

"What Brother Zerec means to say is, The Master can be very persuasive," Nicaro said with a thin smile.

"When do I get to meet The Master?"

"When we return to Sanctuary," Nicaro said.

"When will that be?"

"Several days, perhaps a week. We have much to do before we return home. In the meantime, Brother Dietz will be your escort. You are free to move about the ship, except for the control room and engineering spaces. If we discover you wandering without Brother Dietz, you will be confined to quarters. You are free to talk to anyone who will talk to you. Do you understand these conditions?"

"Yeah, sure, I understand," Sherer said.

"The Brotherhood is breaking bread in the next bay over, so this is a good time to inform them of The Master's decision," Nicaro said. "Come."

Nicaro led the group through a hatch into an adjoining space. The buzz of conversation grew louder when the Knights caught sight of Sherer, and Nicaro held his hands up for silence.

"Brothers, we have an unexpected guest," he shouted. "The Master has granted her permission to join us and learn about our purpose. Her name is Liz Sherer, and she is from the Terra News Network."

Several of the Knights shifted their feet, but no one made a sound.

"Brother Dietz is her escort for her time with us. You may speak with her if you wish, the choice is yours. The Master has decreed that she will carry our message back to the people of Terra Earth, and so it shall be. Praise to The Master."

"Praise to the Master," echoed the group.

Sherer was struck by the shining eagerness she saw in the eyes of many of the men gathered around her. Years earlier, she had done an investigative series on religious extremists in southern Europe, and the Kuiper Knights gave off the same vibe.

These guys are nuts. Dangerous nuts.

The crowd parted as Dietz gestured toward the back of the space, where she saw a table with food and hydration packs piled high.

"We're breaking bread right now. Please, join us."

Sherer picked up a sandwich and hydration pack and turned to follow Dietz. She stopped short when she saw a familiar face.

"Petr!"

"Hello, Liz. How are you?"

"What are you doing here?"

Ystremski touched his blue smock. "I joined the Kuiper Knights. I'm a squire now."

"How did that happen?"

Ystremski looked at Dietz, and they traded smiles. "You say it like it's a bad thing, an accident or illness."

"No, that's not how I meant it. I'm just surprised."

"The ISMC divvied me, and the Knighthood gave me the opportunity to start a new life. I couldn't be happier."

"I saw Abner before I left." Sherer smiled. "His nose looks great."

Ystremski's face darkened. "He's part of the past. I only think about the future."

Dietz cut in. "Ms. Sherer, we should let Squire Petr finish breaking bread. The brothers will be called back to work soon."

As Sherer followed Dietz away, she looked back and saw Ystremski rooted in place, staring at her. She gave him a half-wave, but he didn't respond.

*****

Chapter Twenty-Six

Aboard *Dancer*, Fortis went to see Lakshaw with Anders' message.

"He wants us to wait here for a Fleet vessel?" Lakshaw asked.

"That's what the message says. 'Remain near current position and stand by to transfer the prisoners to a Fleet destroyer.'"

"And then what?"

Fortis shrugged. "He didn't say. Await follow-on tasking, I guess."

Lakshaw shook her head. "Not us. The prisoners. What about them?"

"I have no idea. Hold them incommunicado until our mission is complete, maybe? Prosecute them for piracy?"

"If Fleet were going to prosecute them, we'd have to stick around for the trial. If they do, I'll be lawyering up, because we engaged in a little piracy ourselves."

"I guess they'll hold them. What difference does it make? They won't be here," Fortis said.

"The difference is if word gets out that we're a pirate ship, I'll be forced to change my name and rename *Dancer*, too," Lakshaw said. "Otherwise, I'll be banned from the jump gates, and I'll either starve, or I'll have to take even more sketchy contracts like yours."

"Anders has something in mind, or he wouldn't be diverting a Fleet destroyer out here."

Lakshaw sighed. "This job has been a clusterfuck since it started. Fucking spooks."

Herron poked his head in the door. "Hey, Fortis. Bad news. Mayfield just died. He went into cardiac arrest, and the docs couldn't save him."

"Damn it."

"We need to do something with him and the KIAs we brought back from the other ship."

Fortis looked at Lakshaw. "Any preference on how we handle this?"

"We can't take them back to Terra Earth, or the UNT will quarantine us for hauling potential biohazards. There's an escape hatch behind the engine room we've used for that sort of thing in the past," she said. "Not a lot of space for ceremony, but there's room between the inner and outer hatch for, well, whatever."

"Okay, thanks. C'mon, Herron, let's go get this done."

The Paladins formed up in the cargo bay for the impromptu burial ceremony. The five dead mercenaries were wrapped in sheets and laid out on the deck in front of them. Even the former Space Marines among the Kuiper Knights stood, while the red-clad Knights turned their backs on the ceremony.

Fortis cleared his throat and began his ad lib remarks.

"These men, these warriors, these Paladins, died in battle alongside their comrades in arms. It was a dirty, dangerous job they cheerfully undertook, secure in the knowledge that their brothers were at their sides. Their deaths are a tragedy to those of us left to mourn them, but they died like soldiers, and we are fortunate to have fought alongside them."

A red-clad Kuiper Knight shouted something unintelligible. One of the sentries waded into the group and beat the offender down with several brutal butt strokes.

Fortis continued. "We commit their mortal remains to the mysterious vastness of space to walk forever among the stars with warriors from time immemorial."

He nodded to Herron, who gestured to the Paladins assigned to carry the bodies to the escape hatch. Fortis followed, and after they left the cargo bay, he heard Zylstra dismiss the formation.

The bodies were laid on the deck between the inner and outer hatches. After they secured the inner hatch, Fortis activated the hatch release for the outer hatch, and the atmosphere whooshed out. He waited a minute and closed the outer hatch. When the indicator showed the outer hatch was secure and the atmosphere restored, he opened the inner hatch and saw the space was empty.

The mood in the cargo bay was subdued when they returned. Fortis made a point of telling Herron that the contracts for the five dead Paladins would be paid out to whomever they nominated, and he hoped the mercenaries who overheard him would pass the word along.

In true warrior fashion, the pall of sadness for the dead mercenaries soon gave way to the high spirits of the survivors as members of First Platoon told the stories of their role in the assault on the other ship. Third Squad dominated the storytelling, and their accounts of the fighting to reach the cockpit grew wilder with every retelling.

"After we got to the cockpit, the skipper decided he was going to kick the door," a burly Paladin named Bellore said. "It was a textbook entry. The pilot opened the door just before Fortis kicked it, and they fell onto the deck and got in our way."

Everyone laughed, Fortis hardest of all. The story wasn't all that funny, but the laughter helped dispel Fortis' horrific memories of the killing that had occurred during the fight. He knew it could have just as easily been him in the passageway with no face, or struggling to hold his intestines inside, and the laughter helped him push that realization deep down inside.

It also gratified him to be part of the story because it enhanced his credibility with the Paladins. They were still hired guns, but he thought it was a good sign that they had begun to accept him as more than just a client.

Fortis saw Lakshaw watching from the cargo bay hatch, so he went over to see what she wanted.

"That was a touching send-off," she said.

"I meant it," he said.

"I'm not mocking you," Lakshaw replied. "I thought it was nice. We should all go out so well."

"Indeed."

Fortis' communicator buzzed, and he checked the screen.

Fleet destroyer *Comte de Barras* enroute your position, ETA eight hours. Have prisoners ready to transfer via CdB shuttle. Orders to follow.

* * *

True to Anders' word, Fleet destroyer *Comte de Barras* hailed *Dancer* seven hours later and arrived within sensor range thirty minutes after. The destroyer launched her shuttle as soon as she was in range. A dour-faced Fleet major led a group of personnel aboard *Dancer*.

"Which one of you is Major Fortis?" the major asked by way of introduction.

The Paladins all looked at Fortis, and his face flushed.

"I'm Fortis."

"I'm Major Woodson, of *Comte de Barras*. Take us to the prisoners."

The major's abrupt nature surprised Fortis, but he did as the man asked. When they arrived in the cargo bay, Woodson waved at his men. "Captain Delk, have them loaded aboard the shuttle. I need to talk to Fortis." He turned to Fortis. "Is there somewhere we can talk in private?"

"Sure." Fortis spotted Herron. "Help the captain, please. I'm going to talk to the major."

Fortis led Woodson to the crew's mess, but he didn't offer him a seat or coffee. "What can I do for you, Major?"

Woodson pulled a sealed envelope out of his coveralls. "Message from Fleet Command." When Fortis started to tear open the envelope, the major stopped him. "Your eyes only. Destroy after reading."

"Hmm. Okay." Fortis folded the envelope and stuffed it in his pocket. "Is that it?"

"I don't know what the hell you're up to out here, but you stirred up a shitstorm," Woodson said. "My original orders were to arrest you after I took custody of the pirates, but Fleet Command countermanded those orders two hours ago. As of now, you're still in command of your mission, whatever that is."

"I'm glad to hear that."

"You won't be glad to hear that the sector commander wants you out of here," Woodson said. "Those were her arrest orders that Fleet countermanded, by the way, and she's not happy about it."

"Like you said, they're pirates," Fortis said. "We captured them in the course of defending ourselves."

Woodson held up his hands. "It doesn't matter to me how you captured them. All I know is they're our problem now."

Fortis forced himself not to smile. "Sorry."

"Was that their hulk we passed on the way out here?"

"I don't know. Probably. The ship had a hole in the pressure hull that we couldn't fix, so we abandoned it. Their shuttle is floating around out there somewhere, too."

"Roger that." Woodson studied Fortis for a second. "Do you have anything for me?"

"Negative. How about you?"

"Message is delivered, prisoners are transferred, my mission here is complete. My advice to you is to move closer to the shipping lanes, and next time, call for assistance."

Fortis led Woodson to the main hatch where Lakshaw waited.

"I'm Xenith Lakshaw, master of *Dancer*," she told Woodson. "What are you going to do with those men?"

"That's up to Fleet Command, ma'am," Woodson said. "My job is to take them into custody."

"We're all set, Major," Captain Delk reported from inside the shuttle.

"What about us?" Lakshaw asked. "Don't you need witness statements?"

Woodson shrugged. "That's above my paygrade."

Lakshaw gave the major a skeptical look as he climbed through the hatch and closed it behind him. Once *Dancer's* hatch was secure, the shuttle released.

"Let's go up to the control room," she told Fortis. When they got there, she slumped into her seat. "Doe, spin us around so we can see the *Comte de Barras* on the docking camera."

Fortis saw that the destroyer had turned but hadn't yet accelerated. The image was grainy because of the range, but it looked like the ship jettisoned something before it began to increase speed.

"I knew it!" Lakshaw snarled. "Those bastards airlocked them without a trial."

Fortis stared at the display. "I don't know. It's hard to make out what that is. It could be anything."

"Doe, max resolution and playback," Lakshaw ordered.

They watched the playback, and the picture was a bit clearer, but Fortis still couldn't make out much detail.

"I don't see it," he said. A hard knot formed in his stomach.

What else could it be?

"Maybe because you don't want to," Lakshaw spat back. "You have to admit, it's a pretty convenient solution to the problem."

"The only thing we control is what happens on this ship," Fortis said. "If Fleet Command ordered *Comte de Barras* to air lock the pirates, there's nothing we could have done to prevent it."

Lakshaw's eyes flashed her fury. "That's all I have for you, *Major* Fortis."

When Fortis got back to the cargo bay, the tension was palpable. Several knots of Paladins shot angry looks at him as he joined Herron and Zylstra.

"What's going on?" he asked.

"While you were talking to that major, we almost had a riot," Herron said. "Some of the guys are furious that we turned Space Marines over to the Fleet."

"Ex-Space Marines. Pirates."

"Once a Space Marine, always a Space Marine," Zylstra said with a sneer.

"I'm not happy about it either, but what the hell were we supposed to do? We had our orders, same as *Comte de Barras*."

Zylstra poked Fortis in the chest. "Everything was cool until one of the prisoners asked where those Fleet bastards were taking them, and they responded like this." He made a slashing gesture across his throat. "That's when the pushing and shoving started."

"What are they going to do with them?" Herron asked.

"I don't know." Fortis fixed each of them in a steady stare. "The major chewed me out for taking the prisoners and handed me our orders. Oh, shit!" Fortis fumbled in his pocket and came up with the folded envelope. "Our orders. I forgot all about them."

"What do they say?"

Major Woodson's warning echoed in Fortis' ears.

Your eyes only. Destroy after reading.

"I have to read these alone," he said. "I don't know what they say, but I'll let you know if there's anything in here for you."

"Fuckin' spook bullshit," Zylstra muttered.

"Okay, Fortis. We'll be standing by for whatever, but I hope it's good news. The lads are getting anxious."

Fortis stepped into the passageway and tore open the envelope.

Graham confirmed the target position near FS26098.354.9XHH. Proceed to those coordinates and be prepared to execute assault upon arrival.

He started for the control room to give the coordinates to Lakshaw but stopped. She didn't need to know how they got the target location, so he carefully tore off that part of the message. After a quick debate over how to dispose of the scrap, he shoved it in his mouth, chewed it into a sticky mess, and swallowed it.

Fortis knocked on the control room door and stuck his head in. "Captain Lakshaw, pardon the interruption, but I have received the coordinates of our target."

He handed her the paper, and she raised an eyebrow at the torn section.

"These are in the Free Sector," she said.

"Affirmative. We suspected it would be in the Free Sector. This message confirms it."

She handed the scrap to Doe. "Calculate a course at best speed to the Freedom Jump Gate approaches and passage onward to these coordinates, please."

The AI's fingers danced on the keyboard as he did her bidding. Lakshaw gave Fortis an amused smile.

"I didn't hurt your feelings earlier, did I?" she asked.

"Not at all. I didn't see what you saw, but when I got back down to the cargo bay, some of the men were furious because the Fleet personnel suggested they were going to execute the pirates. They had comrades among the prisoners."

Lakshaw shook her head. "That was an ugly bit of business."

"Two hours to the jump gate," Doe announced. "Thirty-seven hours from the gate to those coordinates."

"Prepare your men," Lakshaw said. "By this time tomorrow, we'll be through the gate and on our way to your target."

When Fortis returned to the hangar, he found Herron and Zylstra in the middle of a loud argument with a large group of Paladins. When they saw Fortis, they surrounded him.

"What's going on here?" Fortis had to shout to make himself heard.

Herron waved his arms, and the crowd grew quiet. "They're angry about what happened with those Space Marines, and they're pissed off because Charlotte sent them on a mission for the UNT."

"What are you talking about?" Fortis' denial was weak, and he knew it. "This isn't—"

"Liar!" Paladins all around him took up the chant. "Liar! Liar!"

Stars exploded behind Fortis' eyes, and the world went black.

* * * * *

Chapter Twenty-Seven

Zerec found Nicaro in the control room.

"One of the teams moving pulse rifles discovered a hatch secured with a high-security lock in the back of a magazine. Are you aware of this?"

Nicaro bristled at Zerec's abruptness, and he shook his head. "No, I haven't heard about it. What's in it"

"You don't know? You were a Fleet captain."

Nicaro rubbed his eyes with his thumb and forefinger. "Brother, I commanded a Fleet destroyer during the Maltaan invasion, but they divvied me before I could move up to a bigger vessel. We didn't have anything like the weapons and systems aboard *Colossus*. You have more time aboard Fleet flagships than I do; what do you know about it?"

Zerec seemed to ignore the barb. "The lock and hatch are helenium, and we don't have any equipment capable of cutting it."

"Hmm. I guess we'll have to wait until we return to Sanctuary, then."

"Very well." Zerec turned to leave, but Nicaro stopped him.

"Whatever it is, if it's worth securing behind helenium, it's worth waiting a few more days for."

* * *

Fortis awoke with a ferocious headache. He was laid out on the cargo bay deck. When he tried to push himself up, he discovered his hands were restrained. His stomach lurched when a wave of nausea broke over him. Through slitted eyes he saw Zylstra sitting on a nearby cargo box.

"What happened?" Fortis' voice was a croak. He held up his hands. "What are these?"

"We had a change of management while you were out," Zylstra said.

"What?" Fortis couldn't comprehend what the mercenary was telling him. "What do you mean?"

"Just shut the fuck up and lay there. Herron will be back soon, and you can talk to him."

Fortis put his head back down and fought to clear the woozy fog from his mind. His whole body was stiff, and he had the uneasy feeling he got after a warp gate jump.

Paladins stood in groups on the other side of the cargo bay. Even in his dazed state, he could see there was none of the usual boisterousness; instead, an uncomfortable air of apprehension hung over them.

Guilt?

He drifted in and out of consciousness until someone pulled him into a seated position. He opened his eyes and saw Herron. The Paladin leader pushed a hydration pack and two pills into his hands.

"Painkillers," Herron said. "I imagine you've got a pretty bad headache."

Fortis hesitated, and Herron scoffed. "If I wanted to kill you, I wouldn't use poison. Take 'em."

He swallowed the pills and sucked down the hydration pack in one long pull. When he was finished, Fortis dropped the empty on the deck next to him. He held up his hands. "What's going on?"

"The lads are angry, Major. We knew who you were from the moment you showed up in Burketown, and it was obvious that Charlotte hired us out on a UNT contract. A paycheck is a paycheck, so we went along with the program until you turned those Space Marines over to that Fleet major and laid that 'orders are orders' bullshit on us. You know they airlocked those guys, right?"

Fortis nodded. "Pirates."

Herron scoffed. "That attitude got you cracked over the head."

"Now what? Cancel the contract and return to Terra Earth?"

"Too late for that. We jumped through the Freedom Gate while you were unconscious."

"We jumped? Lakshaw agreed to that?"

"She's been very cooperative since I explained what would happen to her and her crew if she wasn't. I told her we would turn her loose after she delivers us to Sanctuary."

"She believed you? She seems smarter than that."

"It didn't take a lot of convincing. She's not too happy about what happened with the guys from *Sumida*, either."

"What about Charlotte and Paladin?"

"He'll be angry, but there's not much he can do, is there? Honestly, I think he'll try to pretend we never existed. It's not good for business to admit otherwise."

"What's your plan?"

"We're on our way to link up with a bunch of divvies from a place called Sanctuary. That's where *Sumida* sailed from. The pilot, Kelly, gave us the coordinates before Fleet murdered him."

"So, you're giving up the mercenary life to be Kuiper Knights."

Herron ignored Fortis' statement. "You want to hear something surprising? Kelly said that they grabbed *Colossus*, and she's somewhere near the Leavitt Peripheral."

Fortis raised his eyebrows in feigned surprise but didn't respond.

"Yeah, that's right. Your target is somewhere near the Leavitt Peripheral."

"Do you think you'll be welcome there after what happened with *Sumida*?"

"That's a good question. Zylstra and some of the boys wanted to beat the shit out of you and send you out the airlock, but I talked them out of it. When the Knights hear that we have you, I think we can negotiate something with them, and all will be forgiven if we give you up."

The information stunned Fortis, but he kept his face blank.

"Who are you working for?" Herron asked.

"I don't know."

"I don't believe you."

"What's to believe? I came home from Maltaan and they gave me the choice: take this mission or get divvied." Fortis struggled to focus on the details of his impromptu story. "What was I supposed to do?"

"What was your target?"

"They never told me."

Herron stared at Fortis for a long time as if weighing the validity of his story. "Let me get this straight. You accepted the mission, you came to Burketown and contracted with Charlotte, and then met *Dancer* on SOMO. All of that without knowing what the mission was."

Fortis shrugged. "It sounds hard to believe when you say it like that."

"Why is the UNT fucking with the Kuiper Knights in the Free Sector?"

"I thought maybe *Sumida* was the target when she showed up at the gate. Anti-piracy."

Herron dug into his pocket and pulled out Fortis' communicator. "I find that a little hard to swallow since you received two position updates from someone called 'V' after we hit *Sumida*. They're all near the same place. Somebody called 'T' requested a status report, too."

When he saw the communicator, Fortis knew Herron wasn't buying his story. Instead of piling lies on top of lies, he sat silent.

Herron sighed as he stood up and pocketed the communicator. "Lakshaw tells me we have about forty-two hours before we get to Sanctuary. You should probably come up with a better story for the Kuiper Knights."

Fortis slumped to his side as Herron walked away. His body ached, and his head still throbbed, but his thoughts weren't on his own misery.

They know about V.

* * *

Herron and Zylstra stepped into the passageway to talk in private.

"What do you think?" Zylstra asked.

"Charlotte was right. He's a convincing liar." Herron related his conversation with Fortis. "He blinked when I showed him the communicator. Other than that, I got nothing."

"Give me a chance. I'll get something out of him."

"I understand how you feel, JJ, but our priority must be to deliver him to the Knights in one piece. Whatever secrets he's keeping are worth more to them than getting our revenge. He's our ticket to getting out of this. Maybe they'll give him back when they're done with him."

"You don't want to join up with the Kuiper Knights?"

Herron hesitated for a half second. "Yeah, of course, but we can't show up empty-handed. They will want him, and we need to deliver him in one piece." He changed the subject. "Who's up there with Lakshaw?"

"Nellis. He's trying to beat the AI at chess."

Herron shook his head. "They can't be fucking around like that. We told her not to wake up the AI."

"Okay, I'll take care of it." Zylstra nodded toward the cargo bay. "What about Fortis?"

"We might as well leave him where he's at. He's not going anywhere. He'll be fine as long as nobody messes with him."

Herron watched Zylstra walk toward the control room. The attack on Fortis and the subsequent takeover of *Dancer* by the Paladins had taken him by surprise, and he'd been forced to go along with them. Since then, he could feel his control over the Paladins beginning to slip. Zylstra and many of the others had begun to act without his knowledge, and he needed to work fast to stay ahead of events.

There was nothing about life in the Free Sector with the Kuiper Knights that appealed to Herron. Unlike most of his comrades, Herron had saved some of every paycheck while he was in the Corps, so he hadn't shared their sense of desperation when they were divvied without warning.

Fuck it.

Herron returned to the hangar to wait for events to unfold.

* * *

Nicaro stood next to Zerec and watched the work progress in the cargo bay.

"What do you make of The Master's instructions regarding the mercenaries?" Nicaro asked.

"We will welcome them into the fold, as he decreed. We can always use more experienced men. When do you anticipate our rendezvous with them?"

"Sometime tomorrow afternoon. The long-range sensors were deactivated before we took this ship, so I'm afraid I can't be more specific. They are aboard a converted cargo vessel, and they aren't moving very fast. I sent them an approximate position of where I expect to be on our track along the Peripheral, so they'll intercept us there."

Zerec didn't respond.

"I'm looking forward to meeting their prisoner, Fortis. I recall seeing him during the war bond tour. The ISMC made him out to be some kind of hero."

"Those days are over, Brother Nicaro. Fortis is our enemy now. If the report is accurate, he's living proof that the UNT intends to meddle in our affairs here in the Free Sector."

Nicaro opened his mouth to respond but thought better of it. He had known the former ISMC colonel by name only before The Master had brought them together to hijack *Colossus*, and their relationship had been strained from the beginning. Nicaro agreed with their quest to control the Free Sector, but anything less than complete and utter adherence to the faith was practically blasphemy to zealots like Zerec. He turned to leave.

"I'm headed up to the control room. If you want me, that's where I'll be."

* * *

Ystremski spent the rest of the day working with Barker to move crates of grenades in accordance with Addison's instructions. They hauled cases of good grenades to Cargo Bay Three for transfer off the ship and placed the nine cases of suspect smoke grenades and incendiaries in Cargo Bay Four. After they moved the final crate, they sat side by side on it.

"Do you want to go find Addison and see what's next?" Barker asked.

"Not particularly, but I guess we should."

He kept his head on a swivel looking for Liz Sherer, and he was glad he didn't see her.

He caught sight of Sherer when they broke bread that evening, but he avoided contact with her. She stayed close to Zerec and Nicaro, which kept her far from him and the rest of the squires.

After they finished eating, Nicaro led the Knights in evening devotion before he dismissed them to their berthing compartments. Ystremski danced under a cold shower before he turned into his bunk. After lights out, he stared into the darkness and contemplated his situation.

He had sent several position reports, so he figured Anders knew where he was. He kicked himself for not getting details on an exfil plan; he had assumed he would return to Terra Earth with whatever force Anders sent to capture *Colossus*.

His best chance of maintaining his cover was to avoid anyone he knew from the past, and except for his brief encounter with Bender, he hadn't run into anyone he recognized from the ISMC.

Until now.

For her own safety, he had to keep Liz at arm's length. At some point, the Kuiper Knights would discover he was an agent, and he might not be able to protect her.

Finally, he fell into a dreamless sleep.

* * * * *

Chapter Twenty-Eight

The following morning, Addison told Ystremski and Barker to help the crews who were moving crates of pulse rifles and batteries to Cargo Bay Three. They tied the weapons down and cleared the bay while a shuttle arrived and loaded the cargo. They did this twice before they stopped at midday to break bread, and then they moved two more shuttle loads to the cargo bay in the afternoon. Although Ystremski was strength enhanced to level ten, the crates were large and awkward to move by hand, and each trip from the magazine left them sweating and panting while they waited for the shuttle to depart.

"Where are we, anyway?" Ystremski asked a Knight Errant named Clapp as they leaned against the bulkhead outside Cargo Bay Three.

"The Leavitt Peripheral." Clapp eyed him with suspicion. "Why are you so curious?"

"My apologies, Brother. I've never been to the Free Sector before. I like to learn about new places."

"Just worry about moving cargo."

They stopped work later to break bread. Ystremski made a beeline for the head to recover the communicator to send a current position report. He rejoined the Knights without drawing attention to himself and lined up for his food. Several pages he had worked with that morning nodded in recognition as he picked his way through the crowd to find a spot to eat and drink. Barker sidled up next to him, and they ate in silence.

Before they finished, Addison called for everyone's attention.

"There is a ship due here in one hour. Aboard are almost two hundred new men who will join us and travel back to Sanctuary to enter the Knighthood. When we have finished breaking bread, everyone who is not directly involved in moving weapons to the cargo bay will muster with me. Our task is to ensure there are adequate berthing accommodations for the new arrivals."

Ystremski and Barker traded shrugs as if to ask, *does that include us?*

They rejoined the group moving pulse rifles to Cargo Bay Three, but they only moved one crate before work ceased. Nicaro, Zerec, and a group of other Knights and Knights Errant entered Cargo Bay Four, and the curious squires gathered around the hatch.

Three men dressed in unfamiliar military style uniforms emerged from the umbilical and shook hands with the Knighthood leaders. They were too far away for Ystremski to hear what was said, but it was clear that the Knights welcomed them.

"They must be the new guys," Barker muttered.

The tallest of them gestured to the umbilical and two more newcomers emerged, with a third man between them. They dragged him forward until he stood in front of Zerec. Ystremski jerked when a jolt of recognition and shock hit him.

Fortis!

* * *

Zylstra and the Paladins dragged Fortis aboard the shuttle and crowded in behind him. Doe piloted the craft, while

Herron and several others remained aboard *Dancer* to ensure Lakshaw's cooperation and guard their weapons.

The trip was brief, and Doe expertly guided the craft alongside their destination, which Fortis was certain was *Colossus*. When the umbilical was hooked up, Fortis was pushed to the hatch right behind Zylstra and a handful of others.

The mercenary leader turned and looked at him. "Don't fuck around, Fortis. You can go through the tube awake or asleep, I don't care."

When it was Fortis' turn, he crossed his arms and slid through. Paladins grabbed him at the bottom and pulled him to his feet as he looked around the cavernous space. The large "4" painted on the bulkhead told him it was indeed *Colossus*. Zylstra walked toward a group of people in colored smocks who stood on the other side of the room, and Fortis was pushed along behind him.

"Colonel Zerec," Zylstra said as he extended his hand. "It's an honor and a pleasure to meet you. I am JJ Zylstra, and these are the Paladins.

Zerec gave Zylstra an icy look as they shook. "I go by Brother Zerec these days, Mr. Zylstra. This is Brother Nicaro and Brother Addison."

When introductions were completed, Zylstra gestured to Fortis. "This is Major Fortis of the ISMC. The UNT sent him here to attack you. A gift from us to you."

Fortis recognized Zerec's name, and he knew the former colonel was one of the senior leaders of the Kuiper Knights. His mind raced as he considered his next move. Getting captured was bad enough without becoming propaganda for the Kuiper Knights. He knew too much about the mission to risk interrogation. The Paladin behind him shoved him forward, and he knew what to do.

Go down fighting.

Fortis allowed the momentum from the shove to propel him forward, but instead of stopping short of Zerec, he took four giant steps. He drove his fist into the face of the startled Knight before he landed a roundhouse kick to the knees of the man next to him. He grabbed another man by the smock and headbutted him, and the man screamed as his nose exploded.

The Kuiper Knights recovered from their shock and surrounded Fortis. Fists, elbows, and knees rained down on him from all sides. He kept his chin down and hunched his shoulders to try and protect his head as he punched and kicked in all directions, but the weight of the attack was too much. Fortis was forced down to the deck and men pinned his arms and legs.

"You'll pay for that, you bastard!" Zerec drew back and kicked Fortis in the face. The blow stunned him, and his eye immediately swelled shut. Zerec wound up to kick Fortis again.

"Zerec!" The man whose knee Fortis destroyed with his first kick shouted from where he had fallen to the deck. "That's enough. The Master wants him alive."

"What are you doing?" How can you beat a defenseless man?"

Through his good eye, Fortis watched Liz Sherer rush forward. Two of the Kuiper Knights grabbed her and pulled her away as she screamed and tried to escape.

Liz?

Zerec paused, and Fortis could almost hear the wheels turn in his head. Finally, he lowered his boot.

"You will pay for that, *if* you survive interrogation. I hear the chemicals they use are excruciating. I pray for your survival."

* * *

As soon as Ystremski saw Fortis, he knew there was only one reason the Space Marine would be in the Free Sector. Since he was a prisoner of the mercenaries, Ystremski also knew the mission to recapture *Colossus* had failed.

Does he know about me? Fuck.

The squires behind him surged forward when Fortis attacked Zerec. Ystremski fought his way through the crowd into the passageway outside. He had to come up with an escape plan, and fast.

Across from the cargo bays was a row of hatches with bright red signs.

ESCAPE PODS - EMERGENCY USE ONLY

The passageway was deserted, so he opened one of the hatches and looked inside. The escape pod sat on the launch rails with the hatch open, exactly like he remembered from his many deployments aboard Fleet flagships. When the hatch was closed and the launch button pressed, compressed gas opened the outer door and propelled the pod down the rails and out of the ship. He checked the pressure on the tanks, and relief washed over him when he saw the gauges in the green.

Good to go.

Ystremski ducked back out into the passageway. He could hear shouting from Cargo Bay Four, but he turned for Three. He opened a crate of grenades and stuffed several smokes in one pocket and incendiaries in the other. To make room, he stuck his communicator in the crate. Then he pulled the pins on two smoke grenades and tossed them behind a stack of pulse rifles. When they began to billow choking clouds of red and purple, he threw two incendiaries behind them and headed for Cargo Bay Four.

When he got there, the shouting had died down, and he heard Sherer scream.

"Fire!"

Everyone near the hatch turned and stared at him, and Ystremski pointed toward Cargo Bay Three and choked. Clouds of smoke poured into the passageway, and the incendiaries added a weird bright light to the scene. He bulled his way through the crowd into Bay Four.

"Fire!"

Panic seized the crowd as squires fled down the passageway, away from the smoke. Ystremski pressed himself against the bulkhead to avoid being swept along by the mad rush. He pulled out another smoke and tossed it over the crowd, and the fresh burst of smoke increased the panic to fever pitch. Blinding smoke stung his eyes and burned his throat, but he shoved his way deeper into the bay. Nobody could see as he pulled the pin on an incendiary and threw it as far as he could, where it detonated with a bright flash and burned with white-hot intensity.

Suddenly, Sherer appeared through the smoke. He grabbed her arm and pushed her against the bulkhead.

"Where's Fortis?"

Sherer squinted in confusion and fear. "Petr? What?"

"Abner Fortis. Where is he?"

She pointed. "He was over there somewhere."

"I'll be right back. Get down and stay here."

Ystremski ran at a crouch, dodging Knights and squires alike. He ran headlong into Nicaro, and the two men stood face to face.

"Brother, you've got to get to safety," Ystremski cried. He pushed the leader in the direction of the hatch. "Go now!"

Confusion etched the older man's face, but he nodded and limped away into the smoke. Ystremski pulled out his last smoke grenade, activated it, and dropped it. Then he threw his second to last incendiary across the cargo bay where it exploded with a bright flash.

He waded through the smoke until he found Fortis on his hands and knees, coughing. Ystremski seized him by his shoulders and pulled him to his feet.

"Abner, let's go."

Fortis' legs went out from under him, and he would have collapsed if Ystremski hadn't caught him.

"Fuck this."

Ystremski threw an arm across his back and hoisted the Space Marine across his shoulders in a fireman's carry.

"My turn, dickhead."

Ystremski turned for the hatch. The smoke had begun to dissipate and he could see men in ones and twos making their way for the hatch. Two men in the military uniforms of the newcomers stopped him. The taller of the two, a man with severe scarring across his head, held up his hand.

"Where are you taking him?"

"I need to get him out of here. The space is on fire."

"We'll take him."

The scarred man reached out to take Fortis from Ystremski's shoulders. Ystremski kicked him in the groin with all his strength, and the man let out a guttural scream as he sank to the deck clutching his damaged testicles. The suddenness of the attack took the other man by surprise and gave Ystremski time to slam his free hand into the side of the man's head. His legs wobbled, and he sat down in a daze. Ystremski finished him off with a sidekick to the temple.

Ystremski found Sherer where he had left her squatting near the hatch. He pulled her to her feet and pushed her toward the door.

"There's a hatch straight across the passageway. Hold it open for us."

They picked their way through fallen bodies and entered the passageway in time to hear the first crates of grenades detonate in Hangar Bay Three. Flames and smoke boiled out into the passageway, and a wave of heat engulfed Ystremski. A team of men who were manning a firefighting hose at the hatch screamed in terror as the nozzleman burst into flames. They dropped the hose and ran, and the hose gyrated wildly as high-pressure water added suffocating steam to the already toxic atmosphere.

Ystremski ducked into the escape pod room and dumped Fortis into the pod. He shoved Sherer in on top of him.

"Get in!"

He pulled the pin on his last incendiary, flipped it into the passageway, and secured the door. He dove into the escape pod and slammed the hatch shut.

"Hold on!"

Ystremski punched the launch button on the console. The escape pod rocketed forward as the compressed gas dumped from the tanks. Ystremski, Fortis, and Sherer ended up in a tangle of arms and legs as the pod launched. When the artificial gravity of *Colossus* vanished, they floated free.

Sherer helped Ystremski secure Fortis in one of the seats. "What the hell happened back there?"

Ystremski belted himself into one of the control console seats. "Defective ordnance started going up, so I knew we had to get out."

"Defective ordnance?" Sherer gave him the side-eye as she settled in next to him. "Defective ordnance threw smoke grenades all over the place?"

Ystremski shrugged but didn't respond as he powered up the navigation suite. A virtual display appeared on the screens in front of them. A large, dark planet loomed ahead.

"I don't know where that is, but that's where we're going."

* * * * *

Chapter Twenty-Nine

Ystremski could make out a dark horizon on the sensor screen after the pod entered the atmosphere, but he couldn't see any lights or other signs of human civilization. The resolution wasn't great, but as the pod descended, he began to make out more details. He saw a smear of lights a long way off on the horizon but nothing close by. The surface looked like it was covered with trees until a large open area appeared ahead of them. He touched the screen over the open area and clicked, "Land Here."

Sherer had moved to the row next to Fortis when he began to mumble before they entered the atmosphere. "How's it look?"

"Nighttime. Mostly trees, but I found an open area to land in."

"Good."

"I hope it's not a lake."

She groaned in response. "Why would you say something like that?"

The pod slowed and descended on a survivable glideslope as the autopilot guided them to the designated landing spot, and the surface became more visible. The ground appeared smooth, and uniform lines ran the length of the open area. Ystremski had one final thought before the pod touched down.

A field.

The craft rumbled and shook as it skidded along the furrows and came to a stop. The atmospheric sensors glowed green, so Ystremski twisted the hatch release, and it popped open. A cloud of dirt swirled around him as he climbed from the pod, and he was happy to be out of the cramped vehicle.

"Where are we?" Liz asked.

"A farm, I think. Somebody plowed this land, so they can't be too far."

"Give me a hand with him."

Ystremski climbed back in and lifted Fortis out of the pod. The injured Space Marine groaned and stood with his arms clutched to his abdomen, but he was able to stand up on his own.

"Which way?"

Ystremski couldn't see Fortis' face, but he knew he was hurting. "I think we need to wait a few seconds and give our eyes a chance to adjust." He could already make out more details in the semi-darkness.

Fortis slumped against the pod. "I gotta sit."

Ystremski caught Fortis before he could slide to the ground. "No, you need to stay on your feet." He put one of Fortis's arms around his neck and wrapped his own around Fortis' neck. "I can see some buildings not too far away. C'mon, I'll help you."

Fortis' legs folded and Ystremski scooped him up in a cradle. "I got you, brother. I got you."

"Never a dull moment with you," Liz said as she followed Ystremski across the field. "Thank you. I thought I was a goner back there."

"Just another day in the Corps."

The night air was cool, but Ystremski was sweating before they'd gone fifty meters. The furrows made footing treacherous, and it took all his concentration not to stumble and drop Fortis. The buildings grew in size and definition as they approached, and it relieved him to see one of them was a farmhouse. When they were twenty meters away, a woman's voice with a no-nonsense tone called out from the darkness.

"That's close enough. Who are you and what do you want?"

"We need help," Liz said. "We had to abandon ship, and our friend got hurt. Can you help us?"

"What's wrong with him?"

"I don't know. Please. There was a fire and an explosion, and we had to abandon ship in the pod. He's going to die if you don't help us."

There was a long pause before the woman answered.

"Okay, bring him up, but move slow."

Liz took the lead, and Ystremski followed her up the porch steps. A match flared, and a dim lantern guided them inside the house. After they were inside, the woman turned up the lamp and Ystremski saw a typical living room, with a sofa, a recliner, and a stone fireplace.

"This way."

They went into an adjoining dining room, where the woman cleared the table and lit two more lamps.

"Put him down there."

Ystremski lifted Fortis onto the table and stepped back.

"I'm Linda," Liz said as she offered her hand. "This is Paul."

"Mel."

When Ystremski shook her hand, he found it was calloused, but her grip was warm and dry. Something about her seemed very familiar.

Mel motioned to Fortis. "What happened to him?"

"The ship caught fire, and there was an explosion. The master ordered everyone to abandon ship. We found this guy next to an escape pod, so I grabbed him and punched out."

"Help me get his coveralls off and let's get a look at him."

A floorboard squeaked behind them. Ystremski whirled and saw a tall man holding a huge ballistic pistol standing in the shadows. A shaggy beard and long hair disguised his features.

"Uh, hi," Liz said with a nervous twinge. "I'm Linda."

"What was the name of your ship?" the bearded man asked.

"Distant, uh, Nearness. Distant Nearness."

Ystremski wanted to kick her for choosing such a strange ship name, but it was too late to change it.

"She's a crew ship," Liz added, but Ystremski could tell the man didn't believe her.

He gestured toward the front door. "Paul, let's go talk outside while Mel tends to your friend."

Ystremski walked back out onto the porch on wooden legs and a nervous tingle ran up and down his spine. He was unarmed in the presence of a man who didn't believe their story, and it occurred to him that nobody knew where they were.

"Sit."

Ystremski sat on a bench at one end of the porch, and the man sat in a rocker next to the door.

"My name's Bill Tacker. How about you stop bullshitting me and tell me what the fuck's really going on, Private Ystremski?"

Recognition and relief washed over Ystremski. Bill Tacker was a retired Space Marine, a legend from early in Ystremski's career, and his wife, Mel, had been a surrogate mother to many wayward Space Marines. The last Ystremski had seen of Tacker was just before he was grievously injured during a bug hunt many years before.

"Holy shit, Bill. I didn't recognize you."

A match flared, and Ystremski got a good look at Tacker as he touched the flame to a pipe. Deep scars covered one side of his face, which his long hair and beard had disguised.

"Most don't. The bugs on Ha'aka Ro do good work, don't you think?" The pipe glowed, and the pungent smell of sweet tobacco flooded the porch. "Now, how about the truth?"

"The Corps divvied me," Ystremski said. "I joined the Kuiper Knights to make some money and figure out what to do next. They captured *Colossus*, which was loaded with weapons and gear, and I ended up aboard her. The Knights allowed Liz Sherer aboard as some kind of publicity stunt."

Another wave of pipe smoke wafted through the air. "Carry on."

"A fire started among some incendiary ordnance, and it got out of control, so we jumped in an escape pod and landed here."

Ystremski felt a twinge of guilt for leaving out so much detail, but he didn't know who he could trust with the whole truth. He was almost one hundred percent sure Tacker wasn't sympathetic to the Kuiper Knights, but he might not be sympathetic to the UNT, either.

Almost.

"I wasn't joking when I asked for the truth. You left a whole lot of it out of your story."

Ystremski sighed. "Okay Bill, look, the Corps divvied me, that much is true, but it was a ruse. They did it so I could infiltrate the Knights to find *Colossus* and the weapons."

"Sheep dipped."

"Yeah, exactly. After I found *Colossus*, I thought they were going to send in a Fleet ship to destroy her.

"Instead, Fortis shows up as a prisoner of some mercenaries who were hired to recapture her. The Knights know there's a mole, but they don't know who, so they planned to send Fortis to Sanctuary for exploitation. I couldn't allow that to happen, so I set off some incendiary grenades, tossed a few smokes, and jumped in an escape pod with Fortis. That's the truth."

Tacker shifted his feet and lit another match. "What about Liz Sherer? Do you always travel with members of the press?"

"I don't know how she got there, Bill. She showed up with some of the Knights, but I don't how that happened. You'll have to ask her. Me and Fortis have known her since Balfan-48, and the last place I expected to see her was aboard *Colossus*."

"This other man, Fortis? He's a Space Marine?"

"Affirmative. Major Fortis is one of the finest officers I've ever served with—" Ystremski's voice cracked, and he blinked away the hot tears that threatened to spill down his cheeks. "And he's my best friend."

"Huh." Tacker stood up. "Let's go check on your friend."

Tacker led Ystremski inside where they found Fortis sitting in a dining room chair while Mel dabbed at his wounds. His hands were wrapped and his face was swollen, and he had deep bruising on his abdomen.

"How's our patient?" Tacker asked.

"He's been beat to a pulp," Mel said. "He doesn't seem to be concussed, but I think a couple ribs might be cracked. I think he'll survive. Strange injuries for an explosion."

Liz helped Fortis onto the couch in the living room, and Mel gave him two tablets and a drink of water.

"Pain relievers will help him sleep," she explained.

Fortis was soon snoring softly.

"Petr, come give me a hand hitching up your pod so I can move it into the barn," Tacker said. "We can't leave it out in the middle of the field for the crabs."

"Crabs?"

"Nocturnal crustaceans. The place is infested with them."

* * *

Knight Errant Zerec scowled as two Squires held up expended smoke grenades for his inspection.

"We found these in the cargo bay, Brother Zerec." Zerec turned to Nicaro. "We've been betrayed."

"How many casualties?" Nicaro asked Dietz.

"Seven dead, four wounded, six missing, including the reporter and the Space Marine."

"Six missing. I wonder how many of the missing were saboteurs?" Zerec asked. He grabbed the dead smokes. "Did anyone see who threw these?"

"No, Brother. No one has reported that." Dietz's face flushed. The Knight Errant was talking down to him as if he were a page.

"The first crisis situation we encountered, and everyone panicked." Zerec's eyes narrowed. "How did the reporter escape? You were her escort, weren't you?"

"You were there. The scene in the cargo bay was complete chaos."

"Brothers, we must put our differences aside," Nicaro said. "It will displease The Master to hear that we wasted time bickering instead of fulfilling our mission. What is the status of the weapons transfer?"

"The armorers reported that they have sixty-two cases of pulse rifles remaining, along with spare batteries and battle armor. I have not received a report regarding the remaining grenades. We also don't yet know how the fire in Cargo Bay Four started—"

Zerec snorted. "Sabotage, you idiot!"

Dietz continued as if he hadn't heard the insult. "Everything stored in Cargo Bay Four was suspect and could have spontaneously combusted. We will have a final answer after a thorough investigation."

"Brother, this is madness," Zerec said to Nicaro. "We're wasting time. The fire was an obvious case of sabotage. You say The Master will be displeased if we waste time bickering, but I daresay he will be furious if we allow the saboteurs to escape."

Another Kuiper Knight trotted over to join the group. "Brothers, I have bad news. One of the escape pods is missing."

"What? How?"

The Knight shook his head. "We don't know. A squire searching for the missing Brothers discovered one of the escape pod racks across from Cargo Bay Three is empty."

"The saboteurs have escaped!" Zerec said. "We have to capture them."

"Brother, wait." Nicaro held up his hand. "We don't know if there were saboteurs. As Brother Dietz said—"

"Brother Dietz is a fool, and so are you!" Zerec stabbed a meaty finger into Nicaro's chest. "We have been betrayed from within, and we must respond immediately. I will not stand here cluck-clucking like a bunch of barnyard fowl while our attackers escape. You can stay here and do all the investigating you want, but I am taking the Knights Errant to the surface to capture our enemies."

Zerec stormed away, while Nicaro and the other Knights stared in shocked silence. The relationship between them and the Knights

Errant had always been strained, but their common devotion to The Master and the brotherhood had kept them together.

Dietz cleared his throat. "Brother Nicaro, what do you command?"

"Continue the weapons transfers and clean up Cargo Bay Four. Make a list of the missing Brothers and try to determine who might have been involved in the sabotage." He nodded to the hatch through which Zerec had disappeared. "In the meantime, I will send a report to The Master."

* * * * *

Chapter Thirty

Ystremski and Tacker walked into the barn, where Ystremski saw an eight-wheeled tractor with a large scoop on the front.

"Hey, Bill, where are we, anyway?"

"We're on one of the Upper Hebrides. A day or so from the center of the Leavitt Peripheral."

"A planet with no name?"

"Nobody ever bothered to name the individual planets out here," Tacker said as he took some heavy chains down off the wall and dragged them over to the scoop.

"Is there a space port on this planet?"

"Yep, in Euphoria. That's what we call the capital."

Ystremski helped Tacker heave the chains into the scoop. "Can we catch a shuttle in Euphoria?"

"There's no passenger service out of here." Tacker chuckled. "Nobody comes here to visit."

Before Ystremski could ask more questions, Tacker climbed into the cab and motioned Ystremski to join him.

"Here's the situation," Tacker began. "The crabs aren't really crabs, they're some kind of arachnid. We call them crabs because nobody wants to imagine spiders that fucking big with that many legs and pincers. They're nocturnal, and they're drawn to light and sound. I located a big nest of them about ten meters inside the tree line on the far side of the field you landed on, but the UHDL hasn't had time to help me burn them out."

"What's the UHDL?"

"The Upper Hebrides Defense League. We don't have the ISMC or Fleet in the Free Sector, so a bunch of us formed the UHDL. We help each other out by burning bug holes, protecting against pirates, and that sort of thing.

"Anyway, I watched through my infrared scope as the crabs swarmed out of the woods while you were walking across the field. They were very interested in the pod."

"Why don't we wait for daylight to do this?"

"Is anyone looking for you?"

Tacker's question surprised Ystremski. "I don't know, Bill. I guess so."

"Then we don't want to leave a Fleet escape pod sitting in the middle of my field." The tractor engine roared to life, and the barn doors opened when Tacker pressed a button on the console. He had to shout over the engine. "It will be dark for another nineteen hours, and I don't want to leave it out there any longer than necessary."

The tractor lurched into motion and bounced across the furrowed field. Ystremski caught sight of the pod just before Tacker stopped the tractor.

"Did you turn off the rescue beacon?" Tacker asked as he jumped down from the cab.

"Shit. I forgot."

"Turn it off and then give me a hand."

Ystremski leaned into the pod and turned off the beacon power switch. Tacker dragged the chains over to the pod.

"I want to make a cradle and lift this thing," Tacker said while he worked. "I don't want to drag it."

Ystremski grabbed one end of the chain and wrapped it around the far side of the pod. On the count of three, he and Tacker threw the ends of the chain over the pod and ran around to the other side. After they linked it all together, Tacker edged the tractor forward, and Ystremski hooked the chains with the scoop teeth.

Something bumped into Ystremski's leg, and when he brushed it away, he felt a hard shell and sharp edges.

"Sonofabitch!"

He kicked wildly at the dim shapes gathering around his legs.

"You gonna dance all night?" Tacker shouted from the cab.

Ystremski scrambled up the ladder and plopped into the seat next to Tacker.

"Goddamn crabs, there must have been ten of them on me!"

"Are you sure it was that many?"

Tacker flashed the tractor headlights, and Ystremski saw a seething, writhing mass of crabs blanketed across the field. There were thousands of them.

The ride back to the barn with the escape pod suspended under the scoop was slow, and Ystremski let out a long sigh of relief when the doors swung closed behind them. When Tacker cut the tractor engine, he heard *snick-snick-snick* as claws and feet skittered along the metal walls searching for a way in. Several crabs clung to the pod and tractor.

"Are they always like this?"

Tacker scoffed. "They get worse during mating season." He jumped down from the cab and grabbed a shovel from a wall bracket. "C'mon, give me a hand killing the hitchhikers."

"If there's no shuttle service here, how do we get home?" Ystremski asked as they chopped invading crabs into pieces with their shovels.

"I didn't say there isn't shuttle service, I said there isn't passenger shuttle service. There's no booking office to reserve a seat, but for the right price, you can catch a ride on a supply ship. It might not be a direct flight back to Terra Earth, but you'll get there eventually."

"How far is it to Euphoria?" Ystremski asked as he gathered chopped up crab pieces into a neat pile.

"Fifty kilometers." Tacker shoveled the dead crabs into a two-handled metal bin. "Not that far, but you can't get there from here, and not just because of the crabs. You can't climb the rift." He pointed to a large silver object hanging in the other end of the barn. "For that, you'll need a dirigible."

* * *

Lakshaw stood in the shuttle bay aboard *Dancer* with her arms crossed and an angry look on her face. "You bastard! You said we'd be free to leave!"

Zylstra gave her an amused look. "And you will be. When we're finished with you."

"When will that be?"

"When we're finished." He looked at Herron. "Are you okay waiting here while I take the shuttle down with some of the lads to help Zerec search for Fortis?"

Herron shrugged. "Sure."

What choice do I have?

When *Dancer* rendezvoused with *Colossus* to turn Fortis over to the Kuiper Knights, the shuttle had been packed with ex-Paladins anxious to join their divvied comrades on the flagship. Most of them had ignored Herron when he cautioned against everyone transferring until their weapons and gear were transferred. He had tried to maintain some semblance of order among the men, but his authority had waned as Zylstra emerged as the new leader. When Herron opted not to join the Kuiper Knights, the last bit of his authority over the men had evaporated.

There were four other ex-Paladins who had decided not to join the Kuiper Knights in the Free Sector. The others had ostracized them when they chose to remain aboard *Dancer* with Herron. For a brief time, Herron feared the larger group might act against the five of them, but nothing happened.

"I suppose you want Doe to pilot the shuttle?" Lakshaw asked.

"If I had a pilot rated for atmospheric entry, I wouldn't need him. Unless you want to come?" Zylstra leered as he delivered his double-entendre, and Herron had to resist the urge to punch him.

Lakshaw rolled her eyes and stormed away as Zylstra chuckled.

"How long do you think you'll be down there?"

"I don't know. Zerec, er, Brother Zerec said the place isn't that big, so I don't think it will be too long. I'll be up on comms, so I'll let you know."

Zylstra climbed aboard the shuttle and locked down the hatch. Herron retreated to the shuttle control tower and watched the shuttle launch. When it was gone, he headed for the cargo bay to join his men.

All four of them.

* * *

Ystremski, Liz, and the Tackers gathered around a candle on the dining room table while Fortis snored on the couch in the living room.

"A long time ago, the crust of this planet cracked and shifted," Mel said. "The result was a fifty-meter cliff that stretches from one coast to the other."

"It's straight up and solid rock," Tacker added. "A road would be impossible."

"How do you get supplies in without a road?"

"I had a drop ship bring building materials and supplies in the beginning. Now, we use the pedal-powered dirigible I showed you in the hangar."

"That's how we're getting out of here? A balloon?" Liz asked.

Tacker and Mel laughed.

"It's not as bad as it sounds," Mel said. "It takes some work to get to altitude, but it's easy once you get going." She slapped her thigh. "It's a good workout, too."

Ystremski was skeptical. "Is it big enough for five of us?"

"If two of you don't mind riding in the cargo box," Tacker said. "There's only room for three on the pedals."

"How long does it take to get there?"

"Four hours, depending on the wind," Tacker said.

"Four hours?" Liz looked at Ystremski. "Looks like you're pedaling."

Tacker explained that they couldn't leave until daylight, which was still twelve hours away. He suggested that Ystremski and Liz get some rest. Mel offered a spare bed to Liz, while Ystremski settled into a comfortable chair in the living room next to the sleeping Fortis.

"I'll be fine," he said when Mel protested. "It's not a hole in the ground, it's not raining, and nobody is shooting at me."

Ystremski stared out the window at the dark field and listened to Fortis breathe. He knew the major's injuries weren't life-threatening, but that knowledge did little to ease his worries. They were a long way from home with a lot of enemies standing between them and safety.

Encountering the Tackers was an incredible stroke of good fortune. They could have just as easily crashed into a forest fifty kilometers away and become crab food. Ystremski knew many Space Marines who carried a lucky talisman or swore they were blessed by Lady Luck. Whatever the reason, he knew to push hard when circumstances were breaking in his favor because things would inevitably go wrong.

Fortis mumbled and shifted on the couch. Ystremski considered his friend and shook his head. He'd never seen a lucky streak like the one Fortis had been riding since they'd met years before. No matter how long the odds were, he somehow made it through and usually came out on top.

Ystremski allowed his thoughts to drift to Tanya and the kids. It had seemed cruel to ask her to accept this mission so soon after he returned from six months on Maltaan, but she knew he wouldn't ask it of her unless it was critical. He hadn't been around the Kuiper Knights long enough to learn their ultimate plans for the weapons from *Colossus*, but he knew that eventually it would create problems for the UNT, and the solution would involve the ISMC.

Finally, he slept.

* * *

Dancer's shuttle touched down at the darkened space port in Euphoria and taxied clear of the runway before it shut down. Brother Zerec released his restraint and stood up.

Zylstra got up from the seat next to him. "Brother, I'll be right back."

Zerec scowled as Zylstra went forward.

"We haven't inducted him as a page yet," Addison said, "yet he takes the liberties of a knight."

"Men like him have their uses. Circumstances demand we make certain allowances, but his time will come."

Zylstra returned to the passenger cabin. "We're all set. I'll leave a couple men aboard, and the rest of us will flood the colony. We'll find him by daylight."

The mix of Kuiper Knights and ex-Paladins disembarked onto the tarmac and looked around. Euphoria was a sprawl of prefab warehouses, biodomes, and a wide variety of buildings constructed from local materials. Lights dotted the colony, but there was no apparent nightlife and little else to attract their attention.

Addison threw up his hands. "Perhaps we should wait aboard the shuttle."

"We have nothing to fear in the darkness," Zerec said. "Deploy the brothers and let them become familiar with this place. When it becomes light, they will be that much more prepared for the difficult work ahead."

* * * * *

Chapter Thirty-One

Fortis opened his eyes in the darkness of an unfamiliar room. It wasn't the cell he expected; his body ached, and his head hurt, but he was lying on couch. He used his legs to leverage himself around until he was sitting up, and an involuntary groan escaped his mouth.

"Wha—? What's that?" A man slumped in a chair across the darkened room stood up, and Fortis recognized Petr Ystremski's voice.

"What are you doing here?"

Ystremski rolled his head on his neck and stretched his arms. "Saving your ass, as usual."

"You got any water?"

"Yeah, let me look in the kitchen."

A match flared as Ystremski lit a candle, and Fortis looked around. He saw he was on a sofa in a living room, and the sight confused him. The candle disappeared with Ystremski, and Fortis waited in the dark.

When Ystremski returned, he set a pitcher and two cups on a low table next to the sofa.

"I think this is water." He poured a cup and handed it to Fortis. "Drink it slow."

Fortis could feel the water rehydrating his body as soon as it slid down his throat. He gulped it all and held out his cup for more.

"So much for slow," Ystremski said with a chuckle. He filled Fortis' cup. "This time, I mean it. Slow."

Fortis took another big swallow and leaned back. "Where are we? What happened?"

"It's a long story. Do you remember anything about the mercenaries you hired?"

"Huh." Fortis touched his head. "Yeah, the Paladins betrayed me. I remember that."

"They transferred you to *Colossus* and gave you to the Kuiper Knights. Some of the Knights Errant beat the shit out of you."

"Who?"

"Total fanatics. Way worse than regular Knights. They were going to turn you over to their leader for chemical interrogation after they finished distributing the stolen weapons to all their enclaves in the Free Sector."

"I remember *Colossus*. Some of it, anyway."

"I was on *Colossus*. When I heard you were there and what they had planned for you, I engineered a brilliant escape plan, and here we are."

"You pulled it out of your ass, you mean. Where are we, anyway?"

"We're in the Free Sector in a system called the Upper Hebrides. We're at a farm owned by a retired Space Marine, Bill Tacker, and his wife, Mel."

"How did you end up here?"

"You don't know?"

"The last time I saw you, the Corps had divvied you, and you punched me in the face."

"I'm sorry about that. I had to make it look real, and I got a little carried away."

"Anders said you were sorry."

"He told you about me?"

"He said you were sorry about the punch and that I wasn't supposed to try and contact you."

"Yeah. Tanya and the kids went to North America."

Fortis groaned and laid back down. "All this thinking is making my head hurt worse."

"Relax, and I'll explain. Anders sent me to infiltrate the Kuiper Knights to locate the stolen weapons. Anders sent you to recover them, but the mercenaries switched sides and dealt you to the Knights. Liz Sherer helped me get you off *Colossus*, and we landed here."

"Liz is here?"

"Yeah. She's asleep upstairs."

"She was asleep upstairs, until you two started making all that noise." A candle floated down the stairs and Fortis saw Liz descending. She came over and gave Fortis a peck on the cheek. "How are you feeling?"

"Pretty good, now that I understand what's going on. Except for you. How did you get here?"

"I was chasing a story about stolen guns, and those bastards hijacked my ship. Petr rescued me."

Fortis propped himself up on an elbow. "What's our next step?"

"Like I said, we're at the Tacker farm in the Upper Hebrides. When it's daylight, they're going to help us get to the colony of Euphoria to grab a shuttle out of here."

"Not if they don't get any sleep." Tacker stomped down the stairs holding a lantern overhead, followed by Mel. He walked to the couch and held out his hand. "Bill Tacker."

"Abner Fortis."

After they shook hands, Mel offered hers. "I'm Mel, Mr. Grumpy's better half." She looked at the group. "Since we're all awake, does anyone want breakfast?"

* * *

Anders poked his head in the office door, and Boudreaux waved him over to a chair.

"Do you have any updated locating data on *Colossus*, Nils?"

"No sir, not since the last update approximately thirty hours ago. We received a message twelve hours ago, but it was garbled. I requested retransmission, but we've heard nothing back."

"I'm going to order *Comte de Barras* into the Free Sector to locate and destroy *Colossus*."

The news stunned Anders. "What about our source aboard *Colossus*?"

"It's a shitty deal, but he knew the risks. We have to destroy the planet killer before they offload it."

"Can we send a warning? Give him a chance to get off?" Anders asked.

Boudreaux shook his head. "I'm afraid not. What if he's compromised?"

"General, I—"

"No warnings, General. DINLI."

Anders slowly nodded in agreement. "What about Fortis?"

"Have you figured out where he went?"

"No sir. We haven't heard anything from him or *Dancer*. I sent a message to Charlotte at Paladin, but he hasn't heard anything, either."

"What do you want me to do?" It was obvious to Anders that Boudreaux was losing his patience.

"He might be aboard *Colossus*. Maybe they recaptured her but can't report back."

"I'm sorry, Nils, but we can't wait on mights and maybes. It's time we did what we should have done all along and use the Fleet for more than an expensive taxi service. I'll instruct *Comte de Barras* to do everything within reason to identify who has control of *Colossus*, but we don't have a lot of other options at this point." He locked Anders in an unflinching stare. "It sucks, and I don't like it any better than you do. *De Barras* won't be there for thirty-six hours or so. That gives Ystremski time to get off. Maybe we'll get something from Fortis before she gets there.

"In the meantime, I want you to collect everything we have on the Kuiper Knights. Who they are, how many there are, where they operate from, everything. Something tells me they're not going to take this lying down, and if they have the balls to grab *Colossus*, they might try something else."

"What about the Big Four, sir?"

"We're not going to notify the Big Four about *de Barras* unless they protest."

"They're gonna be pissed off."

"That's a problem for the Ministry of Foreign Affairs. We need to focus on the threat, which is the Kuiper Knights." Boudreaux stood, and Anders followed suit. "Get busy, Nils. We need to get our arms all the way around the Kuiper Knights, pronto."

Anders walked back to his office on wooden legs. The idea of leaving Ystremski and Fortis to their fates went against all his instincts as a Space Marine and a leader, but Boudreaux had left no room for doubt.

After a long moment considering the situation, he picked up his handset and rang Major Rho.

"Major, come up to my office. We've got a big project straight from the top to get started on."

* * *

"We need to prep the dirigible for launch," Tacker said as he led the way to the barn. "It will be daylight in a couple hours, and we need to leave at first light."

"What about the crabs, Bill?"

"Don't worry about them. I'm sure they're gone by now. They usually don't get this close to the house."

Once they closed the barn doors, Mel turned up the lanterns and lit three more. Tacker tapped a large drum with his boot.

"I cook down some of the tobacco crop to extract the oil. The crabs don't like it, so I spray it around the place to keep them away."

"You raise tobacco?" Liz asked.

"The Upper Hebrides version of tobacco. We discovered it by accident when our Terra Earth seed crops failed. It's a broad-leafed plant with a waxy surface that we melt off and collect to repel the crabs. If you strip the wax off the leaves and dry them out, you can smoke it, too. I take it to Euphoria to trade for supplies." He pointed to a square box near the door. "That's what the cargo box is for."

While he talked, Tacker and Mel unfolded a large, reflective, metal bladder and metallic basket with seats and pedals. When they finished, Tacker explained what they were looking at.

"When it gets light and the crabs head back to the forest, we'll drag this outside and spread it out. We'll top off the burner fuel tank with tobacco oil and pressurize it with the hand pump. As it burns, it will fill the bladder with hot air to provide lift. There are seats for three to pedal. The pedals drive a hyper-efficient transmission that converts pedal power to fan power for propulsion. It's possible for two people to generate enough fan power to overcome a twenty kilometer-per-hour headwind, but I don't recommend it." He and Mel traded smiles. "Been there, done that."

"How far to Euphoria?" Fortis asked.

"It's fifty kilometers, so three of us pedaling with moderate effort and two passengers in the box should get us there in four hours or so. We'll have a slight tailwind early in the morning, but it shifts around midday, so Mel and I will have it on the way back."

"This is going to work out just fine," Liz said.

"Maybe, but before we get too far ahead of ourselves, you need to understand something. We'll get you to Euphoria, but you're on your own when we get there. Like many of the people in the Free Sector, the people of Euphoria resent the UNT and their constant meddling. The Kuiper Knights have had a presence here since before me and Mel arrived, and they're a big part of why Euphoria and the Upper Hebrides don't get preyed on like other remote colonies. If people discover that an ISMC officer is sneaking around the Upper Hebrides looking to make trouble for the Knights, and we helped him out, it will be a problem for us."

Fortis, Ystremski, and Liz nodded. "Get us to Euphoria and point us in the right direction," Ystremski said. "That's more than we deserve, and we're grateful for it."

They topped off the burner fuel tanks and filled two spare oil cans. Tacker went over every centimeter of the dirigible to ensure there were no chafed spots or suspect rigging. Mel prepared a pack of food and water for the trip, and when Fortis and Ystremski returned to the house to carry it out, they noticed the sky had grown lighter.

"Let's head up to the roof of the house," Tacker said. "The view is spectacular."

Fortis had a hard time keeping up as he followed the group up the stairs, and he had to stop between the second and third floor. Stabbing pain in his ribs made breathing difficult, and he huffed and puffed to get enough air.

"Are you okay?" Ystremski put a hand on his shoulder. "Let's go back downstairs."

Fortis brushed him away. "Fuck that. I can make it. I just need to catch my breath."

"Good. I didn't want to believe you had become a pussy."

Fortis chuckled and gasped when a finger of agony speared him in the chest.

"If you two lovebirds are finished, you need to get up here," Liz called down the stairs. "It's amazing."

When they got to the top, Fortis saw purple streaks on the dark horizon. While he watched, the purple became blue and red, and then flashes of orange and green shot high overhead.

"Ten years ago, some egghead scientists came all the way from Terra Earth to research the orange and blue flashes," Tacker said. "They theorized that they're gases from underwater volcanoes burning off when they're exposed to the atmosphere."

"What did they find?" Liz asked.

"I dunno. They headed that way with all their gear, and we never heard from them again."

Ystremski snorted and Fortis stifled a laugh to protect his injured ribs.

Tacker pointed down at the field. "Look."

Hundreds of crabs skittered across the field toward the cover of the trees as the sky grew lighter.

"There are more every day," Mel said.

"Yeah. While we're in Euphoria, I'll talk to the UHDL and see if I can get them out here to give us a hand burning out that nest."

Despite Fortis' insistence that he was able to help pedal to Euphoria, the group opted to have Ystremski, Mel, and Tacker propel the dirigible. The climb up and down from the roof had left Fortis gasping for breath while he hugged his abdomen.

"I'll give you a pill to help you rest all the way to Euphoria," Mel said. "By the time we get there, you'll be good to go."

Tacker and Ystremski dragged the dirigible from the barn and laid it out. They fastened the basket and cargo box to the bottom and lit the burners. The craft floated above them a few minutes later as they climbed aboard, and Fortis and Liz curled up in the cargo box. Tacker released the tethers, and they were airborne.

Fortis allowed himself to drift off to sleep.

* * * * *

Chapter Thirty-Two

As soon as it grew light enough to see, Kuiper Knights flooded Euphoria in search of their quarry. They banged on doors and accosted early-risers who were out on the streets, and it wasn't long before the entire colony was riled up.

Zerec and Addison watched with grim satisfaction as the Knights overwhelmed any who protested, crowding around them and shouting in their faces.

A man with a long white beard and a distinct limp approached. "They told me you are the leader. What is the meaning of this?"

Zerec sneered at the man. "We are hunting for some fugitives from the Terra Earth Sector who tried to destroy our ship and kill us. They escaped to this planet, and we are determined to find them. One of them is a Space Marine."

"A Space Marine, here? This is the Free Sector. There are no Space Marines here." The old timer gestured around him. "This is a big planet. What makes you think he's here in Euphoria?"

"You're a fool, old man." Zerec shoved the man away. "Go tell your people we're not leaving without the fugitives, so they better turn them over to us."

Down the street, two of Zylstra's men had a man backed up against a wall. They peppered him with questions as they poked him in the chest and abdomen. When he tried to escape, the mercenaries overwhelmed him with punches and kicks.

"This is getting out of control," Addison said. "The entire colony is going to rise against us if this continues."

"These sheep? They'll do no such thing. They're disorganized rabble who only care for themselves."

* * *

When they got close to Euphoria, the trio stopped pedaling and drifted on the light breeze.

"That's the space port," Tacker said as he pointed. "Everyone lands their dirigibles on the outskirts of the city on this side, so we don't foul the flight path. It looks like there's a shuttle at the space port, so you might be able to get a ride out of here soon. That's good, because everyone will know you don't belong here."

Tacker piloted the dirigible to a soft landing amid the other craft, and Mel hopped out to tie it down. Ystremski held the cargo box lid for Liz, who was slow to crawl out.

"I am so fucking stiff," she said as she stretched and groaned. "Abner is still asleep, I think."

"Hey, Bill. Bill!" A familiar voice got Tacker's attention, and he looked up to see his friend Angus McDonald approaching.

"Walk away!" he whispered fiercely to Liz and Ystremski. "Go now, and don't look back."

Tacker and Mel smiled and walked toward their friend. "Angus, you old bastard, how are you?" The two men shook hands, and Mel gave Angus a peck on the cheek. Tacker saw a fresh welt on his friend's face. "What happened to you?"

McDonald looked around and motioned to the Tackers to follow him. He ducked into a narrow alley and leaned close to them.

"A bunch of Kuiper Knights landed before daybreak and started raising hell all over the colony. They're looking for some escaped prisoners who they say tried to destroy their ship and then came here in an escape pod. One of them is a Space Marine."

"What's a Space Marine doing in the Free Sector?"

McDonald shook his head. "I don't know, Bill. The whole thing is very confusing. All I know is they're pushing people around and beating them if they resist. It might be best if you get back on your balloon and go home."

Tacker frowned. "I came to get some help from the UHDL with a crab hole."

"I'm sorry, Bill, but this is a real bad time for that. I know you well enough to know you won't tolerate their bullshit, but there are too many of them. They have pulse rifles, too."

"Are we in danger?" Mel asked.

"They haven't done anything too bad yet. Bullying, mostly. Some of us have been working hard to keep everyone cool, but I can tell it won't take much for the Knights to escalate."

Tacker couldn't think of anything else to say to delay their departure, so he clapped McDonald on the shoulder.

"Okay, you talked me into it." He looked at Mel. "You ready to leave?"

Her eyes widened for a second, but she nodded. "He's right. We should go."

The trio walked back to Tacker's dirigible, and McDonald patted their cargo box.

"I was hoping this was full of tobacco."

Before they could stop him, he opened the lid and made a disappointed noise.

"Empty."

"Yeah, well, the crabs got into my drying barn and chewed up most of my last crop," Tacker said. He pulled out his tobacco pouch and handed it to McDonald. "Here, take this and enjoy it, and then round up the UHDL and come help me kill this crab hole."

The Tackers climbed back into their seats while McDonald tended the lines.

"Safe flight, folks, and we'll see you soon."

Both Tackers searched the area as they climbed to see if they could spot the trio of fugitives, but they were gone.

* * *

Fortis roused when Liz climbed out of the cargo box. His body ached, but he got to his hands and knees in preparation for getting out. He froze when he heard Tacker warn Ystremski and Liz to walk away and then call out to someone else. The voices faded, and he chanced a peek through the cargo box lid. There was no one in sight, so he heaved himself up and out of the box.

"Psst!"

Ystremski beckoned from the corner of a nearby building and Fortis staggered over to join him.

"That was close," Liz said. "Who was that guy?"

"I don't know. A friend of Tacker's. Where are we going?"

Ystremski pointed back toward the dirigible. "The space port is that way. We saw a shuttle there on the way in. Maybe we can hitch a ride." He looked at Fortis, who leaned against the building and breathed in deep gulps. "Can you walk?"

Fortis nodded. "Yeah, I'm good. Just a little stiff from the ride." He took a step, and his right leg folded underneath him. He would have fallen on his face if Ystremski and Liz hadn't caught him.

"Yeah, you're good all right. C'mon."

Ystremski ducked his head under one of Fortis' arms, and they set off through the narrow streets of Euphoria for the space port. After two blocks, they stopped to give Fortis a break.

"This is a shitshow," Liz said. "Three strangers wandering through the colony are going to draw a lot of attention."

Before anyone could answer, a woman opened the shutters on a window that looked out over the street.

"Are you the ones they're looking for?"

"Hmm, no," Liz said. She looked at Ystremski and Fortis. "Who's looking, and who are they looking for?"

"The men from the shuttle. They're looking for some escaped prisoners. Three prisoners."

"That's not us." Liz sounded ridiculous, and Ystremski snorted, which elicited a groan from Fortis.

"Here, take these." The woman passed some robes out the window. "They'll help disguise your clothes. Stay off the main streets." She closed the shutters.

They donned the robes over their clothes and continued to the space port. A block short of their goal, Ystremski led them into a narrow alley where they hunkered down.

"Stay here and let me scout the area on my own," he said. "If those men from the shuttle are Kuiper Knights, it would be better if they only see one person instead of three, especially if one of us is injured."

"I'm okay," Fortis said. "I just had a kink in my leg from the box."

Liz put a protective arm around his shoulders. "We'll wait here."

After Ystremski disappeared around the corner, Fortis turned to Liz.

"I'm really okay, you know."

"I'm sure you are, but like he said, it's better if they don't see three people sneaking around. Let's hole up here and wait."

Annoyed at his perceived weakness, Fortis nodded. The sleep he'd gotten at Tacker's and in the cargo box had made a big difference, but the pain in his ribs was a constant reminder that he wasn't one hundred percent.

After a short wait, Liz walked down to the end of the alley and peeked around the corner.

"I didn't see anything," she said when she returned.

"How long do you want to stay here?"

Ystremski appeared at the end of the alley.

"What was the name of the ship you chartered?" he asked Fortis.

"*Dancer.*"

"That's the name painted on the tail of that shuttle."

Fortis blinked in surprise. "*Dancer* is here?"

"I don't know about *Dancer*, but her shuttle is."

"That might be our way out of here."

"We'd have to take out the Kuiper Knights guarding it."

"How many?"

"I saw two, so figure four. Maybe."

"Damn." Fortis thought for a second. "If we could bluff our way onto the tarmac, we might make it work."

"Uh, gents. One small problem. We don't have a shuttle pilot."

Ystremski shrugged. "That's never stopped us before."

A few minutes later, they were hiding behind a prefab hangar near the tarmac where the shuttle was parked. Fortis watched the same three Kuiper Knights go up and down the ramp several times.

"I think maybe there's only three," he said.

Liz ducked back under cover. "Only three, but they have pulse rifles."

"What's going on here?"

A loud voice from behind startled them. Two Kuiper Knights in black smocks stood a few paces away with pulse rifles slung and suspicious looks on their faces.

"We came to see the shuttle," Ystremski said as he stepped forward. "We haven't—"

The Knights tried to get their weapons, but Ystremski was on them too fast. He hammered the man on the left with a straight punch to the face. The second man stepped back as he fumbled for his weapon as Ystremski moved in to grapple with him.

Fortis attacked the first man who was crabbing backward as he tried to shake off the effects of Ystremski's punch. The Knight kicked Fortis in his osseointegrated right leg and howled in pain when his shin contacted metal. Fortis landed on top of the man, and they traded short-range punches as they rolled on the ground. Fortis managed a stiff-fingered strike to the throat which left the man clawing at his throat while he struggled to breathe.

He looked up and saw Ystremski had his opponent in a chokehold. The man went limp, and Ystremski held the choke for a few extra seconds before he let the man collapse to the ground.

Fortis rolled free and stood with hands on hips as he gasped for air. He had taken several blows to his injured ribs, and his chest was on fire.

"Are you okay?" Liz asked. Fortis waved off her question.

"What do you want to do with these guys?" he asked Ystremski.

"Tie 'em up and leave 'em here." Ystremski doffed his robe and started to rip it into strips. "Grab their smocks."

Liz and Fortis stripped the Knights of their smocks and Ystremski bound them securely with the makeshift restraints. Fortis saw that the man he'd throat punched had a tattoo of DINLI, the scowling bulldog mascot of the ISMC, on his arm.

"You a Space Marine?"

The man glared over his gag and gave a quick nod.

"Sorry." Fortis hit him with a rabbit punch to the temple and the man fell back, unconscious.

Fortis and Ystremski donned the black smocks and grabbed the pulse rifles.

"I'll go first, then Liz, then you," Ystremski said. "Make it look like we have a prisoner."

"Sounds good."

"Okay then, let's go grab the shuttle."

* * * * *

Chapter Thirty-Three

Fortis felt completely exposed as he trailed Ystremski and Liz across the tarmac to *Dancer's* shuttle. Stabs of pain shot through his body with every step, and he fought the urge to double over. The pain meds he'd taken prior to their flight had completely worn off, and he'd taken several body shots during the fight behind the hangar. Liz heard him struggling and turned around to help.

"Keep going!" Fortis hissed at her. "You're a prisoner, remember?"

Two unarmed Kuiper Knights came out to greet them when Ystremski reached the boarding ramp. They turned around and went back up the ramp when Ystremski brandished his pulse rifle at them. By the time Fortis made it up the ramp, the two men were kneeling on the deck in the passenger compartment with their hands high overhead.

"How many up forward?" Ystremski demanded. They both shook their heads in defiance.

Fortis recognized them as former Paladins, and he stepped in to rake the barrel of his pulse rifle across the face of the nearest one. "How many more forward?"

The injured man squealed as blood spurted from his torn cheek and ruined nose, and the other turned white with shock. Fortis raised his pulse rifle, and the man shrank away.

"One. Just one. P-P-Perkins."

"Is he the pilot?"

"No. The AI is the pilot. Perkins is up there playing chess with it."

"Doe? Doe is the pilot?"

"Yeah. Doe."

Fortis gestured at the Knights. "Watch these fuckers. I'll take care of Perkins, and we'll get moving. Doe knows me from *Dancer*."

When he got to the cockpit, the door was shut. When he tested the knob, it was unlocked, so he burst in.

"Freeze!"

A man in a black smock jumped to his feet. Fortis butt-stroked him in the forehead and he went down in a heap. Doe looked at Fortis and blinked.

"Doe, my name is Fortis. Do you remember me?"

Doe shook his head.

"Where's *Dancer*?"

"*Dancer* is in orbit.

"Okay then, get this thing in the air, and we'll sort it out in space."

"I'm not authorized to take that action. Only Captain Lakshaw or Brother Zylstra can order me to take off."

"We're in kind of a hurry here, Doe. Zylstra would approve, I promise."

"I'm not authorized to take that action. Only Captain Lakshaw or Brother Zylstra can order me to take off," Doe repeated.

"Hurry up!" Liz shouted up the passageway and then stuck her head in the door. "There are more Knights headed this way."

"Tell Ystremski to hold them off." Fortis turned back to Doe and thought for a second. "Is Captain Lakshaw listening on the circuit?"

"I've spoken to her several times."

"Can I use the circuit to call her?"

Doe gestured to the comms panel, and Fortis grabbed the headset.

"*Dancer*, this is, uh, the shuttle. Are you there?"

After a momentary pause, Lakshaw answered.

"Station calling, this is Dancer. Who is this?"

"This is the shuttle. Do you know who this is?"

"Yes, I recognize your voice. How did you get on this circuit?"

"I've got a situation here and I don't have time to explain. I need you to give Doe permission to launch the shuttle and return to *Dancer*."

"I don't understand—"

"Just do it. I'll explain later. Please!"

"Petr said there are forty of those motherfuckers headed this way and his rifle is dead!" Liz shouted from the passageway.

"Doe, this is Captain Lakshaw. Launch the shuttle and return to Dancer at once."

"Yes, Captain." Doe started the launch sequence, and Fortis heard the engines begin to wind up. "Please take your seats and buckle up for safety."

Fortis grabbed the unconscious Kuiper Knight by the collar and dragged him out into the passageway. The shuttle jerked into motion and Fortis fell on his face. He felt a *pop* in his ribs, and a white hot lance stabbed him in the side. He staggered to his feet and made it to the passenger cabin with the Knight in tow.

"Liz, help me with this guy." His vision blurred as a wave of nausea broke over him. "Liz."

Ystremski yanked his pulse rifle away and grabbed the unconscious man by the collar.

"Liz, buckle him up while I take out the trash."

Fortis moaned when Sherer helped him into a seat and fastened his belt. Ystremski returned and took a seat behind him.

"Barely made it, but he's out."

Ystremski barely had time to get his seatbelt buckled before the shuttle accelerated down the runway. The pressure and vibration were agonizing on Fortis' chest, and he chewed his lip to keep from crying out. When the shuttle went vertical, the pain was too much and he sank into blessed unconsciousness.

* * *

The Kuiper Knights finished their sweep of Euphoria with negative results. Zerec questioned several of the colony elders, but they all plead ignorance of any fugitives in the area. The bearded man who had protested earlier was the de facto colony governor, and he made a convincing argument.

"You say these fugitives fled on an escape pod last night. No escape pod has ever landed at the space port, as far as I can remember. We are not friends of the UNT government, and we have no reason to hide their agents."

"They could have landed elsewhere," Zerec said.

The old timer shook his head. "This is a savage planet with many life forms that are deadly to humans. If they came down in the forest, they are almost certainly dead, especially if they landed at night." He smiled at his fellow colonists. "If you don't believe me, you're welcome to head out into the wilderness and find out for yourselves." The colonists laughed.

A Kuiper Knight raced up to the gathering. "Brother Zerec! They're stealing the shuttle!"

"What?"

"The shuttle! They're trying to steal it."

"Who?"

"Some of the brothers."

Zerec heard the engines of the shuttle wind up and took off running for the space port with the rest of the Kuiper Knights behind him. They reached the tarmac in time to watch the shuttle lift off and climb sharply into the clouds. A group of Knights helped two of the battered and bloodied brothers off the tarmac.

"What happened?" Zerec demanded.

"They came out of nowhere," one of the injured men replied. "They were dressed as Knights, and we thought they were with us. Then they attacked."

"Who were 'they?'"

"Two men and a woman. One of them was Fortis."

Zerec turned and found Zylstra. "You left men aboard *Dancer?*"

"One of our leaders, a guy named Herron, stayed behind with a handful of men."

"Call him and arrange for them to greet the fugitives."

* * *

Lakshaw tapped a button on her communicator. "Yak, can you come up to the control room, please?"

After a long pause, during which she could almost hear him sigh, he answered. *"On my way."*

Two minutes later, there was a tap on the control room door and Yak stuck his head in. "What's up?"

Lakshaw motioned him into Doe's empty seat. "Close the door and have a seat."

Yak did as he was told and looked at her expectantly.

"I just got a call from the shuttle. It's on its way back up here."

"Okay. I'll get the bay ready. You could have just told me over the circuit, you know." He studied her face for a second. "What's wrong?"

"Fortis is on the shuttle. Doe couldn't launch without permission, so Fortis called and asked me to order Doe to launch."

"Fortis? Is he one of these cult whack jobs now, too?"

"No, I don't think so. It sounded like a firefight in the background. I think he hijacked the shuttle."

"Huh." Yak stroked his tangled beard. "Do you think Herron and his guys might be a problem?"

"That's why I called you up here. How many of them are aboard?"

"Five total. Herron plus four. They've been hanging out in the cargo bay with their boxes."

Lakshaw flipped through the camera feeds until she came to the cargo bay. The Paladins sat in a circle, engrossed in a card game.

"Do you think we can take them by surprise?" she asked.

"You mean take them prisoner?"

"Exactly. If someone on the surface calls Herron and tells him about the shuttle, he'll probably try to grab it when it returns."

"I don't think we can sneak up on them, and they've got all the weapons."

"What if we confine them to the cargo bay? Can we do that?"

"Hmm. I guess. I've got a portable welder; I could weld the hatch and escape scuttles shut. But they've got explosives, so they can still get out."

Lakshaw examined the cargo bay view. "I see all five of them. Grab your welder and get busy. The welds don't have to be perfect, just enough to keep the hatch shut if someone tries to open it. When you're finished, go to the cargo crane control tower and give me a call. I'll take care of the rest."

Fifteen minutes later, Yak called Lakshaw.

"I'm in the tower, Captain."

"Okay, good. Herron and his guys gave up their card game and broke out some weapons, so I think he might have gotten a data message from the surface."

"What do you want me to do?"

"As soon as I call Herron, turn on the door warning light. Don't open the door, just turn on the light."

"Roger that."

Lakshaw switched to the loudspeaker system in the cargo bay.

"Herron. Herron, can you hear me?"

The door warning light began to flash, and Herron emerged from one of the Paladin cargo boxes. He waved his arms at the camera.

"I can hear you!"

"Cut the light," Lakshaw told Yak over her communicator, and the light went out.

"The shuttle is on its way back from the surface," she announced to Herron. "Your guys are not aboard."

Herron threw up his hands. "I don't understand."

"I think you do, which is why you and your men are gearing up." The rest of Herron's men exited the cargo box, empty-handed but dressed in their tactical gear. "Fortis is on the shuttle."

"What's going on?"

"I guess we'll find out when he gets here. Until then, here's what you're going to do. Return all your weapons to the cargo box and latch it shut. Have a seat and resume your card game. If you make any moves to leave that space, Yak will open the cargo bay door."

The amber warning light began to flash.

Herron and his men traded looks. "This is bullshit, Lakshaw."

"Maybe so, but it's not for long. Until I know what's going on with my shuttle, everyone is going to relax."

* * *

A short while later, the exterior comms circuit came to life.

"Dancer, this is the shuttle. Ready for final approach."

"This is *Dancer,* stand by."

Lakshaw called Yak on her communicator. "The shuttle is here. Can you go operate the shuttle recovery boom?"

"What about Herron and his guys?"

"They haven't moved, but I'll watch them. If they try something, I'll open the exterior door from up here."

Lakshaw brought up the shuttle bay camera on another screen and watched as Yak opened the door and extended the boom. Doe piloted the shuttle to the boom, and they completed the recovery without a hitch. As soon as the shuttle bay door was closed and the atmosphere in the bay was equalized, Yak returned to the cargo crane control tower.

"I'm back up here, Captain."

"Good." Lakshaw watched the shuttle door open. Fortis emerged, assisted by a strange man and woman. Doe followed and gave the "all clear" hand signal. "I'm headed for the shuttle bay."

She met Doe, Fortis, and his handlers in the shuttle bay passageway.

"Captain Lakshaw, this is Liz Sherer and Petr Ystremski," Fortis said. "Friends of mine. I ran into them aboard *Colossus.*"

"Welcome aboard. One moment, please." Lakshaw turned to Doe. "Doe, resume standard operating procedures. Report to the control room and plot a course for the Freedom Jump Gate." After the AI was gone, she turned back to the trio.

"Do you need immediate medical attention?" she asked Fortis.

"No, I'm okay right now."

"He's full of shit," Sherer said. "The poor boy can barely walk. Do you have a doctor on board?"

Lakshaw shook her head. "The best I can offer is an old scanner left behind by a medical team a few years ago. If the jackals at SOMO didn't steal it."

"I have a broken rib." The frustration in Fortis' voice was clear. "Other than that, it's just the usual bumps and bruises."

"Okay then, let's head up to the crew's mess, and I'll buy you a cup of coffee." Lakshaw tapped her communicator. "Yak, anything going on?"

"Nothing, Captain. They're playing cards. One of them asked to use the head by the hatch, but he wasn't gone long."

"Roger that. I'm headed for the crew's mess. Keep me posted."

When they got to the mess, Lakshaw passed out steaming mugs of coffee and sat down.

"This must be one hell of a story. Who's first?"

* * * * *

Chapter Thirty-Four

Fortis, Sherer, and Ystremski took turns telling their stories of how they had arrived aboard *Dancer*. Ystremski went first. He was guarded with the details and only told the captain that he'd joined the Kuiper Knights but had had a change of heart. Lakshaw shook her head in amazement when he described the weapons the Knights seized from *Colossus* and their subsequent escape.

"So, after we landed on that planet, we made it to the colony, saw an opportunity, and grabbed the shuttle," he said.

Ystremski traded looks with Fortis and Sherer, and they nodded in silent agreement to leave the Tackers out of their story.

After Sherer and Fortis told their stories, Lakshaw updated them on the situation aboard *Dancer*.

"Herron and four others are in the cargo bay," she said. "Yak welded the hatch shut so they can't get out."

"What's your plan for them?"

"I'm not taking them back to turn them over to the Fleet. Other than that, I was hoping to get some ideas from you. They're pretty much your prisoners."

"How do you know they're not going to blast their way out with breaching charges?" Ystremski asked.

"Yak is watching them from the cargo crane control tower. I told them if they make any moves, he'll pop the door."

"How long until we get back to Terra Earth? Four days?"

Lakshaw nodded. "Give or take. I'll know for sure when I see Doe's route."

"Are you gonna rotate people in for Yak?"

"Dammit. I didn't think about that."

"How about putting Doe in the tower? An AI doesn't need to sleep, right?"

"That's a good idea. His protocol dictates that he can't open the door because that would kill a human, but he can hit the warning light and call me."

Fortis, who had been listening in silence, spoke up. "Have you told Herron that they're riding home in the cargo bay?"

"Not yet. I'm kind of making this up as I go along."

Sherer chuckled. "These two are experts at that."

"Let me talk to him," Fortis said. "Maybe we can work something out."

"I'm not letting him out of there," Lakshaw said.

"I completely agree. There's no way we'd feel safe. However, they'll be less likely to try something stupid if I explain that they're going to walk away when we get home."

Fortis' words shocked Ystremski. "You want to let them go?"

Fortis shrugged. "Why not? They weren't part of the mutiny. I can't expect five guys to go toe-to-toe with two hundred. Besides, I think Paladin will have something to say about all this." He groaned as he stood up, and Ystremski grabbed his arm.

"You sure you're up for this?"

"Yeah, I'm sure. DINLI. At least we'll have some peace and quiet for the ride home."

* * *

Ten minutes later, Lakshaw and Sherer went to the control room while Fortis and Ystremski crowded into the cargo crane control tower with Yak.

"Welcome back," the bearded cargo master told Fortis as he slid out of his seat.

"Happier than you can imagine to be here."

Yak gestured to the console in front of Fortis. "Standard comms panel. The cargo bay intercom is already dialed up, so all you have to do is push to talk. That yellow button activates the exterior door warning light in case you want to fuck with them, but don't hit the red one next to it unless you want to say goodbye."

"Got it." He picked up the microphone. "Herron. Herron, can you hear me?"

Herron dropped his cards and jumped to his feet.

"Is that you, Fortis?"

"The one and only, back from the dead."

"For what it's worth, I'm glad to hear it. They did you dirty."

"Let's worry about that later. Right now, we need to get a few things straight."

"I'm listening."

"We're headed for Terra Earth, and you're coming with us."

Herron looked around at the other Paladins. "You're not going to airlock us?"

"If you don't make trouble, I have no reason to. If you fuck around—" Fortis turned on the warning light "—I'll open the door myself. If you're lucky, you'll be unconscious before your blood boils." He turned the light off.

"There won't be any trouble. I promise."

"Good. When we get back to Terra Earth, I'll take you down to the surface, and then you're on your own."

"Thank you."

"I know you've got rations in one of your cargo boxes. This is your one chance to get enough for five days. Send one guy in the box. If he comes out with anything other than rations and hydration packs, the lights go on and the door goes up." Fortis flashed the lights again. "We're going home with or without you. It's your choice."

"Yak, Doe is on his way down to meet you," Lakshaw said over an internal circuit.

By the time the AI reached the cargo crane control tower, Herron's man had exited the cargo box with an armload of rations and hydration packs. He spread them out on the deck for inspection while Fortis and Ystremski looked closely for any telltale bulges of weapons or explosives under his clothes. They didn't see any.

"Get comfortable, and I'll be back to check on you later."

The tower door opened. "The captain sent me down to watch the prisoners," Doe told Yak. Fortis and Ystremski squeezed out into the passageway, followed by Yak.

"Yak, I need to make a report to my headquarters," Fortis said. "They need to know what's been happening out here."

"Lakshaw is in the control room. I'm sure she'll oblige you. I gotta get back down below and finish up a repair to the main CO_2 scrubber, or it's going to get awfully stuffy in here before we get home."

"Have you sent a *Colossus* position report lately?" Fortis asked Ystremski as they headed for the control room.

"Two days ago, I told them I found you and then stashed my communicator with the geolocator mode turned on. The piece of shit battery was almost dead, but they might have received a good position within the last twenty-four hours."

"What were you supposed to do after you found the weapons? Find your own way home?"

"You know, we never talked about that. It happened so fast that I didn't really think it through. What were your instructions?"

"Locate *Colossus* and destroy her. I didn't know you were involved; I figured V was a real divvie."

"I am. Was." Ystremski shook his head. "Fuckin' Anders. I don't know how he keeps track of this bullshit. What's he gonna do when he finds out we fucked up?"

Fortis scoffed. "We didn't fuck up. You accomplished your mission. You found the weapons. My mission failed because he insisted on using mercenaries."

"What do you think is the next move?"

Fortis paused at the control room door. "They'll probably do what they should have done from the start. Tell the Big Four to go to hell and send in Fleet units to destroy *Colossus*. She'll have a couple days head start, but they'll find her."

* * *

Two hours after Fortis transmitted their status to Anders, *Dancer* received a reply. Lakshaw brought it down to Fortis and Ystremski in the crew's mess.

Fleet destroyer *Comte de Barras* enroute latest position reported. ETA thirteen hours.

Fortis and Ystremski exchanged looks of surprise.

"Thirteen hours? They must have sent her through the gate two days ago. We were still on *Colossus*."

"Maybe your rich daddy Anders doesn't love you as much as you think?" Lakshaw asked.

Fortis shrugged. "DINLI. We're not worth a shipload of weapons."

"Maybe you're not, but I put a premium on keeping myself intact," Ystremski said.

"Where's Liz?" Fortis asked Lakshaw.

"I let her use my tub, and now she's sacked out in my cabin."

"You have a bathtub on a spaceship?"

"Yes, I have a tub on *my* spaceship. It's a luxury and a huge waste of water, but I'm the captain. As long as the artificial gravity system works, I like to take a bath every once in a while. It's good for the soul."

Yak entered the space with two other *Dancer* crewmembers, who poured coffee and sat at a nearby table.

"I just looked in on Doe," Yak told Lakshaw. "I don't think he's blinked since you told him to watch Herron and his guys."

"How's work on the scrubber going?"

"I just brought her back online, so the old fart smell should start to dissipate pretty soon."

Lakshaw and her crew chatted over their coffees and then went back to their duties. When they were alone again, Ystremski leaned close to Fortis and lowered his voice.

"Did Anders ever mention a super weapon aboard *Colossus*?"

"No, why?"

"When I was aboard the ship, a bunch of the guys who worked in one of the magazines talked about finding a high security magazine with helenium locks. They didn't have anything to cut them, so they're going to wait until they get back to Sanctuary. Somebody said it was some kind of bomb, but the head of the Knights shut down the rumor mill quick."

"Anders didn't say a word to me."

* * *

Six hours later, Lakshaw called them to the control room. She pointed to a contact on the navigation screen.

"That's *Comte de Barras*. Most ships don't include their full identity on their squawk to avoid pirates, but she's not keeping hers a secret."

"It looks like she's going to pass by us pretty close," Fortis said. "Are you going to hail her?"

"Not unless she calls me first. I want as little to do with Fleet ships here in the Free Sector as possible."

Lakshaw no sooner got the words out then the hailing circuit came to life. It was *Comte de Barras*, requesting that *Dancer* identify herself. After she did, there was a heavy silence.

"They just realized who they're talking to," Lakshaw told Fortis and Ystremski. "I bet they're sorry for what they did."

"This is Comte de Barras. *Have a safe journey back to Terra Earth.* Comte de Barras, *out."*

* * * * *

Epilogue

Doe brought *Dancer's* shuttle down to Terra Earth at the Kinshasa civilian space port terminal. Herron and his men hurried down the ramp and disappeared almost before the shuttle stopped moving. Fortis, Ystremski, and Sherer paused by the ramp.

"What's their hurry?" Ystremski asked with a smile.

"It's almost like they don't trust us," Fortis said.

Just then, a convoy of blacked-out vehicles with flashing red and blue lights raced across the tarmac and skidded to a halt. Two dozen heavily armed Space Marines with Military Police armbands emerged and formed a perimeter around the shuttle.

"Should we put our hands up?" Liz asked in a quiet voice.

"I don't think so," Fortis said. "Just don't make any sudden moves."

"Do you think they're here for the Paladins?"

"If they are, they're too late."

A burly Space Marine captain approached. "Major Abner Fortis, I'm Captain Wycoff from the Military Justice Center. Pursuant to orders from Admiral Schein, Chief of the UNT General Staff, I am placing you under arrest for Conspiracy to Violate the Non-Use of Military Force Agreement, to wit; you entered the Free Sector with the intent to conduct military operations."

The captain's words stunned Fortis, and his face burned as the blood rushed to his cheeks.

"What the fuck is this?" Ystremski started forward, and two of the Space Marines stepped between him and Fortis. "This man is a hero."

"Mr. Ystremski, this is a military matter. Please step back."

"I'm Gunnery Sergeant Ystremski."

The captain shook his head. "No sir. You're a civilian now. You're out of our jurisdiction now, unless you interfere."

Fortis offered no resistance as the captain handcuffed him and propelled him toward one of the vehicles.

"I'll look for you," Ystremski called as Fortis climbed in. The captain sat next to Fortis, and the convoy sped away.

"Can you tell me what this is all about?"

The captain shook his head. "My orders are to arrest you and bring you to Lviv, sir. When we get there, everything will be explained."

* * *

After a quick shuttle ride, they arrived at the Military Justice Center in Lviv. The rest of the jailers were as close-mouthed as Wycoff while they processed Fortis into the facility. They collected biometric data and strip-searched him. Fortis' osseointegrated right leg drew some attention, and it took some convincing before they decided it couldn't be removed. Fortis received an orange jumpsuit and plastic slippers, and then he was locked in a windowless holding cell.

He stared at the cell door and pondered his situation. His ribs ached, and his headache had returned, and the cement bunk in the cell offered no comfort. The tiny room was stuffy and the stainless-steel toilet in the corner reeked of pine oil and urine. It had been a long time since he'd last eaten aboard *Dancer,* and his stomach growled with increasing frequency. Even though he knew the entire process was intended to soften him up in preparation for questioning, a doubtful voice whispered from the edge of his consciousness.

I'm really in the shit.

The lock clicked, and one of the guards opened the cell door.

"He's right there, sir."

A familiar Fleet colonel entered the cell. Fortis stared, but he was unable to recall how he knew the newcomer.

"Major Fortis," the colonel said. "Remember me?"

Fortis blinked when it came to him.

"Major Grant? I mean, Colonel Grant?"

Colonel Grant smiled and extended his hand. "The one and same." After they shook, Grant motioned to the bunk. "Have a seat, Major."

Wallace Grant was the same Fleet lawyer who had represented Fortis during his court martial after his cherry drop on Pada-Pada.

"What is going on, Colonel? What are you doing here? Why am I here?"

"One question at a time, Abner. I'm here because some damned fool at the General Staff Legal Office recognized your name and assigned me as your counsel."

Fortis gave him a confused look, and Grant laughed. "I saw your name and volunteered to represent you."

"Can you tell me what's going on?"

"Four days ago, Fleet destroyer *Comte de Barras* entered the Free Sector and destroyed *Colossus,* a former ISMC flagship, in violation of the Non-Use of Military Force Agreement. Generals Boudreaux and Anders allegedly ordered the action, and you've been implicated in it."

"That charge is bullshit, Colonel. I didn't—"

Grant put a finger to his lips and then pointed to the light fixture high in the ceiling above.

"You haven't been charged with anything. Yet. I know it seems like nonsense, but there's a process that must be followed. A criminal board of inquiry has been formed to investigate the matter. They will convene shortly to hear your sworn witness testimony."

Fortis plucked at his jumpsuit. "Do they treat all their witnesses so well?" He took a deep breath and winced. "Any advice?"

"Answer their questions completely. Tell the truth and stick to the facts."

"What about Generals Boudreaux and Anders? Will my testimony be used against them?"

"It's hard to say. They've been charged with allegedly ordering *Comte de Barras* to enter the Free Sector. It's possible that your testimony may become part of the government's case."

"What if I don't want to testify?"

Grant shrugged. "You can't be compelled to testify. If you choose not to, you'll probably sit in this cell until they decide whether to charge you or not, and that could take years."

There was a rap at the door and a guard stuck his head in the cell.

"Colonel, they're ready for you."

* * *

Three hours later, Fortis and Grant returned to the cell. The guards handed Fortis a bag with his clothes in it and left the cell door open.

"That went about like I expected," Grant said as Fortis changed out of his jumpsuit. "It's clear to me that they're not interested in you."

"That's easy for you to say, Colonel. I just spent the last three hours getting grilled."

"You did well." Grant chuckled. "I thought the prosecutor was going to faint when you explained that you were kidnapped and taken into the Free Sector against your will."

"Colonel, I'm no expert on the legal situation surrounding the Free Sector, but it seems to me that General Boudreaux did the right thing by sending in *Comte de Barras*. The Kuiper Knights had begun to distribute the stolen weapons around the sector. Now we know there was a weapon of mass destruction involved, too. I don't understand why he and General Anders are being charged for what should have been our first option."

Grant patted Fortis on the shoulder. "Do us both a favor, Abner. Keep your legal opinions to yourself. As you well know, right and wrong don't play a role in all this. The wrong word in the wrong ear could bring down an avalanche of trouble on your head. Just do your duty, and if anyone asks, say, 'No comment.'"

"Roger that, sir."

The two officers left the building and parted ways. Fortis went to the nearest shuttle stop to catch a ride to the space port. Another blacked-out vehicle, a passenger van, pulled to the curb and the door slid open.

"Major Fortis, come on, I'll give you a ride."

Fortis approached the vehicle. He recognized Admiral Schein beckoning to him.

"It's okay, Major. I'll take you to the space port."

Fortis slid in next to the admiral.

"I'm glad to finally meet you. I've heard a lot about you."

"Same here, sir."

"That was a hell of a job you did out there, Major."

Grant's admonishment echoed in Fortis' ears.

No comment.

"I did my duty, Admiral."

Schein scoffed. "Testimony time is over, son. This is just us talking. Speaking frankly, this whole episode has embarrassed a lot of people who don't like to be embarrassed. Had Ellis Boudreaux told me about his plan to send in *Comte de Barras*, I probably would have authorized it. *After* I cleared it with the politicians. That's the lesson from all of this for a young officer like yourself. Don't be the senior man with a secret."

They rode in silence for a couple minutes.

"Do you have any other questions for me before you head back to Kinshasa, Major?"

"What do I do now, Admiral?"

"What do you mean?"

Fortis stood. "Before all this started, I was the commanding officer of the Intelligence, Surveillance, and Reconnaissance branch. Basically, I was the caretaker of the ISR building. Now that Anders and Boudreaux are being held incommunicado during these proceedings, who do I report to?"

"Return to your regular duties. Go back to your building and be patient. *Comte de Barras* is due to return next week, and the board will want to depose many of the officers and crew. If you don't hear anything in a month, give my office a call, and I'll see what I can do for you."

The van came to a stop in front of the space port terminal. Schein stuck out his hand and they shook.

"These are turbulent times, Major. Keep your head down, do your duty, and you'll be fine. As you Space Marines are fond of saying, DINLI."

"Indeed, Admiral."

"Oh, and welcome home."

#####

About the Author

Paul A. Piatt was born and raised in western Pennsylvania. After his first attempt at college, he joined the Navy to see the world. He started writing as a hobby when he retired in 2005 and published his first novel in 2018. His published works include the Abner Fortis, International Space Marine mil-sf series, the Walter Bailey Misadventures urban fantasy trilogy, and other full-length thrillers in both science fiction and horror. All his novels and published short stories can be found on Amazon. You can find him on Facebook, MeWe, and on the internet at www(dot)papiattauthor(dot)com, or you can contact him directly at paulpiattauthor(at)gmail(dot)com.

* * * * *

Get the **free** Four Horsemen prelude story "**Shattered Crucible**"

and discover other titles by Theogony Books at:

http://chriskennedypublishing.com/

* * * * *

Meet the author and other CKP authors on the Factory Floor:

https://www.facebook.com/groups/461794864654198

* * * * *

Did you like this book?
Please write a review!

* * * * *

The following is an
Excerpt from Book One of The Prince of Britannia Saga:

The Prince Awakens

Fred Hughes

Available from Theogony Books

eBook, Paperback, and (soon) Audio

Excerpt from "The Prince Awakens:"

Sixth Fleet was in chaos. Fortunately, all the heavy units were deployed forward toward the attacking fleet and were directing all the defensive fire they had downrange at the enemy. More than thirteen thousand Swarm attack ships were bearing down on a fleet of twenty-six heavy escorts and the single monitor. The monitor crew had faith in their shields and guns, but could they survive against this many? They would soon find out.

Luckily, they didn't have to face all the Swarm ships. Historically, Swarm forces engaged major threats first, then went after the escorts. Which was why the monitor had to be considered the biggest threat in the battle.

Then the Swarm forces deviated from their usual pattern. The Imperial plan was suddenly irrelevant as the Swarm attack ships divided into fifteen groups and attacked the escorts, which didn't last long. When the last dreadnought died in a nuclear fireball, the Swarm attack ships turned and moved toward the next fleet in the column, Fourth Fleet, leaving the monitor behind.

The entire plan was in shambles. But, more importantly, the whole fleet was at risk of being defeated. The admiral's only option now was to save as many as he could.

"Signal to the Third, Fifth, and Seventh Fleets. The monitors are to execute Withdrawal Plan Beta."

The huge monitors had eight fleet tugs that were magnetically attached to the hull when not in use. Together, the eight tugs could get the monitors into hyperspace. However, this process took time, due to the time it took for the eight tugs to generate a warp field large enough to encompass the enormous ship. It could take up to an hour to accomplish, and they didn't have an hour.

Plan Bravo would use six heavy cruisers to accomplish the same thing. The cruisers' larger fusion engines meant the field could be generated within ten minutes, assuming no one was shooting at them. "The remaining fleet units will move to join First Fleet. Admiral

Mason in First Fleet will take command of the combined force and deploy it for combat."

The fleet admiral continued giving orders.

"I want Second Fleet to do the same, but I want heavy cruiser Squadron Twenty-Three to merge with First Fleet. Admiral Conyers, I want you to coordinate with the Eighth, Ninth, and Tenth Fleets. I want their monitors to perform a normal Alpha Withdrawal. As they're preparing to do that, have their escorts combine into a single fleet. Figure out which admiral is senior and assign him local command to organize them." He pointed at the single icon indicating the only ship left in Sixth Fleet. "Signal *Prometheus* to move at best speed to join First Fleet. That covers everything for now. I fear there's not much we can do for Fourth Fleet."

The icons were already moving on the tactical display as orders were transmitted and implemented.

"I've given the fleets in the planet's orbit their orders, Admiral," the chief of staff informed him. "The other fleets are on the move now. The Swarm should contact Fourth Fleet in approximately ten minutes. Based on their attack of Sixth Fleet, the battle will last about twenty minutes. With fifteen minutes for them to reorganize and travel to First Fleet, we're looking at forty-five minutes to engagement with the Swarm."

"What are the estimates on the rest of the fleets moving to join up with First?"

"Twenty minutes, Admiral. However, *Prometheus* is going to take at least forty-five and will arrive about the same time as the enemy."

"Organize six heavies from Seventh Fleet and have them coordinate a rendezvous with *Prometheus*, earliest possible timing," the admiral ordered. "Then execute a Beta jump. Unless the Swarm forces divert, they should have enough time. Then find out how many ships have the upgraded forty-millimeter rail gun systems and form them into a single force. O'Riley said that converting the guns to barrage fire was a simple program update. Brevet Commodore O'Riley will be in command of the newly created Task Force Twenty-Three. They are to form a wall of steel which the fleet will form behind. I am not sure if we can win this, but we need to bleed these bastards if we can't. If they win, they'll still have to make up those losses, and that will delay the next attack."

* * * * *

Get "The Prince Awakens" here: https://www.amazon.com/dp/B0BK232YT2.

Find out more about Fred Hughes at: https://chriskennedypublishing.com.

* * * * *

The following is an
Excerpt from Book One of Chimera Company:

The Fall of Rho-Torkis

Tim C. Taylor

Now Available from Theogony Books

eBook, Paperback, and Audio

Excerpt from "The Fall of Rho-Torkis:"

"Relax, Sybutu."

Osu didn't fall for the man steepling his fingers behind his desk. When a lieutenant colonel told you to relax, you knew your life had just taken a seriously wrong turn.

"So what if we're ruffling a few feathers?" said Malix. "We have a job to do, and you're going to make it happen. You will take five men with you and travel unobserved to a location in the capital where you will deliver a coded phrase to this contact."

He pushed across a photograph showing a human male dressed in smuggler chic. Even from the static image, the man oozed charm, but he revealed something else too: purple eyes. The man was a mutant.

"His name is Captain Tavistock Fitzwilliam, and he's a free trader of flexible legitimacy. Let's call him a smuggler for simplicity's sake. You deliver the message and then return here without incident, after which no one will speak of this again."

Osu kept his demeanor blank, but the questions were raging inside him. His officers in the 27th gave the appearance of having waved through the colonel's bizarre orders, but the squadron sergeant major would not let this drop easily. He'd be lodged in an ambush point close to the colonel's office where he'd be waiting to pounce on Osu and interrogate him. Vyborg would suspect him of conspiracy in this affront to proper conduct. His sappers as undercover spies? Osu would rather face a crusading army of newts than the sergeant major on the warpath.

"Make sure one of the men you pick is Hines Zy Pel."

Osu's mask must have slipped because Malix added, "If there is a problem, I expect you to speak."

"Is Zy Pel a Special Missions operative, sir?" There. He'd said it.

"You'll have to ask Colonel Lantosh. Even after they bumped up my rank, I still don't have clearance to see Zy Pel's full personnel record. Make of that what you will."

"But you must have put feelers out…"

Malix gave him a cold stare.

You're trying to decide whether to hang me from a whipping post or answer my question. Well, it was your decision to have me lead an undercover team, Colonel. Let's see whether you trust your own judgment.

The colonel seemed to decide on the latter option and softened half a degree. "There was a Hines Zy Pel who died in the Defense of Station 11. Or so the official records tell us. I have reason to think that our Hines Zy Pel is the same man."

"But... Station 11 was twelve years ago. According to the personnel record I've seen, my Zy Pel is in his mid-20s."

Malix put his hands up in surrender. "I know, I know. The other Hines Zy Pel was 42 when he was KIA."

"He's 54? Can't be the same man. Impossible."

"For you and I, Sybutu, that is true. But away from the core worlds, I've encountered mysteries that defy explanation. Don't discount the possibility. Keep an eye on him. For the moment, he is a vital asset, especially given the nature of what I have tasked you with. However, if you ever suspect him of an agenda that undermines his duty to the Legion, then I am ordering you to kill him before he realizes you suspect him."

Kill Zy Pel in cold blood? That wouldn't come easily.

"Acknowledge," the colonel demanded.

"Yes, sir. If Zy Pel appears to be turning, I will kill him."

"Do you remember Colonel Lantosh's words when she was arrested on Irisur?"

Talk about a sucker punch to the gut! Osu remembered everything about the incident when the Militia arrested the CO for standing up to the corruption endemic on that world.

It was Legion philosophy to respond to defeat or reversal with immediate counterattack. Lantosh and Malix's response had been the most un-Legion like possible.

"Yes, sir. She told us not to act. To let the skraggs take her without resistance. Without the Legion retaliating."

"No," snapped Malix. "She did *not*. She ordered us to let her go without retaliating *until the right moment*. This *is* the right moment, Sybutu. This message you will carry. You're doing this for the colonel."

Malix's words set loose a turmoil of emotions in Osu's breast that he didn't fully understand. He wept tears of rage, something he hadn't known was possible.

The colonel stood. "This is the moment when the Legion holds the line. Can I rely upon you, Sergeant?"

Osu saluted. "To the ends of the galaxy, sir. No matter what."

* * * * *

Get "The Fall of Rho-Torkis" now at: https://www.amazon.com/dp/B08VRL8H27.

Find out more about Tim C. Taylor and "The Fall of Rho-Torkis" at: https://chriskennedypublishing.com.

* * * * *

Made in United States
Troutdale, OR
10/09/2024

23607428R00206